OPEN SKIES

Other novels by Thomas H. Block

Mayday

Orbit

Forced Landing

Airship Nine

Skyfall

THOMAS BLOCK

OPEN SKIES

NEW ENGLISH LIBRARY

British Library Cataloguing in Publication Data
Block, Thomas H.
  Open skies.
  I. Title
813′.54[F]

ISBN 0-450-48797-0   04221969

First published in Great Britain 1990

Published by New English Library, ,
a hardcover imprint of Hodder and Stoughton,
a division of Hodder and Stoughton Ltd,
Mill Road, Dunton Green, Sevenoaks, Kent TN13 2YA
Editorial Office: 47 Bedford Square, London WC1B 3DP

Typeset by Hewer Text Composition Services, Edinburgh
Printed in Great Britain by St Edmundsbury Press Ltd, Bury St Edmunds, Suffolk
and bound by Robert Hartnoll Ltd, Bodmin, Cornwall

To someone, somewhere

Heartfelt thanks to good friends, who
show and tell me things I can use.

Ridi, Pagliaccio	(Laugh, clown,
sul tuo amore infranto	over your shattered love.
Ridi del duol che	Laugh at the pain
t'avvelena il cor.	poisoning your heart.)

Canio, Act I

Pagliacci

You may take the most gallant sailor, the most intrepid airman, or the most audacious soldier, put them at a table together – what do you get? The sum of their fears.

Winston Churchill

Prologue

Captain Ned Lange was so furious that he could hardly focus on the array of lighted flight instruments in the airliner's panel – a flight panel that was no more than twenty-four inches directly in front of him. "I've already *told* you once, I want to begin a descent to ten thousand!" Lange said in an emotion-filled voice. "And I want it to begin *right now!*"

"Sure, yeah, okay," First Officer Jay Bridges responded as he shifted himself slightly in the copilot's flight chair of the darkened airliner's cockpit. "Just trying to be helpful," Bridges added, in a tone that was unmistakably sarcastic. "That's why I suggested that we stay at cruise altitude."

"Get me a lower altitude," Captain Lange repeated, not knowing what else to say. It was unlike Lange to lose his temper with a copilot – a highly unusual event for him, something on a par with having his aircraft struck by lightning. Lange hunched forward in his flight chair, his rounded shoulders exaggerating the motion.

"Sure thing, boss," Bridges responded. Yet the copilot made no move towards his microphone to request the lower altitude from air traffic control.

"I've got my reasons to start the descent right now," Lange said aloud, more to himself than to Bridges, as he nervously ran his fingers through his thinning grey hair. *Stay cool, don't let this bastard keep getting to you.* Lange knew that he was making a big deal out of what was ultimately an insignificant decision to begin taking the jet airliner down at that particular moment. He also knew that he really wanted to find some way to work comfortably with this copilot because he disliked any need for personal confrontation. "I want to get below the clouds as early as we can. Maybe we can get a visual approach," Lange said as he continued to try to justify, at least to himself, his mild outburst.

"A visual approach? To Chicago? You must be making a joke, right?"

"No," Lange answered, after taking another deep breath to control himself. Even though this particular copilot's reputation had long preceded him, Lange was still taken aback – shocked, actually – by the young man's continued outlandish arrogance and belligerence. Just like some of the other captains had told him, there was absolutely no reasonable way to work with Jay Bridges. He was nothing but a son of a bitch. Lange glanced across the Boeing cockpit and saw that the copilot had yet to reach for his microphone. "Request that descent right now, please," Lange ordered again, in as calm a voice as he could muster.

"Whatever you say, boss." Bridges reached for the microphone that hung by his side, slowly raised it to his lips, then pressed the button and began to transmit the request. Bridges had, as usual, been intentionally goading this captain, prodding him, pressing the man's obvious limitations and tolerances the way a deep sea fisherman might toy with a hooked sailfish in order to have it squirm just a little longer. And Bridges knew damn well that he was doing it for the same basic reason – the pure sport of it. Annoying captains was a far more interesting way of spending time in the copilot's seat than endlessly scanning flight instruments. This was especially true if the captain was like Lange – an old man who hardly knew how to fight back. For Bridges, this trip was turning into fun. "Chicago, this is Trans-Continental Seventy-one. We are requesting a descent to ten thousand."

"Roger, Trans-Continental, stand by," a tinny voice answered through the cockpit speaker.

Captain Lange kept his attention totally on the flight instruments in front of him, knowing for certain that if he looked over at his copilot there would be that irritating smirk on his face. That would be another frustration that he wouldn't know how to handle. Thank God this was the last segment of today's series of trips and that it was already well into darkness – in the dimly lit cockpit, Lange was spared some of the details of the copilot's constant insolence. Yet just as the young man's reputation had suggested, none of the things Bridges had done seemed quite overt enough to

2

merit an official complaint, at least as far as Lange was concerned.

Lange fidgeted with the autopilot button for a few moments, then pressed it. A low two-tone horn sounded once in the cockpit, to announce that the autopilot had been disengaged. Lange then began to hand-fly the Boeing 737 jetliner, his fingers gently massaging the plastic angles of the control wheel while he held the airliner level at its cruise altitude and airspeed.

The jet was gliding effortlessly through a smooth deck of solid clouds; the world outside the cockpit windows was a constant veil of black. For a few moments, Lange allowed his disquieted thoughts to subside as he sat mesmerised by the very familiar pattern of what the flight instruments and the sensations through the flight controls were telling him about the condition of the airliner under his command. He could feel the undercurrent of power from the engines as it worked its way through the airframe – the ship's pulse – and his thousands of hours of flight experience told him instinctively that all was routine.

"Trans-Continental Seventy-one, descend and maintain ten thousand. Proceed direct to Chicago Heights," an anonymous voice from air traffic control said through the cockpit speaker.

"Seventy-one's going down to ten thousand, direct to Chicago Heights," Bridges answered laconically into his microphone.

Lange smoothly pulled back the twin jet's throttles and gently nosed the airliner into a smooth descent. Normally, at this point he would have been very involved in the technical aspects of what he was accomplishing – watching the hands on the altimeter unwind methodically, scanning the other panel gauges to be certain that they were indicating precisely what he wanted them to.

Yet tonight, Lange felt that none of those technical variables could keep his attention focused for more than a few seconds at a time. No matter how hard he tried, Lange couldn't shake the intense, gnawing intrusion that the young man who sat beside him had become. *He's just a rotten son of a bitch, he's going to make me commit an error. Then everyone will say that it's my fault, even though this bastard was the cause behind it. Damn.* Being personally to blame for a mistake was something that didn't sit well with Ned Lange – it was something that he dreaded even more than personal confrontation.

The Boeing jet was passing through sixteen thousand feet when Captain Lange finally made up his mind about what he would do next. He was, in his mind, a very reasonable and patient man – a respected senior captain with an impeccable safety record and a reputation to match. He knew that he was considered to be over-cautious, even timid, by some of the copilots – but that was something he could live with. Being held responsible for a personal error was something he could not live with, especially with only twenty-five months to go before retirement.

The decision had been made: Lange now felt an *obligation* to report Bridges – an obligation to his fellow pilots, to his company, the airline's passengers and, most of all, to himself. Bridges' insolence was a constant distraction, and anything that caused Ned Lange to be less than totally focused on his duties was something that he would be compelled to deal with, no matter how unpleasant that task might be.

"Eleven thousand," Bridges mumbled, making one of the many company-required callouts that he considered a ridiculous waste of time. If it were up to Bridges he would, of course, not bother with any of those asinine official technicalities insisted on by men like Captain Lange – rules made by doddering old farts who had long ago forgotten how to fly.

"Thank you," Lange responded automatically. Even though it was within his right to remove the copilot from his trip as soon as they landed in Chicago, Lange decided against anything quite that dramatic – ostensibly for the sake of the company and its ability to maintain the published schedule. Lange decided to suffer along with Bridges as his copilot for the one additional segment they were scheduled to fly tomorrow afternoon – a non-stop from Chicago to Miami. But then he would go directly to Captain Davenport's office and tell the chief pilot that he would not, under any circumstances, fly another trip with Jay Bridges assigned to his cockpit. Lange felt that coming

4

from him, the complaint would undoubtedly get Davenport's full attention.

"Levelling at ten thousand," Bridges announced drily. "You want any altitude lower than this, or is this altitude good enough for you?"

"We'll stay at ten thousand."

"Whatever you say, boss," Bridges responded coolly, once again getting in the last word.

Lange ignored him. Instead, he began to think about the descent and landing at O'Hare, the limousine ride to the hotel and – thank God – the moment when he would have the opportunity to close the door on the young man who had sat next to him today from Miami to Philadelphia, Boston, and now into Chicago. *Bastard*. By the time of their arrival back at Miami tomorrow afternoon, Lange silently vowed that First Officer Jay Bridges would mean nothing to him except a bad memory – and he promised himself that this time he would not back down, something that he was inclined to do. Lange would, no matter what, report Jay Bridges to the chief pilot.

"I won't be going to the hotel with you," Bridges suddenly said, leaning slightly towards the captain while he spoke in a raised voice over the ambient noise in the airliner's cockpit.

"Oh?" As much as Lange didn't want to make unnecessary conversation with this copilot, he wanted to take the long limousine ride to the hotel with him even less. "Is that so?" Lange said, as he raised an eyebrow in the copilot's direction. This bit of information might be good news.

"Be sure to tell the hotel jerk at the front desk that I'll check in later," Bridges announced. "I've got business at the airport."

"Sure thing." Lange smiled for the first time since their midday departure from Miami, then glanced up from his flight instruments and out of the cockpit window. At just that moment the airliner popped out of the enveloping overcast and, lying sprawled ahead of them across the entire width of the windshield, the unending array of lights that was the city of Chicago and its suburbs made itself dramatically evident against the blackness of the night sky and the solid overcast above them.

5

"Tell the hotel that I'll be in some time after midnight – and tell them that they sure as hell better not sell my room, either."

"Right." Lange was by now absolutely beaming; he had the airport lights of O'Hare in sight, his copilot wouldn't be taking the long limousine ride with him to the hotel, and by five o'clock tomorrow afternoon the chief pilot would be getting an official report as to what kind of son of a bitch this young man really was.

"Trans-Continental Seventy-one, cleared for a visual approach, follow the USAir jet on a two mile final," the Chicago air traffic controller transmitted.

"Yeah, okay, follow USAir," Bridges transmitted back in a bored voice.

As Lange steered the Boeing airliner towards a landing, he felt proud of himself for making the decision to report the copilot – a decision that was contrary to his basic nature, but one that he now felt an overwhelming obligation to carry out. Captain Ned Lange was quite certain that he was doing everyone a giant favour; First Officer Jay Bridges was simply too ill-suited to continue being employed as a copilot for Trans-Continental Airlines.

The glare of floodlights across the tarmac created valleys of shadow in and around the parked aircraft on the ramp at Chicago's O'Hare Airport. Trans-Continental First Officer Jay Bridges ambled slowly between the areas of reflected light and the patches of dark shadow between them; he glanced at his expensive gold Rolex one more time, trying to make out the position of the hands in the dim glow that reached the spot where he was.

It was almost midnight, which meant that Zarrillo was now nearly half an hour late. Bridges cursed the man, then glanced around again as he wondered which direction Zarrillo might be coming from when he finally did get around to showing up. *That bastard.* Bridges tilted his flight cap further back on his head while he continued to look around the deserted airport ramp.

Although Trans-Continental leased several gates on the east side of the Terminal B concourse, there were only three aircraft currently parked there: the Boeing 737 that Bridges had flown in from Boston nearly two hours earlier, plus two of the company's DC-9 jets. While Bridges had earlier paced around the nearly empty ramp, company mechanics had moved two Trans-Continental Boeing 727s from the concourse gates to the maintenance hangar on the far side of the field; Bridges expected that the mechanics would be back for the other three airplanes shortly, and he hoped that Zarrillo would show up before they did.

Bridges leaned against an unused baggage cart, taking care that he wasn't getting his pilot's uniform dirty. He took off his flight cap, ran a comb through his styled mane of blond hair, then carefully put his flight cap back on.

The ramp in front of Bridges was completely devoid of personnel since it had been over an hour since the last flight of the night had parked and all the duties associated with that incoming flight had long since been accomplished. Motorised tugs, carts, service trucks and vehicles of all types were parked in various spots; everything on the ramp was motionless, except for a cleaning truck approaching out of the darkness on Bridges' left.

Bridges watched as the truck's headlights swept across the black tarmac. The driver was moving the vehicle ahead slowly. Finally, he swung the big truck around at the rear end of the Boeing 737 and manoeuvred the vehicle carefully to a spot beneath the airliner's rear service door. The truck's engine then revved as the driver engaged the hydraulic lift controls that would raise the body of the vehicle above its frame.

Two sets of large steel scissors driven by gleaming silver hydraulic struts slowly lifted the truck body, raising it high into the night sky. Within half a minute the cleaning truck's body was set at the same height as the airliner's rear service door, held up by the raised steel scissors that were part of the truck frame. At that point, the truck's lights and engine were shut down, with the raised body of the vehicle locked upright in its fully extended position about a dozen feet above the truck's cab and tyres. Once again, the ramp area returned to silence and to relative darkness. Bridges looked at his Rolex: it was now three minutes past twelve. *Where the hell was Zarrillo?*

"Is that you?" came a voice from the other side of the baggage cart that Bridges was leaning against.

Bridges turned. "Nice of you to finally show up, goddamnit." He took a step towards the front of the baggage cart, to meet the shadowy figure that was emerging from the other side. "I'm tired, I need some sleep – I gotta work tomorrow, you know. I gotta fly with that asshole Lange."

"Yeah. I know." Louis Zarrillo stepped out of the darkness and into the dim reflected light from a gang of floods a hundred yards away. "But this is important."

"It better be." Bridges looked at Zarrillo; he, too, was wearing his Trans-Continental pilot's uniform, although Zarrillo's jacket had the captain's four stripes on each sleeve rather than the copilot's three. "What trip are you on?" Bridges asked.

"No trip, I came just to talk to you."

"Then why the costume?" Bridges asked, pointing to Zarrillo's uniform.

"Best way to get past security. Best way to get on the ramp." Zarrillo took off his flight cap and wiped away some sweat from his forehead, then shifted his weight nervously from foot to foot as he periodically glanced around in the darkness. He put his flight cap back on. "We don't need to be challenged by some ramp guy trying to make believe he's a cop."

"Hell, we don't need to be *here*, either." Bridges took another step forward. "We could've met anyplace – a bar, a restaurant, a whorehouse . . ."

"Listen, this is important," Zarrillo said again, edging himself a half step backwards to be even deeper into the shadows. "There's problems we've got to talk about. Big problems."

"Big fucking deal." Bridges gave a low, contemptuous laugh. "You always were a chicken-shit – if you didn't have me to hold your hand, you never would've made your first score."

"But there's problems. I . . . I'm not too sure exactly what we should . . ."

"What kind of goddamn problems?" Bridges took one more step forward, around the edge of the baggage cart

8

and out into the open ramp area beside it. "What are you stalling about – so far, you haven't told me a . . ."

From behind Bridges, a man in a dark suit stepped out of the darker shadows and swung down with a metal pipe. The end of the pipe caught Bridges on the left side of his skull; his flight cap was flung aside and rolled several feet across the ramp. As he was hit, the copilot's legs instantly buckled and he fell heavily to the ground.

"Pick him up. Put him in there," the man in the dark suit commanded as he stepped back into the deeper shadows alongside the baggage cart.

"Jesus Christ!" Zarrillo stood over Bridges' body, shifting his glance between where the young copilot lay on the tarmac and where the man who had hit him with the pipe was standing in the shadows. "You were supposed to talk to him!"

"There's no talking to him. We already knew that. Pick him up."

"I . . ."

"Pick him up."

Although Zarrillo did hesitate for another moment, he finally complied. He always did. Zarrillo grabbed hold of Bridges' body, then dragged him over to where he'd been instructed.

"Lay him on that baggage cart. Then get his hat."

"Why?"

"Do what I tell you, dammit. Get in beside him," the man said, ignoring the question as he stepped towards the motorised tug that was connected to the cart. "We're taking a ride."

"Where to?"

The man in the dark suit didn't answer. Instead, he slid into the driver's seat of the motorised tug. The tug's engine was started. The man waited a moment until Zarrillo had retrieved the copilot's flight cap and had come back. As soon as Zarrillo sat down legs-astride on the baggage cart, the man began to drive the tug and cart slowly forward.

From where Zarrillo sat on the baggage cart, he could see that they were moving towards the company Boeing jet that was still on the ramp. Zarrillo glanced down at Bridges

9

and could see, even in the dim light, that the copilot was breathing deeply, heavily. *Stupid bastard, he never knows when to shut up.*

There was a gash on Bridges' head, but he didn't seem to be bleeding too badly. *Maybe now you'll learn.* Zarrillo fumbled with Bridges' flight cap while he thought the situation over; he had long agreed: Bridges was always shooting off his mouth, and he could be jeopardising everything. Evidently, what Bridges needed was to be *shown* that they were serious, that they weren't going to keep taking his shit any more.

The motorised tug jerked to a stop. "Take his body off. Lay it over there," the man in the driver's seat said in a low voice.

Zarrillo blinked. He had just been instructed to lay Bridges on the flat bed beneath the raised portion of the cleaning truck. "Why?"

"It'll look like an accident."

"Oh." Zarrillo slowly nodded. "I see." If anyone were to ask, Bridges would be able to say that he slipped and fell on to the truck bed. That would be his explanation for the cut on his head.

The man in the dark suit said nothing. Finally, he pointed again. "Put him over there. *Right now.*"

Zarrillo glanced around him. The ramp area was still deserted, although he could hear the cleaning crew inside the Boeing as they moved around, the shifts of tone in their muffled voices indicating that they were occasionally going into the raised truck bed to get supplies and then back into the airliner's cabin. "Okay."

Zarrillo tucked the copilot's flight cap under his arm so he wouldn't drop it, then dragged Bridges' body towards the truck. Zarrillo then pulled Bridges across the iron beams that made up the basic frame that the truck's hydraulic lifters were attached to. By the time he had pulled the copilot's body into a position that looked as if the copilot might have stumbled and hit his head, the young man's uniform was covered with grease and oil from the truck frame. "When they find him, he's going to be one unhappy guy," Zarrillo said as he stepped back towards the tug. "I bet that grease on his uniform will get to him more than the bump on his head." Zarrillo didn't believe what he was saying, but he had to say something – the sound of his own voice was comforting.

"Get in."

Zarrillo jumped into the motorised tug just as it began to speed away towards the deeper shadows. "Christ, slow this damned thing down."

"Shut up." The man at the wheel jerked the tug to a stop as he heard the first of several new sounds from behind him.

"What's that?" Zarrillo turned. To his horror, he finally began to realise what was about to happen, what he had become an accomplice to. "God . . . no . . ."

"Be quiet. Enjoy the sight of your problems being solved."

The two men sat in the dark shadows of the ramp as, in the distance, the cleaning truck's engine revved up again and the powerful hydraulic struts began to lower the twin steel scissors from their raised position. The truck bed was slowly descending and, in a matter of moments, it began to crush the unconscious body of First Officer Jay Bridges.

1

I knew that I would be indulging myself when I stepped over to the stereo and pressed the power-on button. The *Pagliacci* compact disc was in my right hand, an unhealthy mixture of mostly gin and a little tonic in my left. I was already suitably mellow without quite being drunk – and that was the perfect condition for seeing Susan, as far as I was concerned.

Susan would probably bitch at me a little if I got too maudlin, but, like I said, I felt particularly mellow tonight. It was at about that time that I decided, what the hell, that I should go all the way and wallow in unmitigated self-indulgence – it wasn't something that I did very often, so maybe one night of it would be good for the soul.

The melodic tones of the opera's prologue filled the townhouse. I pushed the volume up a step – it was only seven o'clock in the evening, too early to worry about offending any of the neighbours. I sat in the far corner of the couch, in the seat that looked out into the darkness of the heavy tropical vegetation behind my unit.

By Miami standards, the weather lately had been damn cool, even for February. After four years in south Florida, any temperature lower than seventy-five degrees Fahrenheit seemed outright frigid to me – and tonight's low would be down below forty. The sliding glass door to the balcony was shut, to keep out the chilling breeze. I toyed with the idea of turning on the furnace, but then decided against it. The heat from the kitchen was enough to keep the townhouse habitable and, besides, I was getting a certain amount of satisfaction out of experiencing mild bouts of personal deprivation. Humans are strange animals.

Susan was due at any moment. I had already finished what could laughingly be called the dinner preparations, considering my limited kitchen abilities. The filets had been seasoned and placed on the platter to be taken out to the balcony grill; the salad was tossed, the green beans were defrosted and in a pot on the stove. At least the wine – a moderate Saint-Emilion – was a little closer to what I assumed Susan was rapidly becoming accustomed to. The bottle was open and breathing, whatever that meant. That was one of those rituals of life I continued to pay homage to, even though I had never seen a shred of evidence that it actually mattered.

Life's a bitch, I mused, in a tone and timbre that melded with the rich operatic singing from the stereo. Placido Domingo – I had seen him at the Met last year – was at that moment waxing lyrical about being wronged by his wife Nedda. It was a sensation that, tonight, I particularly identified with.

Fact was, Leoncavallo's character Canio had more courage than I did because at least he was able to get himself into a state of pure outrage. Even to the point of murder. All I could do was stare out at the shivering palms, drink gin and feel like shit. It was dumb, I knew it was dumb, and I knew that I should stop it. Usually, I did. Not tonight, though. I deluded myself with the thought that my self-indulgence was a personal display of gamesmanship that I could turn off at will. Like hell I could.

The doorbell rang just as Domingo began the aria "*Vesti la giubba*". Timing was perfect. I took my gin with me to the door, as a sort of shield.

Susan was as beautiful as ever. No, that's not true – she was more beautiful than I had ever seen her before. Each time I saw her, that was the feeling I had. Susan smiled up at me, her soft, radiant expression complemented by the luxurious texture of the high-collared black fur coat that she wore. What little resolve I had to remain stoic was blown away by the cool evening breeze.

"Hello, Jack."

"Winter has arrived." I put my arm against hers, ostensibly to fondle the expensive fur.

"Neither one of us could take the cold very well," Susan said as she kissed me on the cheek.

"A lot of people wouldn't consider a forty degree night very cold." I had been rehearsing any one of a hundred clever things to say when I opened the door, but they'd been washed away by the gin.

"A lot of people would be wrong." Susan smiled again, and this time gave that little tilt of her head that showed that she didn't care what anyone thought about anything. She was as independent a person as I had ever met, which was probably why I was still so damned dependent on her. "May I come in?" she asked.

"Why do you think you have to ask?" I stepped aside and she brushed past me, the odour of her perfume filling the hallway. I followed her into the living room, took her coat, then walked over to the bar to make her a drink. Without asking, I put together a vodka gimlet for her, then added more ice, gin and a touch of tonic to my own glass. I headed back to the couch. "Here."

Susan sipped the drink thoughtfully, as if she were sampling a rare concoction. "Perfect, as always. You're the only one who can make these things right."

"That's something." I shrugged, then stood silently. I didn't want to sound like a crybaby. Actually, I was usually accused of being just the opposite – cool, calculating, level-headed. But not around Susan. Being in love with a woman who has elected to take the high road does, I rationalised, give a guy a few liberties with his normal disposition and modus operandi.

"How's the tennis?" Susan asked, as she spotted one of my rackets in a far corner.

"Good. My forehand's getting better. I beat Max last week – solidly, too. Two sets. I'm starting to be able to drive short balls pretty well." For the three years we were married, Susan and I played a lot of tennis, especially after we moved to Miami where we played year round. When she decided to leave, tennis became my main reason for getting up in the morning. It still was.

"Give my regards to Max," Susan said. She sipped at her drink. She was wearing a black dress with a high, loose collar. She had on diamond earrings, several gold chains, and just a hint of make-up. Her dark brown hair was pulled back, with a few strands hanging across her forehead. Pure sex. "I always knew you would beat Max," she added.

15

"Really?" I was acting like a school kid, I wanted to hear more compliments. I sat on the edge of my seat. "Why?"

"Because tennis is a mental game." Susan edged a little closer to me on the couch. "Because you, Jack Sawyer, have the best, most deliberate mind that I've ever come across."

"You're just saying that because it's true."

Susan ignored me and continued, as she usually did. "You play tennis pretty well, but you *think* even better. That's why I've always liked you, and that's why I knew you would eventually beat the hell out of Max and just about anyone else in that crowd. When your skill level gets to even a fraction of theirs, you'll beat them consistently because you're able to out-think them consistently."

"Thank you, Mrs Sawyer." I had surreptitiously slipped her full name into the conversation, just the way a teenage boy sitting in a dark movie theatre might slip his hand around his date's shoulder. Susan was still using my last name, our married name, because she said that she liked the way it sounded; besides, we weren't actually divorced yet, we were only separated.

"And how is work?" she asked, changing the subject.

"The business is coming along." I nodded towards a desk in the opposite corner, the current location of the pretentiously titled Sawyer Investigating Group. All it was at the moment was a heap of bills, mostly for stationery and telephone. When Floyd was killed in an Interstate pile-up just before Christmas, I inherited the files from his private-eye agency simply by taking them – files that were hardly generating enough income for him, a sixty-six year old bachelor who figured that a double-wide house trailer was opulent enough living for any man. Since then, the business had taken a distinct downhill turn.

"Are you doing any flight instructing?" Susan asked. She glanced around the living room of what used to be our home, taking in the details. Hardly anything had changed, except that she had left.

"Yes," I answered directly, without any particular pride. "Part time, at Opa-Locka. I pick up a few bucks and keep my hand in at it, that's all." The piloting part of my life was, as far as I was concerned, behind me. It was another

16

aspect – like my marriage to Susan – that hadn't worked out the way I had expected. Five years ago I was a senior copilot based out of New York for Air East, I was dating Susan and setting up the details for living happily ever after. Early last year Air East went bankrupt. Last summer Susan told me that she *liked* me but didn't *love* me. Last month I turned forty-two. I prayed that bad things really did come in packages of three, because I had really had my fill of late.

"I'm glad you're still flight instructing. It's good to keep it up." Susan sounded genuinely concerned because she was; truthfully, I knew that she really did like me and did want me to do well. Sometimes I wished that I could find something to fault in her, because I supposed that it would make my life a great deal easier. I took a slug of my drink while I listened to the final bars of *Pagliacci*. "The comedy is over," I said as the recording ended.

"What?"

"*La commedia è finita*. The last line of the opera – the comedy is over."

"Oh." Susan looked at the now-silent stereo thoughtfully. "I see." She nodded. "I remember you explaining this story-line to me. The clown, right?"

"Yes. *Pagliacci* – clowns."

"It was very pretty, very dramatic."

"It was. Still is. Some things never change." My interest in classical music and opera was something Susan never really caught on to, although she had tried to appreciate it. On occasion she would indicate that something seemed pretty or was intriguing to her, so I guess it actually was. Susan never lied. She was the most straightforward human being I had ever met.

The gin buzzed through my head. In some ways, it helped me to fumble around with small talk for longer than I might have imagined possible. I hadn't seen Susan for over three months, yet somehow the last time we were together seemed like no more than a few days ago. I put on a CD of Beethoven violin and piano sonatas, then took the filets out to the gas grill on the balcony while Susan finalised things in the kitchen. We sat down to eat. "To your health," I said as we raised the twin glasses of Saint-Emilion – I knew enough to keep the toasting innocuous.

"That, and something else, too," Susan replied. She held her glass raised until I reached across the table with mine. The glasses touched. I could tell from her expression that she was about to say more, that she was about to actually *tell* me something. It was, most probably, the main reason that she had requested that we have dinner together.

"What else?" I asked obligingly, seeing that she wanted me to.

"To your new car." Susan retrieved a piece of paper from the floor beneath her chair, then laid it on the table. "This is the bill of sale. You owe me a dollar."

"I don't have a dollar," I answered reflexively while I ran her surprise announcement through my befuddled thought processes. I had instantly understood what it was all about; title to her BMW, the one I had bought for her two years before.

"BMWs go well here in Coconut Grove. Lots better than the wreck I left you with."

"Nothing wrong with the Ford. It goes forward, backward, all the customary directions. I'm happy with it." I frowned, more out of indecision than for any other reason. Susan had said from the first day she left that as soon as she hooked up with one of the men she had her eye on, then she would get him to buy her a car. That would release our BMW to someone far more deserving. Me. My gut reaction, of course, was to tear up the bill of sale and throw it in her face. If it had been any other woman, I might have done just that. I knew that the odds on my doing that with Susan were somewhere around minus ten. Still, I did have enough pride to want to continue with my resistance. "Like I said, I don't have a dollar."

"Let's not argue about this. This was our deal from the beginning."

"It was *your* deal," I protested, although hardly convincingly. "Besides, how can you be so sure that you're getting a new car?"

She reached for her handbag, took out a set of keys and dropped them on the table. Rubber-coated keys, denoting

18

expensive vehicle. Rubber keys don't clatter when they hit a table, like my Ford keys do – they thump instead. The sound that the dropped keys had made had melded well with the violin interlude at that moment coming from the stereo. "A new Mercedes sports car," Susan announced.

"In your name?"

"Of course."

"What colour?"

"Red."

"Red. Naturally. No question about it. That's fitting. I should've guessed."

"Don't be too catty." Susan smiled; she always allowed me that much, that I could make references to her being a whore if I wanted to. It always amazed me how much she really didn't care what anyone thought of her. Not anyone, me included.

"Who gave you this new *blitzkrieg* machine?" I asked, with more anger in my voice than I would have predicted.

"A name that wouldn't mean anything. Names are unimportant." Susan took a deep breath, then looked at me plaintively. She was once again going to try to make me understand, which we both knew would not be an easy task. Impossible, actually. "There's nothing new that I can tell you," she began.

"Then maybe you shouldn't begin." I glanced down at the paper that she had put on the table and, all at once, I realised why I didn't want the BMW back. I didn't want it back because while she still had it, she had something of *ours*. If she took her name off the title and gave the car back to me, that would be one less tie that we had to each other, one less thread to bind myself to her. Sick, sick, sick. I should have my goddamn brain cut out or, better yet, my heart.

"Of all the men that I've liked in my life, I've liked you the most."

"Thanks," I responded coolly. Inside, my guts were throbbing.

"You know what I mean, and you know that it's true. You also know that the other part of me – what we've both labelled as my lacking – is a fact, too. I've just never been in love with

19

anybody, not in the way people talk about being in love. I thought once that perhaps I was in love with you, but time has shown both of us that I was wrong. Dead wrong. You were the closest to me, but I still wasn't in love with you."

"You didn't give it enough time," I said in a neutral voice.

"I gave it too much time." Susan picked up her wine glass and drained it. I reached across the table with the bottle of Saint-Emilion and filled her glass again. Château Labrie, '77 – I should have bought something better. "Maybe if I had left sooner," Susan continued, "then I wouldn't have hurt you as much as I did. That's my biggest regret."

"I'll live."

"Of course you'll live. Both of us will live. It's a painful experience, but it's for the best for both of us. You and I will always be friends. I'm sorry that you're still in love with me, and I wish that I were in love with you – but that doesn't change anything."

"Are you enjoying yourself with this guy?" I pointed to the rubber keys on the table. *La commedia è finita*. The comedy was definitely over. I wondered how Leoncavallo might have melded the concept of a set of rubberised Mercedes keys into *Pagliacci*.

"Don't get mad," Susan said.

Evidently, my face was too easy to read, at least for her. "I'm not mad," I lied. I had suddenly become mad as hell – a healthy sign, really – although the bad news was that I could already feel my swells of anger begin to ebb away. That had always been one of my basic problems with Susan, that I couldn't stay mad at her for any length of time. That, plus the fact that I was still so damned much in love with her. Why in God's name were human beings subject to this kind of nonsensical emotion? It was a mystery to me.

"I've done something else for you, too," Susan said. She pushed her green beans around on the plate, eyeing them carefully, occasionally sequestering the next one she had selected for the trip up to her mouth. I could tell from her eating pace that she was going to leave at least half her food. There would be no clean plate award for Susan tonight. "But the other thing I've done for you is no big

20

deal," she continued, after she had swallowed the next green bean from her designated sequence.

"I've got lots undone. Every little bit helps."

"I suppose that's true." Susan took another sip from her Saint-Emilion, this time as a cover gesture while she mulled over exactly how she was going to broach whatever was on her mind. Finally, she spoke. "I had an opportunity to recommend your investigating business to a man I met at a party. He promised that he'd call you to set up an interview."

"This isn't the Mercedes-man, is it?" Even while I asked the question, I could feel my face flush – a combination of anxiety and anger. I certainly needed to get some investigating business pretty soon or I was going to wind up very thin; on the other hand, I didn't really think that I could be extremely professional towards the man who was Susan's current interest. If I did do some work for this creep, it would probably be best that I not bring a loaded gun into the same room that he was in.

"No." Susan grinned. "Not him." She had anticipated my question, and was obviously happy that she had the proper answer. "I did meet this potential client at a party in Palm Beach that my, ah, friend had given," she continued, "but that was the only connection. The client's name is Elmer Woodruff." Susan beamed at me, tipping her hand that she had saved the best part for last. "Woodruff is a Vice President for Trans-Continental Airlines – he's the airline's most senior executive here in Miami."

"Oh." I sat in a stupor, not knowing quite what to make of it. The final moments of a Beethoven sonata were playing; the tempo had picked up markedly, the violin carrying the essence of the lilting melody while the crisply voiced piano provided dramatic background. I waited until the score had ended before I opened my mouth again. "This doesn't have anything to do with me getting an airline job, with me flying for them, does it?"

"Just the opposite."

"Good. I've got no intention of getting my name on the bottom of another seniority list, of locking myself in a cockpit with people that I don't like, to fly airplanes I don't basically enjoy, so that I can fly to places that

I don't care about." I was bitter about having spent so much of my life in a frustrated attempt to have a career as an airline pilot. Deregulation, bankruptcies, seniority limitations, inter-company animosities, government meddling, the countless bureaucratic restrictions, plus a list of other aggravations had long ago turned that job totally sour for me.

"I know how you feel." Susan put down her fork and pushed her plate aside. She reached across the table and took my hand. "As soon as Elmer Woodruff started talking to me, I could tell that he was looking for *you* – the only thing was that he didn't know your name yet."

"Did you tell him that we're still married?" I asked. "Technically speaking, of course." I squeezed Susan's hand in return; it was soft and warm. Her fingers lay malleably against mine.

"Actually, yes."

Our eyes locked on to each other's. "What did he say about that?"

"I told him about us since he already knew what my last name was. Besides, I think it kind of intrigued him that a separated couple would be looking out for each other's interests."

"It intrigues *me*."

"The talk about you, me, our marriage, was what got the conversation with Woodruff going. But what made the ultimate difference to him was *you* – your qualifications, your experience, your credentials."

"Did you tell him about my qualifications with green beans?" I nodded towards her pushed-aside dinner plate, a scattering of isolated beans among chunks of unwanted filet. "You really should eat all your dinner – beautiful women in red Mercedes are starving in China."

"Woodruff should call at any time now, to set up the interview," Susan continued as she ignored my verbal digressions. She did, however, keep holding my hand. For a grown man to be thankful for that was a pitiful display on my part, and I loathed myself for it. After a short pause, Susan spoke again. "He was sketchy with what his problem was, but evidently it requires some discreet investigation concerning some of his flight crews."

22

"Wonderful." The news was good, but all I could think of at that moment was Susan. Her perfume floated across the short distance between us; she held her head at a slight angle and the long lines of her neck were absolutely intoxicating. The final Beethoven sonata had finished playing and the disc player had shut itself down. We sat in absolute silence for a minute or two, and all I could hear was my own heart beating. *You're losing control of yourself.* But the liquor that I had already consumed had made me care even less about losing control. I knew that at that moment I had two basic paths to choose from – one that was measured, sane and sober, the other far less so. A little voice inside me told me to stop, but a far bigger voice inside me told the little voice to drop dead. "How about an after-dinner drink?"

"Even though I haven't finished my green beans?"

"Especially so."

"You've talked me into it." Susan gently untwined her fingers from my grasp.

"You get the drinks, I'll put on music."

Susan steered herself towards the bar. "What would you like?" she called back.

"A surprise," I retorted, a double entendre at the very least. While she was fumbling with glasses, I impulsively pulled out an Ella Fitzgerald disc. I now could see quite clearly where I was headed, but I also knew that I couldn't make myself stop – like an out-of-control skier hurtling down a narrow, nearly vertical slope. I put the Ella Fitzgerald CD into the player just as Susan came up behind me with the drinks. What the hell, if I was going to indulge myself I might as well do a complete job of it.

"Amaretto on the rocks," Susan announced as she handed mine over.

"Nectar of the Italian gods." Ella was singing Gershwin selections. The first cut was "Someone to Watch Over Me". Ella's velvet voice filled the townhouse, and also filled the open spaces inside my head that weren't already occupied by gin, Saint-Emilion and now Amaretto. After another sip I put my Amaretto down and stepped closer to Susan. Susan took one more sip of her drink, then put her own glass down.

"Jack." She put her hands up on my shoulders and we

swayed gently, at quarter tempo, to the music. "You've got to let me say what I'm going to say," Susan announced softly, "and without interrupting me."

"No."

"Yes." She kept her hands on my shoulders while she pulled herself closer. "I don't love you, but I sure as hell like you an awful damn lot." She paused as Ella's song ended. We waited for the next one to begin. It was "Embraceable You"; Susan squeezed me a little tighter, this had always been one of her favourites. "I like everything about you, your curly hair, that crooked tooth of yours, the way you think and feel and look and talk."

"So why don't we . . ."

"Stop. Don't interrupt." She put on a mildly scolding expression, which melted back to her smile a few moments later. "I like you better than the guy who gave me the Mercedes." She stopped again, this time to gauge the effect.

My demeanour remained absolutely non-partisan, in stark contrast to the turmoil in my insides; my interior regions were a quaint blend of fear, love, lust, and a good measure of drunkenness. I was dreading what she was going to say next and, at the very same time, I couldn't wait to hear what it would be.

"So this is where it's really at," Susan continued. She, too, was obviously feeling the drinks. "I'm looking around, seeing what's out there, seeing what I can do, seeing what I can wind up with. Hell, if I'm not in *love* with anyone, then why shouldn't I try to get the best deal that I can, huh?"

"Like your red car?" I had, at best, mixed emotions about this dialogue.

"Exactly." Susan sighed. "I know it sounds horrible, but it's something like – career planning." All at once she began to laugh; even to her, her explanation had sounded pretty ludicrous.

"It's hard to take you seriously when you're obviously not even taking yourself seriously," I responded in an all-knowing tone. I was, once again, intending to get ultimate mileage out of that freshman psychology course I had taken several hundred years before.

"I take this seriously, I just can't explain it correctly when

24

I've had so much to drink," Susan answered. She kept her hands on me, her eyes riveted to mine. "But what I do know for certain is that the last thing I want is to hurt you any more than I already have. That's why I try to stay away from you, so that you don't hurt any more."

"I don't hurt any less when you're away."

Long pause. "Maybe." With that, Susan pulled herself a little closer.

"The idea I'm getting at this moment is that you're afraid that you're leading me on. That no matter what, there's no long-term reason for me to be encouraged. Am I right?"

"Sort of."

"The extension of that logic," I said, in my most analytical tone, pretending to be discussing a Mister John Doe rather than my aching, vulnerable self, "is that if I'm weak and give in, then I'll hate myself in the morning?"

"In a manner of speaking."

"Oh." I made a mental note to tell my academician friends that someone should do a doctoral thesis on sexual role reversals in the latter part of the twentieth century – I wanted to know if I was the only one experiencing this sort of thing, or if male-as-jilted-party had become as common as Influenza B. "I see what you're saying." I nodded my head slowly, thoughtfully. "But since I'm a big boy, why don't we just let me make up my own mind. Is that okay?"

Susan shrugged, then smiled. "You're the boss." She was hanging on tightly when Ella Fitzgerald began to sing another Gershwin selection, this one with an apt title: "Who Cares?" While the refrain line was sung, Susan and I were busily knotting ourselves more firmly together – my arms were tightening around her waist, while her hands were toying with the nape of my neck. Even though the music was still on, we both had already ended the façade of dancing. We were standing rock-still, our faces inches apart.

We stared at each other for quite some time before we finally kissed. Our lips fitted together like two proper pieces of a puzzle, reminding me how damned well we had always done that sort of thing. In short order we had steered each other to the couch, and both of us were working hard at stopping ourselves from pressing ahead too quickly. Hands, arms, bodies, smooth skin, warmth. We fumbled with buttons, snaps and zippers, helping each other with our clothes until we were both naked, the garments lying scattered around us like shell casings from a gun battle.

Susan pressed me down on my back, and I willingly complied. "Jack, I can't wait any more," Susan said as she manoeuvred around until she was just the way we both wanted her to be. It was soon obvious that the depth of our passion would easily outlast the Ella Fitzgerald disc. It was a good thing that I had had the foresight to set the disc player to automatic repeat.

2

It would be a cliché to say that I hated myself in the morning but, unfortunately, it was true. Susan had left around 3 a.m. in a taxi – actually, a limousine – that she had made previous arrangements with. The Mercedes-man would be paying for that, too, I expected.

I had given my reluctant goodbyes at the doorstep, then resisted the temptation to go out and kick the tyres on my new-to-me BMW. Instead, I had one more drink, then went directly to bed. I slept fitfully, with dreams about being passed at high speed by a big red Mercedes. So much for the subtleties and innuendoes of the subconscious.

I woke up in a cold sweat at seven fifteen. I decided that my psyche had been cleansed enough for one night, thank you, so I crawled out of bed and went through a full morning ritual in hopes that a shave, shower and breakfast would cheer me up. The eggs stared back at me in mocking contention, and I could, I swear, hear them snickering whenever I turned to pour coffee. The little voice in me was scolding me unmercifully about being an absolute fool the night before, while the big voice who had driven me to it was conspicuous in its absence. Evidently, the big voice only came out late at night, under the prodding of alcohol. That was good to know, although I wondered if I ever actually *learned* anything from these kinds of experience.

After breakfast I sat at my desk and rummaged through a short but growing stack of unpaid bills, then shoved them aside. The previous weekend I had finished my only current job – a domestic surveillance – which I had wrapped up when the suspect-husband had, in fact, done his shuffling around town. One roll of film shot past my camera's telephoto lens and the assignment was done. Now, nothing. I sat quietly for a few moments then glanced over at my answering machine.

27

I was surprised to see that the red light was blinking – there was a call on it.

I punched the buttons and listened. Elmer Woodruff, the high muck of Trans-Continental Airlines. He had called the night before, some time between the Saint-Emilion and the Amaretto. He wanted me to call him this morning at his office, any time after eight. It was 8.06, so I dialled his number. Two rings later, Woodruff himself answered. I was impressed.

It was short and sweet. Woodruff told me that he might be needing a private investigator who understood the piloting side of the airline business. If I was interested I should immediately haul my ass out to his office for a discussion – although, to his credit, he did explain that last part in slightly more civilised terms. Deciding that playing hard to get might not be the best tactic at that particular point, I told him that I'd be on the way before he heard the telephone click. He said that would be okay.

But then I dallied by dialling one other number. "Max," I said, not needing to identify myself to the powerhouse that I played tennis with at least twice a week, "I need you to sell my car."

"The Ford?"

"Yes. Put it on your lot, give me whatever you think I should have out of it after it sells." Apart from being a decent-yet-muscle-bound tennis player, Max had the ultimate persona of a double-dealing used car salesman. But for his close friends, he suspended his normal behaviour patterns and became totally and scrupulously honest. To those who knew him, his occasional bouts of honesty were a display of affection that could bring tears to our eyes.

"That Ford ain't worth much. I'll do my best. You gonna be needing another car?"

"No. Susan was here last night, she gave me back the BMW."

"No fooling?"

"Yes, no fooling." I was getting restless, Elmer Woodruff was waiting. "I need you to pick the Ford up at my place, the keys will be under the front mat. I'll sign the paperwork at the courts tonight."

"Okay. But then you gotta tell me how you got the BMW back from Susan."

"Sure," I answered. I hung up, wondering what in hell I could say to make the BMW deal sound a little more palatable to my macho friends. I shrugged, then headed outside.

It was a cloudless sky and still a bit chilly. The forecast for today was clear and breezy with a high in the seventies. It was the kind of weather where people in the north think they've died and gone to heaven, while Florida residents whine and snivel at how crummy Mother Nature is treating them of late. Position, as they say, determines perspective.

I slid a key under the old Ford's front mat, then turned to the BMW. The white 735i sat gleaming in the morning sun; Susan had even had the car washed and waxed for me. For a moment I wondered if her Mercedes friend had helped her. Not his style; his chauffeur probably did it while he and Susan sipped apéritifs on the veranda.

I unlocked the door to the BMW and slid inside. On the centre console were three new sets of compact discs: the operas *Rigoletto* and *Carmen*, and Tchaikovsky Symphonies numbers Four, Five and Six. Attached to them was a note from Susan which read, "Listen to these CDs *on the way* to jobs! Get inspired! Work hard! Be successful!" Okay, fair enough. I unwrapped the Tchaikovsky set of CDs first, wrestling with the bubble-plastic it was wrapped in for an annoying amount of time until I finally got the discs out. To my mind, a man would be rich enough when he could hire someone else to fight his battles with modern packaging. Finally, I started the BMW, slipped the CD into the player, and took off towards Miami International Airport.

The Coconut Grove section of Miami was a strange blend of extremes, rich and poor, historic and modern. The east end of the Grove was artsy-craftsy and expensive as hell; the west end was poor and black. The townhouse Susan and I had bought was geographically halfway. I wheeled around the tight streets in the BMW to the accompaniment of Peter Ilich Tchaikovsky's first movement of the Fourth Symphony. The single theme that dominated the Fourth Symphony was stated quickly by the horns and trumpets, and the BMW's marvellous custom sound system – a radio, a CD player and a powerful amplifier coupled to seven speakers – picked up all the nuances. Thank you, Susan, I managed to say to myself, in spite of the thoughts about what she might be doing on the veranda with the Mercedes-man. Compared to the radio I had in the Ford, this sound system was the difference between a casual stroll and a four minute mile.

I turned north on 37th Avenue. The traffic was light, and the 735i jumped nimbly between the packs of cars as I quickly got accustomed to it again. Responsive steering, marvellous acceleration. No wonder it was the official yuppie staff car. Miami International Airport loomed ahead, and I concentrated on working myself towards the building where Woodruff said his office was.

Trans-Continental's administration office was near their hangar at the northwest corner of the field. I parked, then took my shoulder-holstered .38 pistol out and locked it in the car's glove compartment – there was no sense tempting the airline's security personnel into a shootout at OK Corral. I then turned to the BMW's internal security system to punch in a code, just like I used to do. I started to put the digits of my birth date into the machine but then stopped, realising that those digits were exactly what someone else – Susan – would assume I would be utilising to disable the BMW's ignition system electronically. Using our birth dates was our old method.

But then I stopped myself again, realising that *Susan* was the one who had voluntarily brought the car back to me – which meant that she probably had no designs on stealing it. Then I paused one more time as I grudgingly admitted to myself that if Susan even *hinted* at wanting the car back, then I would probably give it to her anyway. Crazy, man. I shook my head in self-disgust, but then punched in my birth date digits all the same. It was, I swore, my final act of unrequited love for the day. I would now make every effort to put Susan out of my mind.

I walked slowly towards the entrance of the administration building. Behind the administration building was the Trans-Continental hangar, and alongside that overpowering edifice of non-architecture was one of their Boeing 737 jets. The airplane had just been pushed outside and was in the process of being towed to the terminal building.

The morning sun danced off the airliner's silver wings and tail; the multi-hued red strip along the length of the fuselage provided a pleasant contrast. It was a neat-looking machine – and exactly the same model of Boeing jet that I had flown for Air East before that grossly mismanaged company had elected to take its financial swan dive.

"Woodruff – I've got an appointment," I said to the ancient pelican who guarded the double doors to the inner sanctum. After giving my name, rank and serial number, the hired cop had me cool my heels while he telephoned upstairs to discover if I really would be allowed in. I spent my waiting time thanking God that I no longer worked for an airline.

"Elevator to the third floor, end of the corridor, room 301," the old man grunted after he had laid down the telephone.

"Right." I tried to work on my mental attitude all the way up the elevator and down the corridor. Positive imaging, they say, can do wonders. But my thoughts kept drifting back to last night and how I had literally held Susan in my hands, in spite of my resolution not to let it happen. What I needed, I knew, was a job to immerse myself in and, maybe, a little more self-control.

Room 301 was the last room on the left – the corner office, of course. The outer door was open and an attractive blonde sat at a big desk. Behind her was another door, the one behind which Mister Big undoubtedly resided. The blonde gave me a once-over as I walked in. I smiled self-consciously. "Jack Sawyer. I've got an appointment."

"Yes. Mr Woodruff is expecting you." The blonde rose from her seat and stuck out her hand. "I'm Tracy Cummings. Executive Secretary."

"Nice to meet you," I mumbled. I took her hand in mine, all the while trying to decide whether to shake it, squeeze it, hold it or kiss it. I hated modern moments like these because they're always no-win – if you give them back a wet fish then they say you're a wimp, if you pump 'em solid they say you're a macho creep, and if you do something in the middle they'll say you have no personality at all. Strictly no-win. I gave her my half-a-flounder, half-a-weight-lifter response and prayed that she wasn't the one who would be doing the hiring.

"You can go right in," she said, pointing to the closed door. "Can I get you some coffee?"

"Would you?" My response came out more as a question than a statement and, even worse, it was a question that could somehow be related to implications of the feminist movement. That was, of course, not actually what I had meant. The blonde laughed, although not long and hard enough to make me feel like a total fool. Tracy's demeanour was my first clue that she might not be heavily steeped in those qualities that made too many of the women I had met since Susan's departure into such a royal pain to deal with. Or was I all too often just reacting to the fact that I was a bachelor again when I really didn't want to be? Probably a little of both. "Could I rephrase myself?"

"If you'd like." Tracy kept smiling.

"I would. What I meant is that I'd be very pleased to have coffee. Just cream, no sugar."

"My pleasure." Tracy took a half step towards the exit. "You'd get coffee for me, wouldn't you?" she suddenly asked, seemingly as a continuation of the joke.

"Get you coffee? No way."

"No?" She now looked a little taken back. A little leery, too.

"No coffee. I'd bring Saint-Emilion."

"Oh. How nice." Her guarded expression faded and her smile reappeared. "In crystal?"

"Pure Baccarat."

"Lovely." Tracy laughed, wholesomely. She was nearly my age, tall, thin, with an oval face and pleasant if not overwhelming beautiful looks. A competent lady – or at least that was the appearance that she had so far exuded. I had, of course, been fooled many times in the past since my judgment in those matters was notoriously weak. "Please tell Mr Woodruff that I'm bringing in more coffee for him, too," she added.

"Right." I watched Tracy leave the room, then turned and opened the door to the inner skunk works of Trans-Continental. As I stepped across the threshold, I tried not to focus on how badly I needed whatever this job might turn out to be.

A bald-headed man occupied the desk in the centre of the office, and he immediately surprised me on two counts; first, by wearing a tight-fitting, open-collared sports shirt, and second, by having his feet up on his desk. I was wearing a navy blue jacket, a burgundy and blue paisley tie and an over-starched Ralph Lauren shirt. Clearly, I had over-dressed. "I'm Jack Sawyer."

"Elmer Woodruff." The man in front of me had not been brought in by central casting because his deep tan, burly features and short, stocky hands made him look more like a sixty year old alligator wrestler than a corporate high executive. Woodruff was a full head shorter than me, but he gave the impression of having bellied up to more bars than I had to date, or probably ever would. If I were an alligator and I saw him coming, I'd head the other way. "Jack, you call me Elmer, okay?"

"Sure thing." We locked our outstretched hands together, and for an instant I thought that he wanted me to Indian-wrestle. Instead, he pumped our hands a few times, then let go – his blonde secretary had probably already let him know that I was under suspicion of being a wimp. "Tracy says that she's bringing you more coffee," I reported, figuring it was okay to use her first name since I was also supposed to use his.

"Good. Sit down."

As I did, Woodruff launched into a narrative about how charming Susan had been, and how refreshing it was to see a divorcing couple who could still be pleasant and objective about each other. I mumbled some reinforcing platitudes here and there, and then said a few things in support of myself as the perfect solution to his problem – whatever in God's name it might be.

"Okay, fine. You've obviously got the proper background for the job."

I nodded affirmatively, to show a high level of self-assurance. Sitting across from Woodruff for a while, my closer inspection of him showed me that I had been wrong about his baldness – Woodruff was not totally bald, he had two thin fields of snow-white hair to trim out the mountainous peak of tanned scalp that rose majestically above his deeply valleyed brow. Rand McNally could learn a few things from this man's features. "So what, specifically, can I do for you?" I asked, sensing all too well that this was not a fellow who intended first to chat about the weather.

"Not a great deal, hopefully."

"Not a good start. I can't make money doing less than a great deal."

"In this case, maybe you can."

"Then, in this case, I might be interested." Our cryptic conversation was brought to a halt by Tracy, who walked into the inner office with two cups of coffee.

Tracy handed Woodruff his coffee first, a large mug of steaming black. She then turned and handed me a smaller mug. "Just cream," she said.

"Thank you," I answered, trying to be smooth, taking the cup from her fingers without removing my eyes from her face.

"You'll have to show me how you do that some time." Tracy nodded towards my fingers, which were wrapped around the mug.

I understood her point. "It's an old family secret. We never watch what we're doing. We never watch what we're saying either, for that matter, as you've already seen. It takes lots of practice."

"I'd bet."

"Okay, down to business." Woodruff swallowed half his hot coffee in one gulp. "This is my problem," he said, facing me, "you tell me what you think."

I sat forward in my chair, trying to give the impression of absolute attentiveness.

"A copilot from our Miami base was killed during his overnight stay in Chicago a few weeks ago. Police are investigating – an accident is their official verdict – but I think it might go deeper than that. What I want is someone to dig around and see if they can find anything. Think you might be interested?"

I gave a go-ahead signal with my hand to indicate that I wanted to hear more, although my heart was already sinking. At best, this seemed like a dead-end job.

"Okay. First, let us tell you something about the victim." Woodruff nodded towards Tracy as he sat back in his chair.

34

Tracy took a file off the corner of his desk and began to read aloud from it. "First Officer Jay Bridges was hired by Trans-Continental three and a half years ago. He was based in Washington DC for the first eight months of his employment, then here in Miami since then. He was a copilot on Boeing 737 equipment. His file is full of derogatories . . ."

"What's that mean?" I interrupted.

"It means he was a son of a bitch," Woodruff chimed in. "Bridges made a science out of being obnoxious. He was widely disliked, to say the very least. He was a so-so pilot, but he was really excellent at being a prick of a human being, especially towards people in authority positions who weren't inclined to fight back very hard. He was always showing off to whoever would tolerate it, driving everybody nuts."

"So how did he stay employed?"

Woodruff leaned forward in his chair, towards me. "And you're supposed to be an ex-airline pilot? Why don't we test your credentials by letting you answer that question for us."

"The union," I answered quickly. I made a mental note not to ask Woodruff any more rhetorical questions. While I knew that airline pilots needed a union to prevent managements from exerting too much profit-oriented influence in the cockpit, I also knew that the unions always became ardent defenders of the lowest common denominator in their ranks. Unless a fellow like Bridges did something that was unquestionably and overwhelmingly against the rules, his foibles – laziness, an anti-company attitude, sloppy work habits – would never get him thrown out the door.

"Go to the head of the class," Woodruff said. He motioned for Tracy to hand him the file, then glanced over it for a moment. After a while, he looked back at me. "Well? What do you think?"

As much as I hated to say it, I figured that I had to. "I can't see what I can do for you. An obnoxious copilot gets killed in Chicago. An unfortunate occurrence, but hardly the bailiwick of a private investigator."

Woodruff snorted, an expression that was half laugh and half a grunt. "But I got a hunch that this is not just an accident." He stopped and stared directly at me. There was

35

no additional response, other than that look of intensity in his eyes.

It was time to make a show of perception, no matter how unsure I might be of what I was about to say. "I can tell that your hunches aren't wrong too often," I said, figuring that flattery was as good a start as any. "It's the coincidence angle, right?"

"Absolutely." Woodruff's face lit up and, as it did, the Grand Canyon on his forehead illustrated a graphic lesson in the theories of plate tectonics. "Of all our pilots to meet with a violent death, Bridges was the king of the probables."

"What was the accident like?" I asked.

While Woodruff explained in gory detail what the lowering of a few thousand pounds of iron and steel can do to a human body lying beneath it, I asked a few additional questions about why Bridges was walking around the ramp in the middle of the night and who was operating the truck's lift controls.

Woodruff's answers supported his position that "accident" seemed like an unusual word for what had occurred in Chicago that night. "Lots of coincidences. A few too many, I would think."

"Yeah, but it's not just that. Not only was Bridges a pain in the ass, but he also showed a few other traits that made me think that this mountain is made out of landfill."

"Like what?"

"Like he lived too damned well, considering his salary. His increase in wealth was sudden, too – within the last year or so. He's had three new cars in twelve months, and just moved to an expensive condo in Lauderdale. He's also been throwing lots of cash around."

"No dead rich uncles lately?"

"No," Tracy said. "None that we could find."

"And tell him what you've heard on the line," Woodruff said, gesturing for Tracy to continue. I knew that the phrase *heard on the line* meant the gossip being bandied around among the line's pilots and flight attendants. This turn in the conversation might also mean that Tracy had once been a flight attendant herself – that was how she still had contacts out there. Yet for a reason I hadn't quite put a finger on yet, Tracy didn't look like the flight attendant type to me.

"This is just rumour, of course," Tracy began. "But for a few months before he was killed, Bridges was hinting around to the few crew members who would still talk to him that he was into some kind of super-smart deal. It was making him rich. Lots of easy cash."

"Naturally."

"Right. Nothing he said was specific," Tracy continued, "but there were enough general hints that it caused a few of the crews to come to me."

"Why to you?" I asked, unable to keep my curiosity at bay any longer. I didn't know the organisational chart of Trans-Continental, but it was an odds-on bet that the flight crews had no official connection to this side of the airline's general administration. Discontinuities in her story were an express train on a local track to me.

"I knew a number of the flight crews." Tracy paused and glanced at me. She sensed correctly that I wasn't satisfied with that open-ended explanation. She took a deep breath, then added more. "My late husband was a captain."

"Oh. Sorry." My express train had been throttled back; flight crews would go straight to her because they knew her, and because they knew that she had direct access to the ear of the company's exalted pukka sahib. "But I imagine that those flight crews who came to you weren't Bridges' best pals."

"Yes, that's true," Woodruff answered before Tracy could speak. "That's why we didn't do much except watch Bridges from a distance."

"Did you discover anything?"

"Not one blessed thing. Bridges did his job, then went home – stopping now and then just to piss off a few people. But we never found even the slightest bit of evidence that he was making this extra money at the expense of the company."

I mulled this over in silence for a few moments, trying to make my sheer bewilderment appear more like introspective analysis. Finally, I spoke. "Okay, Elmer," I said, using his name because it was so ill-suited to him that I had already developed an affinity for it, "let's say that Bridges was involved in some kind of deal with a few undesirable characters, and that these undesirable creeps finally decided to knock him off. Even if this is true, what's the point of running after these people? I mean, beyond the normal attempts at assisting the police effort. What I'm trying to say, Elmer, is – quite simply – what's in this for you?"

"I'll skip the part about my concern for my fellow man and my moral indignation at what I assume is a violent crime. Instead, I'll jump directly to the hell I'll catch if it later comes out that Bridges' actions and murder were somehow linked to the airline."

"What kind of hell will you catch?" I asked, doing my impersonation of Perry Mason baiting a witness.

"Corporate hell." Woodruff leaned forward on his desk and his voice dropped a few decibels. Clearly, I was about to hear something that Elmer didn't often share with most other mortals. I put on my priest-in-the-confessional face and listened intently. "Corporate hell is the worst kind of hell there is. No visible flame, but lots of heat. If it comes out that Bridges – and maybe others here – are involved in some sort of criminal bullcrap, the adverse publicity and general bad press will rattle cages right to the top. It'll wind up on *my* shoulders. Remember, I'm responsible for the whole goddamned Miami base here, and any bad vibes are going to have *my* name firmly attached."

"You mean that the corporate hierarchy expects you to know about all the actions of every one of your employees?"

"No, although I'm sure they'd like me to. What I'm worried about is the possibility of this being the beginning of a whole network of problems. If it comes out that half the mechanics are smuggling diamonds or half the pilots are running dope, upstairs is going to say that I was obviously asleep in my corner office rather than minding the store." Woodruff waved his arms expansively around the room.

"I see your point." The grand pukka sahib was right; he *did* have a nice office – well worth trying to keep.

"All I want you to do is scout around, snoop around, and be damn sure that this Bridges thing was an isolated incident. Frankly, I don't give a shit if he *was* murdered, just so that the murderers aren't on the company payroll.

I'll pay you a weekly retainer and expenses so I can rest assured that no unpleasant surprises will be waiting for me on some future Monday morning. You can do whatever you think is required. Just be able to tell me – honestly and with certainty – that nothing's about to blow up in my face."

"It's a deal," I said quickly, before I could think of any reason to say otherwise.

3

I could feel Tracy's eyes on me as we rode in the Trans-Continental company bus that was taking us from their hangar offices to the terminal building on the far side of the airport. Studiously, I continued watching a British Airways Boeing 747 in the distance. The huge jumbo jet had just taken the active runway and was beginning its takeoff roll. "Amazing machines," I commented, mostly to fill the silence.

"My late husband once explained to me the reason why jumbo jets look to be flying so darned slow. Do you know why?"

"Not really," I answered. The 747 lifted off in what appeared to be a near-hover. "It's something to do with their proportions, I'd guess."

"Right." Tracy turned more in her seat so she could face me directly. "He said that the human eye judges speed by the time it takes an object to move across its own length. Since a 747 flies at about the same speed as most other airline jets, its longer length makes it appear much slower."

"Is that why I got more speeding tickets when I drove a small sports car?" I turned myself around to face her fully. She had a friendly, inviting expression, the kind of expression that compels a person to say more than they really want to about whatever the topic might be. At that moment it occurred to me that Tracy would make a wonderful criminal interrogator; when she was done, she could turn the hapless sap over to an executioner before he realised the significance of the confessions he was being duped into making. "Now I drive a big old Ford. The cops just seem to yawn when I speed by."

"I thought you told me that you drove a white BMW."

"A recent change." I had forgotten that while Tracy was

40

having me signed on as an official Trans-Continental consultant after Elmer hired me a couple of hours before, one of the many forms she had me fill out related to my car and the necessary parking sticker for it. I had also forgotten that the prerequisite of being a good liar was having a good memory. I certainly had no intention of getting into the sordid details of the story about Susan, me and the BMW.

"Oh." Tracy nodded with an appropriate hint of scepticism.

"What was your late husband's name?" I asked, figuring that now would be as inappropriate a time as any to broach the subject. What I didn't know, though, was why I cared to ask the question at all. Curious, I suppose.

"Carl."

"Married long?"

"Four years, four months."

"How'd he die?" Somehow, the fact that we were sitting side by side in a bouncing bus made me seem at least partially eligible to ask personal questions.

"Cancer."

"Oh." I paused to search for an appropriate reply. Tracy's eyes were locked on mine. Her eyes remained in pure neutral. After a few moments I realised that I couldn't think of anything fitting, so I said the only thing I could think of at all. "That's bad."

"Yes. It was very bad." Tracy waited, as if she were deciding whether or not to add any more. Finally, she did. "It'll be two years next month. Carl was forty-four. From the time we learned about it until he died, it took a little over a year."

We both lapsed into silence again as we swayed with the motions of the vehicle. Now that we had come out of a narrow side road, the bus driver had taken to sudden spurts of acceleration and heavy braking as he weaved in and out of the mounting midday traffic. Once, a few of our fellow passengers gasped as the driver pulled in front of a big red Cadillac. "Think he's late for lunch?" I asked. I gestured towards the small Latin man behind the driver's wheel.

"More than likely, he's late for a rendezvous with Heaven." Tracy shrugged, then smiled in a knowing way.

41

"The company chews these guys out all the time, but I guess it's a boring job. I guess it's the only excitement they get."

"I suppose." The parallels in the conversation had caused me to think of a quote I had once heard somewhere – that boredom, not cancer, was the biggest disease known to man. I had already learned enough about Tracy to know not to volunteer that theory.

"Here we are," Tracy announced. The bus driver made one more sharp turn in order to pull up to the entrance of the Trans-Continental portion of the terminal building. He then jammed on the brakes and nearly skidded the bus to a stop. As we shuffled off, the driver grinned up at us. Tracy turned back to me. "Just like we said, he's doing battle with boredom. He's a real showman."

"That's absolutely right," I agreed. *Worse than cancer?* Maybe, maybe not. I turned and looked at the terminal. It was sloping ramps to kerbside check-in spots, with glass and concrete on the front. The midday rush was in full progress. The public address system droned on in a female voice about a gate change for the St Louis flight. I followed Tracy through the automatic doors, then stood in the lobby.

"The main check-in area." She waved her hand at the counters that lined the walls. "Behind the partitions are offices and supervisors who deal with passengers and ticketing. None of this should be of any use to you, but your identification card will get you in anywhere you want."

"Okay." I followed her towards a door in the rear wall, passing several shops that sold newspapers, magazines and gifts.

"This is the only elevator in this section, it runs from the basement on through to the second floor offices. The basement has the baggage facilities, plus a crew lounge and the flight planning area. It also has the employees' cafeteria – something that I suggest you try to stay away from if you value your appetite."

"I'm an airline expert, I already know about employee cafeterias." I gave her a conspiratorial nod as we got into the elevator. We rode up to the second floor in silence.

"The office I took for you is on this end," Tracy said as we stepped out of the elevator and stood in the long, windowless corridor. "On the opposite end are the crew scheduling and flight attendant supervisor offices." Tracy wheeled around and I followed her. She pointed to a closed door. "Captain Davenport, the divisional chief pilot. Do you want me to introduce you, or to say anything to him? I've already come up with a cover story that should be good enough to . . ."

"I want to be introduced," I interrupted, "but no cover story. We tell everybody, straight out, that I'm looking into the affairs of Jay Bridges regarding illegal activities involving airline personnel." I'd been thinking about an appropriate opening tactic for this job, and, by a process of elimination, was left with this one. Like the man said, when all else fails, you might as well try the truth.

"I can't believe that you'd want to do that," Tracy said.

"I do." Since the job was basically one of flushing out anyone who might have been involved with Bridges, spreading the word loud and clear that I was snooping around might work; it would be in the same vein as a hunter banging a drum while walking through the woods. "The more people who know what I'm here for, the better."

"Are you sure?"

"Absolutely." I could see what Tracy was thinking – that banging a drum in the woods was a good idea when you were dealing with birds and squirrels, not such a good idea when you were potentially dealing with tigers. A valid point, but one that I couldn't afford to dwell on. "Well, I've got to take a few chances," I answered. I shrugged.

Tracy stopped dead in her tracks. She glared at me. "That sounds pretty macho. Even worse than that, it sounds pretty damned stupid."

"There's nothing else I can do. There's nothing else to go on," I said as we stood in the empty corridor.

"Hardly enough reasons to risk your life."

"I don't intend to risk my life," I answered predictably, wondering for a moment if I really would be taking too much of a chance by letting people know so early on what I was here for. Tigers could bite, I reminded myself – but, then again, I still had a few of my own teeth. "Spreading the word is just a tactic – I certainly intend to be very careful."

"It sounds too dangerous."

"At the moment, not only do we not have a single clue but we also don't even know for certain that *anything* had been going on. If I poke around and make it seem as if I already *know* there's a snake under the rock, then maybe we can get the damned creature to wiggle. Plan B is that if there's no snake at all, then this deep intrigue is a moot point anyway – right?"

"It still seems to me that you're walking into a threatening situation totally blind," Tracy responded, although with a far mellower tone than the one she had used a moment before.

"A little blind, yes." I gave her that much because, clearly, Tracy's concerns were about me. I had an obligation to convince her that I had the situation under control. "The reason Elmer hired me for this is that I'm a professional, I know what I'm doing," I said, wallowing in my own glory. *Jack Sawyer: A legend in his own mind* filtered into my thoughts. It was, I figured, good to be a legend to someone – and at the moment, inside my own skull was the only place. That would have to do for the time being. "That's why your boss didn't ask you to take on this job – he was smart enough to see that he needed a professional to do it."

"I suppose."

"You'll have to trust me that this is the best way," I said, as convincingly as I could. Was it really the best way, I wondered? If *best* was synonymous with *only*, then it actually was. I wasn't about to let a good job slip through my itchy fingers just because I was clueless about how to find an opening clue. "Okay?"

"Okay," Tracy answered, nodding slowly. Her motions showed that she would accept it, but she sure as hell didn't like it. She started walking forward again. After a few steps, Tracy turned to a door, took out a key and opened it. She swung the door open, then stepped aside for me to enter first.

The room was small. Three chairs, a desk, a lamp. The kind of hell to which an interior decorator would be relegated to spend eternity. "I can see why Elmer wants to hold on to his corner pad."

"This place was too big for a phone booth so we decided to let you use it."

44

"What was it before? A holding pen for the criminally insane?" Not only was it gloomy, it was *used* gloomy.

"No, although you're close." Tracy smiled. "It was an office for check pilots. Staffing was cut down some and this room was left over."

I pointed to the telephone on the desk, which sat beside a computer display screen. "Does it work?"

"Yes. Extension 6847 on the company line. Dial 91 to get an outside line. Elmer says no calls to your overseas relatives."

"None of them will speak to me."

"Here's a company telephone book," Tracy continued as she pulled out a small folder from her handbag. "My number's on the very top." She smiled blatantly, which made it impossible to tell whether she was leading me on or pulling my leg.

"What about this computer?" I ran my hand across the top of the dark display screen; the casing was dusty enough to write my name on.

"A crew management computer." Tracy pulled out another booklet from her handbag. "Here are the keystroke codes for pulling out all sorts of information."

"Show me." I pushed two chairs to the front of the computer screen and motioned for Tracy to take the seat in front of the keyboard.

"Here," she said, after she had flipped open the code booklet and turned on the screen. "I'll call up the record of Bridges' last flight."

"Prophetic." I waited while she punched in the appropriate code and the black screen filled with green letters and numbers.

"As you can see, Bridges' flight terminated at O'Hare at nine fifty-two in the evening."

"Which was two and a half hours before Bridges himself was terminated at O'Hare." I laid a finger on the computer line that indicated the dead copilot's final trip. Above his name was the name of the captain. "What about this Ned Lange?"

Tracy laughed, in a way that would have been very disconcerting if she were laughing about me. "Ned Lange

45

is the absolute *last* man on the planet to be involved with Jay Bridges in any kind of shaky deal."

"Why?"

"Because . . ." Tracy paused for a moment, searching for the appropriate words. "Because he's a little old lady, that's why. We get ten page letters from him if the crew bus goes through a yellow traffic light. He's very careful, very conservative, very concerned about doing everything *exactly* by the book."

"Oh." I drummed my fingers on the edge of the computer screen. I had known a few captains at Air East just like Ned Lange, and they were certainly as far from potential murderers as people could be. On the other hand, sometimes people change, or sometimes they get into situations over their head. "You're probably right, but I'd still like to check it out a little further."

"You're the boss." Tracy stood up from the computer screen. "How about a visit with Chief Pilot Davenport? If you're still crazy enough to want to tell the world why you're here, Davenport's probably the next logical person for you to meet."

"There's no time like the present." I followed Tracy through the door and down the short walk to the chief pilot's office. She entered first, said a few words to a secretary in the outer office who was sifting through a pile of correspondence that was taller than she was, and the two of us marched into a corner cubicle that had evidently been designed for the chief.

The inner office was exactly like the chief pilot's office at Air East had been – a big desk and a few overstuffed chairs in front, a couple of filing cabinets with airplane models perched on top, some airplane photographs hung on the walls. On the back wall was a bulletin board overfilled with computer messages and notices, most of them yellow with age.

"Hello, Tracy. What can I do for you?"

The man at the desk was thin, with a gaunt face and dark eyes. He was wearing a dark, expensive suit. I guessed his age as early fifties, as much by the tactical retreat of his hairline as by any other means. As Tracy said a few appropriate words that would lead us into introductions, I was careful to maintain my expression in the neighbourhood of nonchalant.

46

As my dear mother had always said, first impressions were the lasting ones.

"So you're a private investigator," Davenport said as he reached out his hand while barely rising from his chair.

"Yes." I stepped forward the extra yard to shake his barely stretched-out hand; my nonchalant expression had melted into a slight smile, something I hoped would be intriguing without being infuriating.

"Well, now." Davenport glanced at Tracy, then back at me. "Is there anything . . . in particular?"

Tracy stood silent, knowing not to volunteer anything beyond the simple truth she had told so far – that Elmer Woodruff had hired me to do some in-house investigating. She was going to let me fill in the details – dig my own grave, from her point of view – in my own fashion. Tracy was a smart lady. "Bridges. First Officer Jay Bridges," I said.

"I should have guessed." Davenport looked down at his desk, then back at me. "Do you know what's missing from the top of my desk for the first time in probably three years?" he asked.

I had always hated game shows, so I didn't bother to answer. I had a sneaking suspicion that William Davenport didn't offer much in the way of prizes anyway.

"The Bridges file," Davenport answered himself, after he saw that I wasn't interested in becoming one of his contestants. "That little bastard – excuse my language, Tracy – was the biggest ongoing personnel problem that I had. He was non-stop trouble, although never quite enough for me to build a strong case so that the union wouldn't be able to get his job back. The only reason I could take that file off my desk was that the stupid little jerk finally managed to kill himself. Now you want to talk about him. You'll have to excuse my lack of enthusiasm."

"Elmer seemed pretty enthusiastic when he suggested that I check into some of the things Bridges had been doing around here." I watched a tiny reaction pass across Davenport's eyes before the darkness in them washed that glimmer of attentiveness away; being on a first-name basis with the senior vice president was something of a bugle call to Davenport's ears, as I figured it might be.

47

"Like what?"

"Like . . . some information I've gotten . . . about dealings . . . airline people might be included . . ." I waved my hand in a gesture indicating that there was much more but I chose not to reveal anything at the moment.

"Oh." Davenport blinked, then frowned. "What is it that you need from me?"

"Help, in an ongoing way."

"Please be more specific." Davenport squirmed – it was obvious that he wasn't used to being treated with anything other than complete deference.

"Sure." I casually sat on the corner of his desk, pushing back a few of his papers as I did. The desk was too neat anyway, it needed some rearranging. "I've got to do a lot of poking around to get to the next names that I'll need," I said, wondering if I sounded more confident than I felt. I glanced over at Tracy, whose expression gave no indication that she knew I was putting out a great deal of recently contrived fiction. I looked back at Davenport. "My temporary office is just a few doors down the hall. I'll need to come in here and go through your files and, maybe, to talk to you."

"When?"

"Lots. Any number of times during the next several days."

"I'm a busy man."

"That's good to hear." I shifted my rear end a little, and a few of Davenport's neatly stacked papers fell off the desk and floated gently to the floor in varying degrees of swooping flight. The theories of aerodynamics were alive and well in the chief pilot's office. "I intend to be a busy man, too – very busy, until I get this job wrapped up."

Davenport was obviously displeased, yet he was smart enough to know that he didn't have much room to man- oeuvre. "How about if I assign someone to you, someone who was familiar with Bridges?"

"One of the pilots?" Since I was intending to exploit that angle first, I needed a conduit into the pilot ranks.

"Yes."

"Fine."

Davenport stepped up and moved around his desk and brushed past Tracy and me without any additional comment.

After he had left the room, Tracy spoke in a voice low enough so that no one in the adjacent rooms could hear. "You were lots nicer to Elmer."

"I liked Elmer."

"Then I take it that you don't like Davenport?"

"Nolo contendere. Elmer hired me, so I like him the best. I'm loyal to whomever pays me first."

"Or pays you the most?"

"No. I strictly use the first payment principle, cash on the barrel head. A man's got to have some sense of ethics, you know."

Tracy smiled. "Sounds like you should have been a lawyer."

"Yeah, I missed the boat on that one. Those people *really* know how to like." Our tête-à-tête was interrupted by the return of Chief Pilot Davenport, his dark eyes looking darker, his gaunt face looking more gaunt. Walking a few steps behind him was a black man wearing a blue shirt, grey pants and a paisley tie. He had a large, somewhat overweight frame, short, frizzy hair and a thin moustache.

"This is one of our check pilots, Captain Ishmael Reese," Davenport said as he began the introductions. Reese smiled at Tracy, whom he obviously already knew, then he reached across and pumped my hand.

"You want to know about Bridges?" Reese asked, after he glanced over at Davenport to see, in a sense, that he had permission to speak.

"Yes. Lots of stuff. Lots of digging. I want to fill in some of the blanks, then we go on from there."

"I don't know about the blanks, man, but that suits me just fine."

"I take it that you weren't fond of First Officer Bridges."

"Spoiled white kid."

"Well spoken and to the point. I'd have to say that his record seems to agree."

"When do you want to start? The chief here says," Reese added while he made a half nod towards where Davenport stood, "that doing whatever you want is my job until he says otherwise."

"I want to start right now, Ishmael."

49

"Call me Izzy."

"Sure thing." I slid off the corner of Davenport's desk, taking a few more papers with me. Maybe, in some deep recess of my mind, I was getting back at all the chief pilots I had grovelled to for so many years. I walked out without saying anything else to Davenport, my arm around Izzy's shoulder. "Hey, that's a great-looking tie you've got there," I said, glancing down at his paisley.

"Yeah, you too," Izzy said, looking at my tie. "You know, paisleys are back in again, man. All us cool dudes are wearing them. I knew you was one of us when I first looked at you."

"Thanks." Maybe my dear mother was right, and first impressions do mean a great deal.

4

"So how's the new job going?" Max Bergman asked as he towelled himself off. The perspiration was running along the lines of his jaw and down his neck, disappearing beneath his faded green tennis shirt.

"Stop trying to distract me. I'm going to close you out, right now." After I took another drink of water, I glanced over at Max. For the first time, I noticed the faded, nearly illegible lettering on the front of his shirt. "Is that the shirt we got from that tournament in Boca?" I asked. "Mine shredded a long time ago."

"Yeah, from Boca." Max grinned impishly as he tugged on the front of his soaking wet shirt. "These things last longer if you don't take too good care of them."

"Is that so?"

"Yeah. You wash your stuff too much, that's the trouble. If you take too good care of something, it don't last."

"Spare me the details." I picked up my racket and wiped the residual moisture off the handle.

"Women are the same way, too. Take too good care of them and they don't last, they don't stick around."

"Right." Max was making his standard speech about how I treated the women in my life; we had both been through this routine so many times that neither one of us noticed that the other wasn't listening to a damned word of it. We had become an Abbott and Costello routine in tennis clothes. "I'd take your advice more seriously if you knew how to play tennis. But I notice from the score," I said as I pointed to the flip cards beside the court, "that I'm up again. In just a few minutes that'll be three times in a row that you've lost to me."

"Four more points to go." Max stepped back on to the court, flipping his racket casually from hand to hand. "Four points can be lots of points."

"I know they say it's not over until the fat lady sings, but I think I hear that corpulent soprano calling your name."

"We here to talk, or we here to play? Your serve." Max tossed the balls to me and took his position behind the baseline.

"Okay, six games to five." I had already resolved to play smart but extra hard this game, I sure didn't want to let my victory slip away by being too cautious and allowing the set score to get to six-all. If I did, then Max would have the momentum going into the tie-break. "Here we go."

My first serve was crisp and deep to his backhand. Max punched back a good cross-court return that barely cleared the net. I covered it with a forehand shot down the middle, and we sparred back and forth with some light exchanges for a few strokes. When I caught him leaning left, I hit a sharp-angle forehand that nicked the edge of the sideline and bounded out of his reach. "Fifteen-love."

My second serve took a good bounce and jammed him. Max hit his return into the net. "Thirty-love."

My next serve was mediocre, and I was barely able to retrieve Max's shot deep to my backhand. Even then, I popped the ball too high over the net and Max pounced all over it for an unreturnable smash. "Thirty-fifteen."

"I told you it wasn't over yet," Max said casually over his shoulder as he ambled back to the baseline.

I ignored his obvious attempt at gamesmanship as I took my position. I took a few deep breaths, then began to play. Another good serve was followed by another good return, and we bounded all over the court chasing down balls that might have normally been too much of a placement for either one of us to deal with. It never ceased to amaze me how much better most people played when they really got into the points.

I watched Max scoop up a mid-court half volley and push it softly over my head. Yet, for some reason, all of that exchange was now happening in what seemed like less than the normal pace – it was like a movie of a tennis match that was being shown at half speed. That sense of slow motion enabled me to analyse the shot and make a decision: I decided that I would be better off going back than jumping for the ball. I sped towards the back court.

The ball was descending now, but I wasn't watching it. Instead, I concentrated on the baseline; I was using the backcourt line as my pivot point. When I reached the baseline I spun around, the ball hit the court and bounced up softly but a little further to my right than I had guessed it would. I lunged towards it, flicking off a wristy forehand. I hadn't been able to hit the ball squarely so it had very little pace on it – yet it still managed to clear the net. Max dived for the dying ball, but he missed it. "Forty-fifteen."

We each walked back to the baseline slowly, both of us breathing heavily, wiping off the sweat. Double match point. Yet tonight, the sense that being ahead usually triggered in me – be cautious, wait him out, let him make the error – didn't occur. Instead, I felt an urge to press the issue, to *take* the point rather than have it given to me by him making an error.

My serve hit right where I wanted it to, deep on the forehand side of the box. Max hit his usual reply, a low cross-court. I had already taken a step in by the time his shot cleared the net, and I focused on taking the ball on the rise and putting it down the opposite line. But rather than thinking it through or forcing my body through the motions, I let it happen by simply concentrating on the goal rather than the method.

I could feel my body uncurl as I stepped into the shot. My legs were slightly bent as I met the ball, and I thrust up into it with all my weight and balance. My stroke, too, was complete and without a hint of hesitation from the backswing to the follow-through. The ball sailed off the strings of my racket, cleared the net by a foot, then accelerated down to smack hard against the pavement well inside the opposite baseline.

"Holy shit." Max stood with his mouth open. I had, from just about as far away as possible, hit an unreturnable shot, a clean winner. More important than that, I had done it at match point – I had done it when it had really counted. "Where the hell did you get *that* shot from?" Max asked as we both walked towards the net.

"I don't know. I just let it happen." We shook hands and walked to the sidelines.

"You sure beat me tonight." Max smiled. "Maybe that fat lady *was* singing."

"Maybe."

It was just about at that moment that I saw the man or, more specifically, saw the glimmer from the court lights as they bounced off the pistol in his hand. "Down!" I pushed Max behind the water cooler just as the first shot exploded in the quiet night air; the bullet passed inches away from me, ricocheting off the metal pipe that held up the canvas awning between the courts.

"Shit! Who's he after?" Max said as he got up from where I had pushed him. We both huddled behind the water cooler.

"You sell any bad cars lately?" While I spoke, I scanned around the edge of the empty spectator area where the man with the gun had been. Naturally, he was already gone – but where to? Which side of the darkness surrounding the edges of the lighted court had he disappeared in? They were questions worth betting your life on.

"Can't be my bad cars. The only bad car I got on the lot is your Ford. It ain't been moved yet." Max paused, scanning the darkness surrounding the courts. "What do we do?"

"Not sit here." I broke into a headlong sprint towards the rear gate. I could hear that Max was no more than a step or two behind. I was betting that the man with the gun had come from the parking lot and, after he missed with his first shot, I suspected that the parking lot side of the darkness was probably the direction that he would step back towards.

Another shot rang out, and it kicked up a piece of the pavement ten feet to our right. The angle told me that I had guessed correctly, that the man was on the wrong side of the court to get a clear shot at us. "Here!"

I rolled through the open gate and on to the grass, with Max just a half step behind. My white BMW was straddling the grass just where I had left it – my usual parking spot, closer to the court we normally used rather than in the parking lot. I yanked the door open, then pulled out my pistol from beneath the driver's seat.

"Now what?"

54

"My turn to serve."

"What do you want me to do?"

"Get in the car, start it up. Lights off, but be ready to go."

Max eased himself towards the driver's door. "Keys?"

"In the ignition."

"Be careful."

"You can bet on it." I moved quickly around the grass area and positioned myself near to an open spot at the fence while I waited for Max to provide the diversion that I needed. Within a few seconds the interior light in the BMW flashed on briefly as Max opened the door and climbed into the driver's seat. I assumed that the gunman's eyes would be drawn towards the light, and I used that moment for moving through the gate and around the back side of the court.

The dark court windscreens covered me as I edged my way ahead, hardly breathing, listening for any sounds that would give me a tip as to which way the guy was. There were four courts built into this complex; the only court in use tonight had been ours. Except for me, Max, and some guy who was trying to kill us, the place was deserted. With the court lights still on, it was a little too bright behind the windscreens to make me comfortable so I moved quickly to the end of the path, to the deeper shadows.

Still nothing. I had no view at all of Max and the BMW, and I was beginning to worry about that fact when all of a sudden I spotted the guy – medium height and build, dark wavy hair – as he moved cautiously along the fence that led to the parking lot. He was, evidently, attempting to circle back towards where he thought both of us still were. I crouched down behind one of the small bushes that lined the path I was on.

When the man got as close to me as I thought he would – there was an intersecting path at that spot and he could have gone either way – I stood up. "Hold it!" But even as I aimed my gun at that shadowy blur of a figure in the distance, I knew that neither one of us had clear enough sight of the other to make the likelihood of a hit anything other than dumb luck.

I could see that the guy I was covering was pretty experienced at these sorts of things because, without the slightest hesitation, he spun around, fired a wild shot in my general

55

direction, then dived behind the low row of bushes on his side of the path. Realising that I was the only one of us still standing – not an enviable position to be in – I decided to do likewise. The grass and twigs on the ground stuck to my wet tennis clothes as I rolled far enough out of the way to make my location a mystery to the guy who was after me.

I crawled forward slowly, in the direction of the parking lot. By now I figured that since this guy had lost his key advantage – surprise – he'd be bagging it at any time now. For all he knew, my tennis partner was Rambo and I was the equivalent of a Gurkha regiment.

I edged around more low bushes. My sneakers and white socks were covered with wood chips and mulch. By the time I reached the parking lot I began to wonder about my logic since the gunman was nowhere in sight.

I thought about heading back to where I had left Max, but then decided against that, too. Max didn't get to where he was in life by becoming a stoic target – he would have enough common sense to get himself, as they say, out of harm's way. Then, for just an instant, I caught sight of the gunman as he dashed from one deep shadow to another. My theory had been confirmed, the guy was headed back for his car. I worked my way ahead as quickly as I could, to a spot near the entrance of the mostly empty parking lot.

There were two cars parked at the other end. One of them would be Max's, but I didn't know which since he always drove whatever he had on his sales lot that he was in the mood for at the time. From what I could see in the darkness, the car on the right was small and foreign, the car on the left was a big American highway yacht with four doors and a hood the length of a small aircraft carrier. My problem was that there was about fifty feet of no-man's-land between me and the vehicles, and the two cars were spread far enough apart to make it impossible to cover both of them at the same moment.

It was time for me to flush the tiger out of the woods again, a metaphor that I was getting painfully accustomed to. Maybe Tracy was right, that this method of changing a situation's status quo was getting too risky. On the other hand, I needed this job pretty bad, and the guy with the gun whom I had chased back to the parking lot was the only solid clue that I had come across to date. My rational mind concluded that I was, purely for the sake of business, understandably reluctant to let this son of a bitch who had tried to kill me and my best buddy slip through my fingers. The rational mind is a wonderfully accommodating device, I reflected – always giving us whatever reasons we need for doing whatever we basically feel an emotional urge to do anyway.

It was a pretty sure bet that the guy I was looking for was sitting in his vehicle just waiting for me either to make a move in his direction or to beat feet. The question was, which car was he in? I could go back to find Max, but there wasn't time for that.

In this situation I knew that I was only going to get one choice of target. I could disable either of the vehicles with a well placed shot or two. But as soon as I started firing, then – if I had guessed wrong – the gunman would know where I was and what I was up to. That would give him a free pass out of the parking lot, or a distinct advantage if I were dumb enough to try engaging in a full-scale firefight from my exposed position in the middle of an empty expanse of tarmac.

The little foreign job on the right was neither sporty nor exotic – just one of those cheap imports created to get folks back and forth to the dry cleaners and the kid's piano lessons. On the left, the Queen Mary with tyres also didn't represent Max's style, although it did seem more of a possibility. Maybe Max had a heavy date later tonight and he needed a big back seat? Maybe.

The die was cast. I moved at an angle to my right and, by process of elimination, lined up on the foreign car. I glanced around just to be sure that no itinerant tennis players had shown up in the area, then squeezed off two quick shots. The shots exploded loudly and left a ringing in my ears. Both bullets hit their mark, and the two tyres on the left side of the foreign car bottomed out to their rims. I heard the car's engine start and I lined up for another shot at the engine block once that lamed vehicle began its swing towards the exit.

But instead of the foreign car moving, the behemoth at the other corner of the lot sped ahead! *Damn it, Max.* The big, dark-coloured car left two streams of burnt rubber as it accelerated, lights off, towards the exit.

I jerked myself around and tried to set up for a quick shot at the disappearing target. I pulled the trigger again, but I knew it was purely a gesture of frustration on my part. The bullet probably hit the car somewhere, burying itself harmlessly in that rolling pyramid of metal. My only clue was scurrying around the corner at high speed and well out of sight a full minute before Max finally appeared, on foot, to my left.

"He got away," Max said as he surveyed the scene.

"Yes, he got away."

Max pointed to his little foreign car, which was listing hard to port, its deflated rubber spreading out obscenely beneath its rims. "Why'd you want to shoot up my car?"

"You drive a car like that, you deserve to have it shot up."

"Yeah, probably."

"I've never seen you drive such a piece of junk before."

"I was late, and it was the closest car to the office door."

"Damn."

"Yeah." Max nodded. "Damn." He looked around the area, then towards the exit where the big car had disappeared. "Hey, I think I see something. Hold on." Max trotted away into the distance, picked up something from the ground, then trotted back.

"What is it?" I asked as he approached.

"Mirror." Max held up the shattered remnants of the big car's side mirror – I had evidently hit it with my last shot.

I took a few pieces of the mirror in my hand. "Two tyres for a side mirror. Not much of a trade on our part."

Max nodded slowly, then peered out into the darkness. He turned back to me. "I figure that this guy owes me for the two tyres. I'm sticking with you until we find him."

"You don't have to, I'll find him myself."

"I've seen you operate on him so far. I ain't impressed. I'm sticking."

"Suit yourself. But what about your business?"

"Everything's under control at the lot. My new man needs

58

a little room so he can learn a few things on his own. It's the only way a guy ever learns, right?"

"Right." I wasn't going to disagree with Max – if he wanted to help, I'd be thankful. Besides, the guy we were after had shot at him, too. That sort of made all of this his business, too, if you cared to follow the convoluted logic that I was currently subscribing to.

"Anyway," Max added as we turned around and headed back for the BMW, "I don't have to worry much about the lot for the next few days. The only car I've got that'd be tough to sell is your Ford."

"I'm not worried about you selling my car," I answered magnanimously. That was me speaking, the guy who had just shot out my best friend's tyres.

"What I really want to do is to sell your old Ford to the guy who took the shots at us," Max said as we walked around the courts and back towards my car. "It would serve him right."

"The ultimate in poetic justice," I responded.

"Yeah. Poetry stuff. I'd like to do that to him, too."

5

We drove the BMW back to my place. All the way, Max and I were engaged in analytical conversation pertaining to the manifestation of violence we'd been subjected to. Putting it another way, we argued about whether the guy who had recently tried to make us into history had, in fact, been after him or me.

Max's theory about the guy possibly being the husband of one of his recent soirée partners was, on the surface, as plausible as my hunch that the shooting had to do with the Trans-Continental Airlines investigation; yet the angle of *coincidence* always tipped the scales for me, so I was pretty gut-sure that the shots had been inspired earlier that day by my very own loud mouth. "As far as the idea that this creep was an anonymous hustler looking to scoop up our gold Rolexes, I'll remind you that we're two big guys strutting around in athletic clothes. Even Miami muscle can find easier pickings than that."

"Yeah, I guess." Max shrugged.

"Besides, a random hit takes all the challenge out of it. We need some hatred here to get our boilers stoked."

"My steam's up, man, don't worry about it," Max answered with a scowl.

"Does it make any difference if that clown was after me rather than you?" I was getting warmed to the notion of Max helping me on this job, but I didn't want to get his services under false pretences. The more I thought about it, the more I *knew* that those shots had been for me.

"Naw," Max answered quickly, showing that he had already considered that possibility, too. I suspected that, macho elements of his pride aside, Max also felt that I had been tonight's target of opportunity. "If he wasn't one of my ladies' husbands, some day he will be. Then you'll owe me one."

"It's a deal." We took the rest of the short ride in silence. When I made the final turn on to the street where my condo was, I spotted the red Mercedes immediately. "Christ."

"What?" Max sat further upright, scanning around nervously. "Do you see the guy's car?" he asked.

"Worse." I pulled in behind the red Mercedes sports car. The damned thing gleamed, even in the dull street lights. "Susan."

"Yeah?" Max took a few seconds to gather his thoughts. He had always liked Susan, and had always blamed our break-up on me being just a little too soft to handle her. Fact was, he was probably more right than wrong. But that, as they say, was yesterday's rain. "Did you invite her over tonight?" Max asked.

"More or less." I left out the core fact that I hadn't *actually* invited Susan over, that she was in a sense always invited. Susan still had – at my moronic insistence, for that matter – her own key to the front door.

"Good. She can help us."

"I'll bet." I parked the BMW behind her car, then followed Max into the condo.

Susan was in the living room. She was curled up on the couch, sipping a tall drink and listening to Ella Fitzgerald. The lamp in the corner covered her with a glow of soft yellow light. "If I Gave My Heart to You" was playing, and on that particular cut Ella sounded a little more nasal than she usually did. Susan smiled at us as we walked in. "Hi. How was the tennis?" she asked.

"Good to see you, babe," Max answered. He walked over and kissed Susan on the cheek. "He was lucky tonight."

Susan nodded sympathetically to Max. "You going to get him the next time?"

"Sure thing, babe."

"Max, what can I get you to drink?" I said. Susan was wearing dark slacks and a cream-coloured blouse. Her hair was slightly messed, just enough to be properly ravishing. While I waited for Max's answer, I realised that I had yet to say a single word to her – or her to me, for that matter. Even during our waning years together, we still had the married life rituals down pretty well.

61

"Beer."

"Okay."

"No, wait. Make it a scotch on the rocks. A double. I earned it tonight."

"By losing?" Susan glanced between the two of us; something, she knew, was up.

"He lost at tennis, but he won during the post-match gun fight."

"Oh, oh. You making bad line calls again, Jack?"

Whenever she used my name, I still tingled a little – names, after all, were very personal things, so I liked it when she fondled mine. "Plenty of bad calls, but that wasn't what started it. Some anonymous person lurking in the bushes didn't care for my tennis outfit. He tried to make a few ventilation holes in it."

"Really?"

"Max has the flat tyres to prove it."

"What?"

"Max will tell you what happened while I get our drinks." As much as I didn't want to, I took a step away from Susan and towards the bar. "Susan's already got a head start on us," I said over my shoulder to Max, "so we'll have to do some quick guzzling to catch up."

Max proceeded to tell her about the after-match altercation. I noticed that he left out any possibility that the hit man had been after him – evidently both of us had become firm subscribers to the theory that it was my personal ambience that the unknown creep had been attempting to eradicate. "Here's your drink," I said as I stepped back towards where Max had slid on to the couch next to Susan. I had poured myself a mostly-gin, and had already got below the tops of the ice cubes. I knew from that warm feeling inside – I was drinking on a pretty empty stomach – that I needed to slow up my consumption rate if I intended to do any serious thinking tonight.

"That gun fight sounds pretty terrible." Susan's brow had the classic furrows in it when she was concerned, and she had them now. I was pleased to see that.

I sat in the chair across from her and Max. My eyes lingered on her furrowed brow. A pleasant sight. "Not so terrible. He did, after all, miss."

"He might not miss the next time."

"True."

"What are you going to do about it?"

"Drink gin." I took another slug of my drink; I was already beginning to get more water than alcohol out of the glass – my tongue was telling me that it was almost time for a refill.

"Drinking gin doesn't sound like much of a defence."

"An excellent point. Maybe I should stop drinking. Maybe I should give the subject some serious thought." I put my now-empty glass on the table between us with an exaggerated flourish; there's nothing like a public gesture of turning away from demon rum to make a man feel self-righteous.

"Serious thought is nice, Jack, but that might not be enough. Not against some crazy guy with a gun."

"Perhaps you've forgotten that my thought process is a venerable and impenetrable shield." Just then, the doorbell rang. My heart immediately sank; I knew in a flash who was at the door. Damn.

"You expecting someone?" Max quickly got up from his seat and edged towards the side wall. He was obviously thinking that more than his tyres were about to have bullets put through them.

"It's okay, I know who it is." Actually, it wasn't okay at all, but there was nothing at that point that I could do to stop it. *Damn, damn, damn.* I got up and stepped towards the door, knowing now what I had forgotten about because of the after-match excitement: Tracy was supposed to come over, ostensibly to discuss the Trans-Continental case. I opened the door.

"Hello. You having a party?" Tracy gestured towards the two cars in the driveway.

I glanced out at the white BMW and the red Mercedes – it was, at the very least, a nice display of affluence for the neighbourhood. Tracy's car was parked in the street directly behind my BMW. It was a grey Porsche. By yuppie standards that meant she would fit into our ad hoc group pretty well – except that I was already wondering exactly what the dynamics of the group would turn out to be. "Not really a party. It depends on how you look at it."

"I'm willing to take a peek, if you'll invite me in."

"Sorry." I ushered Tracy through the door, took her coat, then steered her towards the living room. "This is Tracy Cummings," I announced to the upturned duo of faces in front of me. I didn't know what else to say. No one else was speaking. "From Trans-Continental Airlines. She's Elmer Woodruff's executive secretary."

"Oh, how nice to meet you!" Susan said enthusiastically as she jumped up to greet Tracy. The two women shook hands. "I'm the one who made the introductions between Elmer and Jack. Sort of, anyway."

"You must be Susan." Tracy had a funny little smile on her face. It was the sort of smile that I would have preferred not to have seen. "I've heard a lot about you."

"From Elmer, or from Jack?" Susan always managed to maintain an absolutely neutral countenance while she asked questions that from anyone else would have been far too gauche to consider. It was another of her personality traits that was wonderful to observe in action. Sometimes.

"Both, actually." Tracy glanced towards me for a brief moment, then turned back towards the two of them. "And you are . . .?"

"Max Bergman. Just a friend."

"Max is my usual tennis partner," I added. I watched Max give Tracy a dead-fish handshake. I was glad to see that I wasn't the only man around who handled it badly when a pretty lady stuck out her claw. "And we're all here, more or less, on Trans-Continental business."

"Really?" Tracy looked even more sceptical now than she had since the introductions had begun. "How could that be?"

"Well, tonight Max and I were on the receiving end of several rounds of ammunition. Fortunately, they were badly aimed."

"Really? You were shot at?"

"Yes. And a few of the details make us think that the bullets probably had the Trans-Continental logo on them. That's why Max came back with me. Susan is here because . . ." I paused and gestured towards her, since I didn't have the faintest idea why Susan had picked tonight to show up at my place. I figured that, like the old expression went, since

64

she had buttered her bread it would be only right if I let her sleep in it.

"The truth is that I wanted to see how Jack's job with Elmer was going."

"Oh," I said. That news was pleasant enough. Susan had again answered a question without the slightest bit of guile in her reply – as if it were perfectly normal for a divorcing wife to be concerned about her husband's business career. Maybe it was. Maybe if I got married and divorced more often, I'd have a better feel for the situation.

I looked around at the group. Susan smiled radiantly while Tracy nodded knowingly and I shuffled my feet awkwardly. Max looked puzzled. The Ella Fitzgerald CD had come to an end, and the silence was overwhelming. No one made a move for what seemed like hours, but was probably less than half a minute. Then I cleared my throat and found the courage to speak. "Max has offered to help me on the Trans-Continental job. He's got a stake in it, now that this guy – whoever he is – has taken shots at him, too."

"Yeah." Max nodded vigorously while he rocked back and forth on his heels; I could tell that, finally, the conversation had taken a turn to his liking. Macho stuff. Testosterone was the lubricant that greased the wheels of his life. "I ain't going to take that stuff lying down. Not me."

"And I want to help, too," Susan added. "I've got some . . . free time . . . these next several days. This is a big case, and I want to see you do well with it. That's the least I can do for you."

I was a little hesitant to look over at Tracy, who was, after all, one of my current bosses. Instead, I addressed the group at large. "I won't pretend that I couldn't use the help, but let me remind everyone that this isn't a parlour game or a movie script. There are flesh-and-blood bad guys out there who have shown an annoying propensity to shoot at real people with real bullets."

Tracy took a step in my direction, although she spoke loud enough for everyone to hear. "I don't know what Elmer will say about all of this."

"You mean this gang of mine?" For that matter, I didn't know what to say about them myself. Now that I thought

65

about it, I realised that there was enough developing grunt work in this job for each of them to contribute something without running any personal risks. Since Max was my best friend, and since I couldn't get Susan out of my mind anyway, I might as well have the two of them along. "Elmer hired the Sawyer Investigating Group. I just want to be sure that he gets a big enough group considering the money he's paying."

"That makes sense. Sort of," Tracy answered.

"Do you really think so?"

"No, but so what?" Tracy smiled when she spoke, and it softened her features and made her look even prettier. A competent, pleasant lady.

"I like your honesty." I now realised that Tracy played in a totally different league from Susan – Tracy was wholesome rather than super-sexy, practical instead of provocative. Yet there was no denying that she was attractive. And intelligent. "You're part of the group, too," I said, venturing out into what I feared was a potential verbal abyss. "At least I hope so. I'd like you to be."

"Oh, yes. Please. We all would." Susan took a step towards Tracy. She laid her hand on Tracy's shoulder. "Jack knows what he's doing, but there's a great deal to this sort of thing. I'm sure that we can all play an important part."

"Yeah," Max said. "We'll all be able to help." He turned to me. "I'm getting another drink. You want one?"

"Right." I nodded towards my empty glass on the table; Max scooped it up.

"How about you, Tracy? A drink?"

"Well . . ." Tracy ran her hands along the sides of her skirt. She glanced at me.

I could tell that she wanted me to say more, so I did. "You're part of the investigation anyway, from the feeling that I got from Elmer. But now I want to put you officially on my payroll. A dollar a day, plus all the booze you can drink. How about it?"

"Isn't that something of a conflict of interest, if I work for both you and Elmer?"

"Probably. But conflicts can add spice to your life." I looked at Tracy openly, wondering whether I was only being glib – or if I was actually trying to tell her something about the

66

nonsensical relationship between me and Susan. Between me and the world. All of it, more than likely.

"So conflict is part of what you're offering in your employment package?" Tracy asked. She was pretending to be serious.

"Sure. Lots of conflict." Tracy had cancer in her life, and I had conflict. I wasn't so sure, as far as end results went, that the two were very far apart. *Cancer. Conflict.* They were both outside influences that could shake a person to their very core. Perhaps Tracy and I had a great deal in common after all. Shared misery as the bromide for what ails you. "I offer you conflict of interest, a dollar a day and all the liquor you can drink. Really quite a generous contract for your services. What do you say?"

Tracy glanced around the room again, her eyes lingering for a brief moment on both Susan and Max. Finally, she turned back to me. "I'd say, how about making me a vodka collins?"

"And I'd say that it would be my extreme pleasure. Welcome aboard." I made a beeline towards the bar to seal our newly expanded relationship symbolically. Since Susan was already the engine of my sinking ship, that conceivably meant that Tracy could be the rudder. To continue the metaphor, Max was the first mate. The shipwreck that my life was in was getting pretty crowded. Would that be good or bad? I didn't have time to figure it out because I was too busy baling water.

"Jack, hold on," Tracy said.

"What?"

She smiled, then ran one hand through her blonde hair as if she were straightening it out from a wind. "Since we're going to be here a while, you might as well make me a double."

6

It was eight fifteen in the morning when I stood directly in front of Elmer Woodruff's desk with my hands at my sides. To my left was Tracy, and to my right were Susan and Max. Elmer sat in his swivel chair and rocked back and forth vigorously. The chair squeaked, and we all pretended not to notice. There was a less than pleasant expression on Elmer's face. "So that's the situation," I said. I had explained my plan – the group's plan from last night, really – and now I needed the Pope of Trans-Continental to give his blessing.

"Jesus Christ," Elmer answered. It was as if he had read my thoughts; religion was evidently going to be today's unstated theme.

"But I'm going to need some help. Really." I noticed that I was sounding less assured and more pleading than I cared to. I looked at Elmer with an expression that I hoped would be taken as determination. Elmer was wearing the same kind of tight-fitting, open-collared sports shirt that he had worn the day before, although today's version was solid grey. The colour of his shirt matched the look I was getting from his face. "This is turning into a big job. A complex job."

"That's bullshit." Elmer strummed his fingers on the edge of the desk.

His answer struck me as less than encouraging. The only thing I'd been able to predict accurately this morning was that Elmer wasn't the sort who'd wear the same shirt two days in a row. "I'll admit that what I'm saying might sound like an exaggeration, but there really are a lot of things to do. Things that I'll need help with." I spoke to him in a soothing, accommodating tone in the hopes that I'd be able to placate him with my sheer charm. So far, my charisma seemed to have had exactly the opposite effect.

"I hired *you*, not a goddamned army." Elmer squeezed his

lips together and looked around at the others in the group. I noticed that only Susan, of the four of us, looked directly back at him for any length of time. "Nothing's going to stay *confidential* if we're going to have a *gang* snooping around, for chrissake. We've got to keep this quiet. Damn quiet."

"Elmer, I'm afraid that you're just plain wrong." I decided on reversing my tactic to something of a frontal attack, since I was getting nowhere by being discreet. Discretion was something that I was probably out of practice with anyway. "It's already too late to keep it quiet."

"Yeah. Thanks to you." Elmer's frown went from medium to high grade.

"I had no choice."

"Bullshit."

"I had no choice," I repeated. I glanced beyond Elmer, out of the window. The view from his office was mostly of the tarmac ramp behind Trans-Continental's hangar. The ramp was empty, except on the far right where I could make out the wingtip of one of the company jets. But from where I stood, too little of that airplane was visible for me to identify the type.

I found myself spending the next half minute of the discernibly pregnant silence that hung between Elmer and me in an attempt to figure out what type of jet it could be from just the tip of its wing. If I hadn't had that diversion to occupy my thoughts, I might have put my foot in my mouth clear up to my knee. As it was, I was already swallowing ankle high.

"This whole business is getting goddamn ridiculous. This is definitely not what I had in mind when I hired you for this goddamn job."

I was right, religion would be our undertone. It was time to call up the image of the antichrist. "The reason you hired me was that you didn't know what to do next. Now you're telling me that what I'm doing isn't what you had in mind for me to be doing next. Since we seem to be on a hunt for bullshit this morning, I'd like to be the first to say that I think I've found some." I was getting bolder because it sounded like I was just about to lose the job anyway, and I didn't want to look like a wimp in front of Max and the ladies.

Elmer glared at me, but said nothing.

"I agree with Jack," Tracy announced. Her voice filled the void in the room, giving our two-man comedy a freshened direction. "I know that this isn't what you wanted when you started this investigation, but now it's the only way to go."

"Why is that?" Elmer stood up from his swivel chair, turned around and stepped up to the window. He faced the empty Trans-Continental ramp, with his back to us. "Go ahead, Tracy. Explain yourself. Convince me." His voice was cool, but it lacked the biting edge that it had had a minute before.

"Jack convinced me last night." Tracy was speaking to a turned-away Elmer – something she was evidently accustomed to. I visualised an entire soliloquy with Elmer pointed in another direction. Very dramatic. "Like Jack already told you, he didn't really have a single thing to go on at the beginning. He sent the word out that he already knew a great deal."

"So I've heard – from any one of a dozen people," Elmer answered. He continued to look out of the window.

"For good or bad, that was enough to get someone excited. Excited enough to get that someone to take shots at him last night."

Elmer turned to face us again. "Someone got excited all right – but maybe it was *someone else* who got excited." He nodded to himself a few times, then turned to me. "What about other clients? Maybe it's someone from one of your other clients' cases who did the shooting."

"I'm not working any other case that's got enough heat in it to boil an egg – never mind to kindle up an attempted murder. Not a chance."

"How about old cases? How about if someone's holding a grudge, or maybe looking for revenge?"

"Old cases are ancient history," I said, omitting the fact that there weren't many of them to speak of. There was no sense besmirching my fragile reputation, I might need it intact some time in the future. "The only thing unsettled from my old cases is usually my bill."

"Then how about another episode of Miami kill-and-plunder?" Elmer took a step towards where the rest of us

70

stood – a step that I hoped was symbolic of his change of mind and mood. On the other hand, maybe he was getting close so he could rip the Trans-Continental identification badge off from where it hung conspicuously on my jacket from a little plastic clip. "Maybe those shots had nothing to do with the Trans-Continental investigation at all." Elmer nodded to himself again, obviously pleased with his current analysis. "That could be it, too." He turned to Max. "You were there, too, Mr Bergman. What's your opinion?"

"Max. Call me Max."

"Okay, Max. You call me Elmer."

"Sure thing, Elmer." Max paused for a few seconds after the reintroductions to gather his thoughts. In spite of the delay, I had confidence in what Max was about to say because I already knew his opinion and I also knew that he was good with people – talking reluctant people into things was, after all, how a car salesman made his living. "We talked over that idea for a long time last night."

"Oh?" Elmer looked a little disappointed; he had clearly expected that perception to be strictly his own.

"Yeah. And it didn't make any sense at all that it was anything but a hit job on Jack. There was only one guy out there against the two of us, plus we're dressed in tennis clothes. That maybe means that we don't even have our wallets, you know?"

"Oh. Yeah." Elmer slowly nodded in agreement.

"And we're big guys, dressed for running, and most of the time we were fifty feet apart on different sides of the tennis net. That ain't an easy group to try to rob, you see what I mean?"

"Yeah. I see what you mean." I could see that Elmer was warming up quickly to Max, as I could have predicted. Both of them had a great deal of on-the-job learning in common, and both knew how to use it. If this conversation kept going much longer, I expected the two of them to make plans to go bowling together. "But what about the shots?" Elmer asked. "What do you think about the shots?"

"They were too close to me, that's true," Max continued. "But they were *really* close to Jack. Unless that creep had never fired a gun before in his life, Jack was the guy's target. Definitely."

"I hate to hear that," Susan said. She was standing beside Max, and she stepped towards Elmer as she spoke. Susan looked just as radiant now as she had last night – especially after Tracy and Max had left and she asked me if she could stay. My perfect mood from our evening together would still have been intact if she hadn't reminded me over breakfast that our current pattern of liaisons was a temporary arrangement until the Mercedes-man returned from a trip to Europe. At that point I probably should have thrown her out for good; instead, I made omelettes, bacon and coffee. "That's why we've got to help Jack," Susan continued, "to make it as safe as possible for him."

She looked over at me, but I continued to pretend to be looking only at Elmer – there was only so much open-heart surgery I could take before lunch. "Like I said before, I could use the help."

"Jack's in a dangerous position," Susan added.

"But so am I," Elmer replied. "Especially if it comes out that all of this was an exercise in lunacy on my part." He shook his head slowly again, then stepped behind his desk. He sat down and rocked back and forth a few times. The chair creaked; it definitely needed oil. There were probably five hundred mechanics and two thousand gallons of oil within a hundred yards of where we were standing, yet I knew that the chair would never get one ounce of lubrication. Half a dozen squeaks later, Elmer looked up at me. "Okay, Jack, I'll go along with it. It's too late for anything else anyway."

"You won't regret it," I answered, accepting his approval before he had a chance to renege.

"Regret it? I regret it already. But we might as well go full steam since enough people already know what you're here for. Besides, maybe you're right. Maybe there's no other way. Tracy?"

"Yes?"

"Get the proper identification tags for Max and Susan." Elmer gave them a welcome-aboard gesture by waving his hand. "Then let the word circulate that everyone who works for this goddamn airline better be cooperating fully with this special investigation. By the way, the investigation team also includes you, Tracy. If that much attention doesn't get the cockroaches out of the cabinets, there's nothing more I can do."

"It will," I said.

"Right. And if it doesn't, you can help me find a new job." Elmer glanced around his office, a place that I could tell he dearly felt at home in. I would hate to be the one who made him lose his great view of the empty tarmac ramp.

I took a deep breath, then turned towards the group. "Okay, let's get to work." I then led the enhanced Sawyer Investigating Team out of Elmer's office. Hopefully, we were headed into a nefarious world of treachery and deceit that was just waiting to be effectively sleuthed by one newly minted professional and three rank amateurs.

7

I was into my temporary office in the Trans-Continental terminal building a little after nine o'clock. Tracy was taking Susan and Max through the identification card process at the hangar, so that meant I would be on my own for a while. After spending most of the last two days with an ever-growing confederation of helpers, I felt pretty lonely after just a few minutes of being locked in the dreary environment that Tracy had selected for me. Maybe that was her plan, I mused to myself; maybe she was exhibiting some level of attraction to me and thus wanted me to feel lonely. More likely, it was pure self-delusion. Each of us is, indeed, the centre of our own universe.

I knew that, in an increasing way, I liked Tracy. I also loved Susan and had great affection for Max. Having all three of them on this job was mingling it into an amorphous body of emotion that was more on my mind than it should have been. It was getting my internal gyros a little out of whack.

Middle age was, I could now vouch from the inside, a rocky road for men. Women, too, probably. Coming to terms with the facts of human existence could be a depressing dilemma as the years went by. On the other hand, I could now use a portion of my remaining time on earth to try to find an attempted murderer with Max, to make a pass at Tracy, or even to track down Susan's new boyfriend if I cared to. Options abounded.

I shrugged, then got back to work. I fiddled with the company crew management computer for a while longer, until I had extracted all the data that I was looking for and made a note of it on the pad of useless information that I kept for each case. Finished with that, I picked up the telephone and asked Izzy Reese to come over to my dreary office.

"Nice day, huh?" Izzy said as he closed the door behind him a few minutes later.

"Hard to tell in here." I waved my hand around the gloomy room, then motioned Izzy towards a chair. He was wearing a blue shirt with brown pants and another paisley tie – this one even wilder than the last. He had left his jacket back in his office. Today, I was wearing a typical honky's ensemble: a white shirt, a striped blue-and-brown tie, dark brown slacks and a camel jacket. "That's another great paisley, Iz. Wow."

"Hey, man, it's in the blood, you know?" Izzy eyed my clothes for a minute. "Guess you've got your image to keep up," he said with what would pass as an all-knowing smirk. "If you're going to rub shoulders with the high folks, it's good that you put on their uniform. But I do dig your desert hairs."

"Yeah, the camel jacket is a favourite." Izzy settled into his seat while I shuffled some papers. Finally, I looked up. "How's things going with Davenport?" I asked.

Izzy smiled. "You got his attention, I'll say that. Once you left yesterday, he buzzed around me like I was his rich white uncle. He was very concerned that I was doing all the stuff you asked me."

"Naturally, he wanted to know exactly what that stuff was."

"Naturally." Izzy nodded. "I told him, of course, since you wouldn't have been so bold about it yourself if it was any kind of secret. I figured that you wanted him – and anyone else who asked, for that matter – to know."

"Figured right. Guys that wear paisleys are brighter than most."

"Even guys who only *sometimes* wear paisleys can be pretty bright." Izzy pointed to my striped blue-and-brown number. Our mutual admiration society had grown increasingly vocal, and the pleasant sensation it triggered in me gave me the sudden urge to rip off my own tie and set it on fire. "Anyway, I went through the computer records and got the list," Izzy said. "Like I figured, not too many."

"Just as good. The smaller the haystack, the easier we'll spot the needles."

"I think it was Tonto who once said, what you mean *we*, white man?"

It was my turn to smile. "Okay, Iz. I'll confess. I consider you on the inside. You is one of *we*."

"Me and Davenport?"

"You, me, my staff, Tracy and Elmer. That's the army, period. If I omitted anyone's name, I assure you that it was strictly by design." I waited for Izzy's reaction; none was visible. Finally, I continued. "Do you want to hear about the battle plans?"

"Lead on, General." Izzy touched his hand to his forehead in an abbreviated salute. "I await your orders."

"First, I've got to tell you about our staff. Susan and Max will be along in a little while. He's my best friend, she's my, uh, wife – although we're separated." I had hesitated just long enough during my confession to Izzy to display convincingly just how uncomfortable the situation made me.

"Sounds like an interesting group. Sounds like interesting group dynamics."

"Yeah, sometimes." I laughed, then continued. "Anyway, those two can help with the legwork, and whatever kind of sifting we'll need through the information that we come up with. Elmer will remain aloof from our operation unless we really need him. Tracy will keep Elmer informed, and do whatever else she feels like doing since she's sort of the king's emissary in our merry band."

"Fine with me."

"So tell me about the list you came up with." I had asked Izzy to compile a list of pilots and flight attendants who had flown with Jay Bridges at least half a dozen times in the past year. Whatever the dead copilot had been up to, it made sense that he might have spun some of his magical web over whomever was hanging around him.

Izzy laid down on the desk the computer run that he had brought with him into the room. "One captain, one female flight attendant."

I glanced down at the printout but didn't recognise either of the names. "What do you think?"

"I think that I could've fingered these two without the help of the whirling electrons. Computers are overrated toys."

"Don't tell IBM."

"They forgot to ask me. Anyway, the involvement of

these two folks with Bridges was, as they say, common knowledge."

"Common and carnal knowledge?"

"Yeah, some of that stuff too. Paula Tate, our female flight attendant friend of Bridges, was the grand carnee. She's an absolute hummer." Izzy laid a folder on the desk. "Here's her file."

"Worth reading?" I opened it up and ran my thumb through the stack of papers without really looking at them – I had faith that Izzy knew more about almost everything than any of the company computers could tell me.

"Naw." Izzy wrinkled his nose, making it an even wider protuberance than Mom Nature had designed it to be. His thin black moustache disappeared somewhere between his pendulous lips and bulbous nose. "On paper, she was just another sky waitress. In person, you'll see the difference."

"I'm all ears." I had also asked Izzy to have the folks on his friends-of-the-deceased list come in for a meeting with me as soon as possible; I already knew him well enough not to have to ask if it was arranged.

"She's next door."

"Then let the games begin." Izzy got up and walked out to get her while I glanced through her file and scribbled a few notes on my pad. After I picked up details from her personnel record, I glanced at the computer run that showed how many times she had flown with Jay Bridges. She had flown with Bridges an increasing number of times during the summer and early fall, then a great number of times from November until just before he was killed. But Paula Tate was not part of the crew on Bridges' last flight to Chicago. I picked up her file again and was looking at her picture when the door opened. She walked in.

"I'm Paula Tate. I hear that you want to talk about Jay."

"Yes. Please sit down." She closed the door behind her; Izzy had stayed away, having the good sense to leave us alone. As she walked up to the desk and sat in the chair in front of me, I pretended to be studying her file. In reality, I was trying to stare at her through those little holes in the edges of computer-run paper that make it possible for the machine to spit out reams of useless information at high

77

printing speeds. After a few moments I got tired of being surreptitious, so I laid down the computer sheet and looked at her directly.

Paula Tate was obviously accustomed to being stared at; she had a pleasant, unconcerned expression on her face as she stared straight back at me. The two of us sat for our portraits for what must have been half a minute while we each took in the details. From my perspective, her details were vexing – she was a gorgeous woman in her mid-twenties, with a radiant face and smile, shoulder length golden-brown hair, and brown eyes. My male prejudice told me that she was just too damned beautiful to be a murderer – which was a hell of an unprofessional way to begin an interrogation. Still, no matter what else Jay Bridges might have been, his taste in women seemed on target.

"I wasn't on Jay's last trip," Paula stated matter-of-factly.

"Yes, I've seen that." I pretended to look at the file some more, before I finally looked up. "Did they tell you what I'm here for?" I asked. There was, after all, no sense fishing if I didn't bait the hook.

"Sure. That Jay was probably into something illegal, and that he was killed in Chicago. That black pilot hinted that it wasn't an accident like we were first told." While she spoke her dimples grew larger, and I had the impression that we were talking about her dating preferences, not a potential murder. Still, she also gave the impression of being very aware of what she was saying.

"And what do you think?" I said.

"About what?"

"About Jay. About him being involved in something illegal. About him being murdered."

Paula smiled at me. "Well . . . who knows, you know?"

As silly as her words had sounded, I could tell that she knew exactly what she was saying and to whom she was saying it. That incredible collection of female genes sitting in front of me was pulling my chain, toying with me. It was time for me to do the same with her. "You don't sound terribly remorseful about poor Jay."

"Hey, you know, he's already dead. Right?"

"No question about it."

78

"So let's get right down to the basics, okay?" she said conspiratorially.

Paula had leaned forward in her seat a few inches; I did likewise to match her body language – another thing I had learned from college psychology. "Suits me just fine."

"It's no secret that Jay and I were good friends."

"Very good friends. Very good friends indeed. That's what I've been told."

Paula laughed for a brief instant at my last remark, in a way that made me feel slightly dumb for the overtones of moral reproach that I had couched the words in. "So go ahead," I continued, trying to regroup. "Tell me about your good friend Jay."

"Even though we were good friends – parties, sex, that kind of thing – I couldn't say that I knew a great deal about him. We had good times together, but we weren't together all the time."

"Did you live together?" I felt like a peeping Tom, but I was groping for some way to get her out of the comfortable groove that she was rolling along in. Either I was a worse interrogator than I thought, or she was damned good at this sort of thing. Probably both.

"We only lived together on airline trips." Paula smiled again, and it wasn't the least bit a self-conscious smile. "We had a good time on trips, we stayed in the same room, we partied. Having Jay along on an overnight was more fun than, say, watching television in the hotel room or going out on a food frenzy with the widebodies."

"Widebodies?"

"Yeah. The fat, old queens who have been in this job too long for anyone's good – including their own. All they can think about is strapping on a feed bag in faraway cities. It's their main reason for living, I guess. For me, there's lots more to life than watching your rump get two inches wider every year."

"That's a tough position to argue against. I don't think I'll try."

"I didn't think you'd try. You look like the kind of guy who understands more than he lets on. Am I right?"

"If I said yes, I'd be lying to you. Just wishful thinking

on my part." While I was soaking up the compliments being showered on me by the number one lead in my hunt to find a murderer, I was, deep down, increasingly torqued off at myself for allowing my ego to be so easily manipulated. I could see now that Paula Tate was a real artist, and that men were her lumps of clay. Still, that didn't make her a murderer – what I desperately needed was the kind of information that I suspected she was an expert at withholding. "So you and Jay stayed together, slept together, and yet you say that you don't know much about him? Is that right?"

"I know that he liked Bourbon on the rocks, the Miami Dolphins and playing blackjack. I pretty much knew what his sexual preferences were." Paula smiled again, this time conveying the unmistakable impression that even she was growing weary of the nolo contendere aspects of our tête-à-tête. "But I didn't know if Jay was Democrat, Republican or a Communist. I didn't know anything specific about his other girlfriends, but I knew that he had them. Even more important from your point of view was that I didn't know a damned thing about what he did when I wasn't with him."

"Really? You had no idea? Yet you knew enough to know that he had other girlfriends?" I was getting nowhere fast and that was obvious to both of us. Paula knew more, and she also knew how not to say it.

"Sure, he had other girlfriends. I had other boyfriends. So what?"

"Did he ever mention the subject of money to you?"

"Of course. All the time. He liked money even better than he liked sex. And Jay liked sex quite a lot." She smiled again, this time in a way that made me want to wring her neck. My male ego was being bruised by the concept that Paula was selling things wholesale that should, by my superficial appraisal, have been collector's items. On the other hand, I really didn't know what her price was. Maybe she took a low down-payment, but her interest rates were phenomenal. "With all that sex, you'd think that you would have learned a little more about Jay – you know, pillow talk, that kind of thing."

"Not everyone talks during sex. Some people don't even talk afterwards."

The first thought that went through my head was that sex education was a subject that Paula was obviously well qualified to teach. I shook that thought aside; it was too cheap a shot. Besides, I knew that I was just licking my wounds at, so far, being bested during this pseudo-investigation. "Your friend Jay had lots of extra money. Surely you must have noticed that he lived a great deal better than most copilots. You never asked him where it came from?"

"Is there a reward for knowing the answer?" Paula looked across the desk at me with a little smirk that said it all; she wanted to know what her cut would be.

"Are you asking for a reward for turning in evidence in a potential murder case?" I asked pretentiously. "I don't think that the police or the courts would think much of that." I suppose I was trying to frighten her into blurting something out, but as soon as I said it I knew that I was manoeuvring on quicksand. I was wasting both her time and mine but I didn't want to let her go because, first, I was enjoying looking at her and, second, she had rubbed against my male tendencies enough for me to want to give her a hard time.

"Don't be silly, I'm just making a joke." Paula was completely composed; she was a good actress delivering a set of well rehearsed lines.

"It's nothing to joke about."

"You're absolutely right. I shouldn't make jokes about things like that." Paula kept a neutral expression on her face, without the slightest hint of apprehension or annoyance. She looked like she was willing to spend the rest of the day chatting with me if I really wanted her to.

"We already know most of what we're looking for," I lied, "so none of this matters. I'm just a little surprised that you won't help us fill out a few of the missing pieces. I'd like to think that since the two of you were lovers, you'd want to help."

"Sure, that's what I'd expect you to think. Your generation makes a big deal about who they sleep with. My generation doesn't. Jay and I were ships in the night. We had some good times. That's all I knew. It's too bad that he's dead because he was fun. That's all I can tell you."

We make a big deal about who we sleep with. The image

81

of Susan, naked, lying on the bed, waiting for me, floated through my mind. *Susan waiting for me.* Mercifully, the image faded after a few moments. "There are worse things to do in life than trying to help people that you've made love with."

"That's a tough statement to argue against. I don't think I'll try," Paula responded. She was trying to flatter me by using my previous line, but it came off as a taunt.

"Yeah." *Make love, be in love, be loved.* Somehow, none of those trite words and phrases ever seemed to fit the feelings, at least as far as I was concerned. I was now thoroughly aggravated and completely skewed from the direction my thoughts should have been focused on. I said a few more words, gave her my card and asked Paula to call if she thought of anything. She said yes while, of course, actually meaning no. Hell no.

The truth was that, at least for the moment, I needed her a lot more than she needed me. That's a crummy negotiating position to be in, which was why she was so smug and I was increasingly irritable. Besides, I was getting tired of being lectured at by a beautiful girl young enough to be my proverbial daughter – especially about subjects to do with love. In that category at least, I was something of a combat veteran. I was also tired of being outsmarted by her. When she left, I sat back and thought the whole scene over several times.

"Is your preference to burn wood alone, or can anyone join your bonfire?" Izzy asked when he opened the door and peeked in.

"Throw on a log, I'm down to glowing embers."

"She's a hummer, just like I said, huh? I was going to warn you more, but I figured you needed to learn for yourself."

"She took me for a roller-coaster ride. She knows lots, but says nothing. I suspect that she has a good idea where Jay's money had come from, but she saw no reason to tell me."

"So your personal magnetism didn't work? Does that also mean that you didn't have enough dough to offer her a bribe?"

"As your soul brothers would say, right on."

82

"The brothers don't say that kind of thing any more, man. Only ageing honkies use those expressions these days."

"Thanks, I needed that." I stood up and stretched for a few moments, trying to get the blood moving again. There's something about being mentally pummelled by a pretty young lady that makes a middle-aged man feel like crawling into a dark cave and hibernating. On the other hand, there was still Susan, Tracy, Max and my growing pile of unpaid bills. I decided that – as they say on the spiritual TV channel – I should be turning towards the more upbeat, positive aspects in my life. By doing that, praise the Lord, I would be reaffirming myself, giving my soul a sense of direction. Hallelujah. "Okay, then let's get some joy in our lives. Let's get back to our hunt for a vicious, cold-blooded murderer. Who's next on our agenda?"

"We're backing up in the outer office, we've got two to deal with."

"Who?"

"Captain Ned Lange and Captain Louis Zarrillo. Want me to make a suggestion?" Izzy said.

"I guess it's pretty obvious that I could use a few."

"Don't be down on yourself, I'm still betting on the paisley-tie crowd." Izzy fingered his own tie for a moment. "But here's what I suggest. Let me talk to Lange. He really don't know shit – but it'll take him at least two, maybe three hours to tell you so. Guaranteed."

"Lange. He was the captain on Bridges' last flight?"

"Yeah. Odds are stronger that Elmer Woodruff or me were involved with Bridges before Lange would've been. Don't waste your time on him, he just happened to be on Bridges' last flight. Somebody had to be. Who it was really means nothing."

"Right on," I said.

"Maybe I was wrong, maybe that expression does have a chance of making a comeback. Next time we're eatin' barbecue, I'll check with the brothers." Izzy wrinkled his nose and, once again, his tiny black moustache disappeared beneath the folds of his brown skin for a few moments. "But one thing we can get out of Lange is a powerful transmitter to the troops. If you want, I can press the law-and-order button

83

and issue forthwith the jive about knowing most of the details about what bad had come down with Bridges. Old Ned will be happy to broadcast that message through the crewroom for us."

"Sounds effective. Do it."

Izzy stood up. "And I'll send Zarrillo in. You deal with him."

"I think you're telling me that he's worth an extra glance." While I spoke, I looked down at the computer printout that Izzy had brought me earlier; Captain Louis Zarrillo had flown with Bridges five months out of the last twelve. While a few of his flights in that period had a different copilot, the great preponderance of them had Bridges in the right seat. "Lots of exposure to our boy," I said as I tapped my hand against the printout.

"Yeah. Exposure." Izzy headed for the door. "One thing more you should know," he added. "I saw your new friend Paula as she cornered Zarrillo in the corridor. She spotted him on her way out. Made a beeline in his direction."

"Maybe they're old friends."

"Maybe they sang in the same church choir."

"I'm getting your point."

"Yeah. And they were having a soul-mate kind of talk, if you know what I mean. Zarrillo had a big frown on his face, and Paula-baby had a big and growing grin. She kept stepping up closer to Zarrillo, and he kept edging further down the corridor. She was the *pursuer* and he was the *pursued*. By the time they saw me, they had edged themselves half the way towards the elevator."

"They told me in detective school that those kinds of things can sometimes mean something. I think they called them clues."

"Right on," Izzy said as he flashed the palms of his hands at me in a with-it gesture. He then opened the door and left.

I glanced at Zarrillo's file for a few moments, making notes in my pad from the data on the sheets. The door opened and Zarrillo stepped into the room. He was in his captain's uniform, his stylised black hair flowing carefully from under the edges of his flight cap, his uniform with its gold stripes appearing neat and authoritative against his reddish Latin-American complexion and a mouth filled with brilliantly white teeth. My very first impression was that the man should have been the lead character in a toothpaste advertisement. "Thank you so much for coming, Captain. I hope this doesn't interrupt your day too badly," I said as the two of us shook hands.

"I have very little time that I can spend with you, I'm afraid to say." Louis Zarrillo checked his wristwatch. "My crew check-in time is in fifteen minutes."

"I can have Izzy Reese call downstairs to say that you're here, if you'd like."

"No, I'm sorry. I have to be downstairs in fifteen minutes. To review the flight plan."

"I see." We both sat. I fumbled with papers for a moment while I jostled with those all-important additional first impressions. What would dear Mom say about Louis Zarrillo? Although she'd probably phrase it more delicately, the bullshit about his needing to be downstairs precisely at official check-in time to review the flight plan was pure Hollywood. In reality, it would take only a few minutes of the allocated one hour before departure to see that today's routine flight was being handled in the same routine manner as it was every other damned day of the week. Clearly, Mom would point out that Zarrillo wanted to get away from me as soon as he could. He wasn't on the hook yet, but I could feel the float of my fishing line beginning to bob up and down. "This is about Jay Bridges."

"Yes. That's what I've been told." Zarrillo blinked a few times, then assumed a position of studied casualness. I made a mental note to tell Paula Tate that she could make a few bucks giving Zarrillo lessons in how to appear calm in the face of potential adversity – something he was clearly ill-prepared for. "But there's very little that I can tell you."

"Your name came up simply because you had flown with Bridges in the past." I tapped the computer printout. "Just like a dozen other captains. We're just looking for any little clue, something he might have said, a casual word or phrase that might help us wrap this investigation up." After speaking to Paula, dealing with this man seemed to call for the opposite tack – I was reassuring him rather than trying to frighten him.

If I frightened him any more, I had the distinct impression that he might decide to faint.

"No, he said nothing. Nothing at all. We hardly spoke, except for official duties, of course."

"Of course." I could picture Zarrillo and Bridges conducting their official dialogues: *Roger, wilco, over and out.* Captain Louie was trying to make me believe that he had sat within a few feet of a copilot for five of the last twelve months and never said a word to him. The manure was getting pretty deep on his side of the cattle fence; it seemed to be time to turn on the electric prod. "But I was wondering how come you seemed to fly with Bridges so often. Unless the company records are in error, you had flown with him several months in a row."

"Well, yes, that's true." Zarrillo did the classic squirm in his seat while he flashed his pearly whites. Clearly, he was biding his time while thinking up a suitable retort. "I wondered that myself, why Bridges kept flying with me," he finally continued. "I knew that he had trouble with some of the captains, and I had no particular problems with him. Maybe that's why he kept putting himself on my trips."

"That makes sense," I said, knowing damned well that it didn't. Bridges wasn't the sort to lie low for months on end, and a captain who didn't want to keep working with a particular copilot could handle that problem in any one of a dozen ways. The way the pilots' bidding system worked, both those guys had to *want* to keep flying with each other or they never would have got together for so many months in a row. "Okay, then. Sorry to bother you, that's all I'll need."

"No problem. Sorry I couldn't be more help," Zarrillo said as we shook hands. He wheeled around and exited posthaste, leaving me no opportunity to say anything else if I were so inclined.

But I wasn't. What I was inclined to do was to sit down and give serious thought to this morning's perplexing puzzle: why was Captain Louis Zarrillo lying to me.

8

The knock on my office door brought me back to reality. "Come in," I called out as I glanced at my wristwatch. It had been nearly a quarter of an hour since I'd begun meditating on the lies of Captain Louis Zarrillo. *Tempus* did indeed *fugit* when you didn't know what you'd be doing next.

The door to my dreary office opened to reveal the sort of vision that a man could use when he's not doing particularly well at his chosen profession. In the doorway, smiling at me, were Susan and Tracy. Standing behind them was Max, who was wearing his usual neutral countenance. "Good to see you folks. I could use some help and encouragement right about now."

"Things not going well?" Susan asked. Her sympathetic expression made her appear sexier than ever.

"Not terribly." I waved the ladies towards the two open chairs in front of my desk. Max, seeing no place to sit after he stepped into the room, elected to lean against the side wall. "Make yourselves at home. Before we begin, I've got one more person to get." I picked up the telephone and dialled Izzy's number. He answered it on the first ring. "Tonto, this is the Lone Ranger. You still got Lange in there with you?"

"I should've put a money bet on it," he answered. "Coulda won some easy cash."

"If you bet with me and win, you're going to have to take an IOU."

"That's okay, you're good for it."

"I know that Lange's right in front of you, so I'll make this brief. Is there any sign of his end of the conversation drying up in the immediate future?"

"Naw."

"Getting anything useful?"

"Not a shot, no way."

87

"Have you already gotten around to pressing that law-and-order button we spoke about? Is Captain Lange ready to sally forth and spread the gossip that we already know lots more than we actually do?" I glanced up at my three cohorts in the room and winked. Even though they didn't know who I was talking to, I could see that they were happy with the direction of the conversation – it was something of an indication that our army was indeed on the *move*.

"Yeah, that's all been done," Izzy replied matter-of-factly. "Is there anything else?"

"Yes. Use this phone call as your excuse to get Lange out of there. Then come back here to my office as soon as you can, we're getting ready to come up with strategy."

"We could use some. I'm on the way."

I hung up the telephone and turned to Tracy. "That was Izzy," I said. "He'll be here in a minute, then we'll review our situation and come up with a plan."

"Who's Izzy?" Susan asked.

"A check pilot who's been assigned to help us."

"Is that something that you requested?"

"Sort of." I left out any discussion of Chief Pilot Davenport, since I wasn't too sure how he fitted in yet. "Anyway, Izzy sends out good vibrations, so, out of need, I made the assumption that he's a good man."

"He is," Tracy said.

"Glad to hear that. Since we needed someone from the pilot corps as part of our group, Izzy was my choice." At that moment the door opened and Izzy literally waltzed in – he was a big man and somewhat overweight, but he manoeuvred his frame gracefully and with an economy of motion. Without a word from me, Izzy said hello to Tracy and then introduced himself to Susan and Max. Everyone shook hands and smiled amicably. Izzy did a miniature carioca step to manoeuvre himself against the side wall next to Max.

"This is the entire team, fellow ballplayers, with the exception of the boss. Elmer can be thought of as our team manager." At the mention of the boss's name I felt a little rumbling in my gut; I knew that as far as Elmer was concerned, we were approaching the late innings and our team was still hitless.

88

"I guess we're ready. The question is, ready for what?" Susan asked.

"Good question. We'll get to that in a minute. First the rules. Simple ones, no need to take notes." From my seat behind the desk I scanned the expectant faces in front of me. Susan, Max, Tracy and Izzy. It was a good line-up – hopefully, enough of a line-up. "There have to be no secrets between any of us. We've each got to throw everything we know or suspect out on the table. Then maybe someone else in the group will be able to build on it."

Tracy nodded. "Good idea."

"Yes, it is. And that reminds me, I'll need someone to nudge me later so I can remember to tell you folks my feelings about Chief Pilot Davenport." There was probably no point in sharing my first impressions of Davenport but, what the hell, it would make me feel good and give a prime example of sharing useless information.

"Okay."

"Rule number two is no acting on your own. Remember, if our hunches are right then we're dealing with dangerous folks who have already killed at least one man. They've also, we're pretty sure, taken shots at Max and me."

"Yeah." Max shuffled his feet where he stood. "Bastards," he mumbled towards Izzy, who mumbled a similar epithet back in agreement.

"Final point," I continued. "Although it's really a rehash of what I've already said. Since we're basically operating in the dark, everyone should throw in anything they can come up with no matter how foolish or pointless it might sound." Now I had all the excuses I needed to say nasty things about Davenport and every other chief pilot I had ever dealt with – the pay for this job might not have been tops, but at least the potential for personal satisfaction abounded. "At this point, nothing should be considered as a waste of our time since time is the only thing we've got going for ourselves."

"Does Izzy know about everything that happened at the tennis courts?" Max asked. I could tell from the way he phrased the question that Max had already fully accepted Izzy as one of us.

"Yes, he's been told about our night on the town. But

something that hasn't been shared yet is what Izzy worked on this morning."

"Oh?"

I gestured palms open to Izzy to indicate that he now had the floor. He took half a step forward and began relating his suspicions about whoever had flown the most with the late Jay Bridges in the past twelve months, and how he then confirmed that information with the company computer.

When Izzy finished, Susan asked a question. "I assume that you've already set up interviews with that stewardess and captain?"

"Yes." Having the correct answers for Susan's questions was something that always made me feel good. "Not only set up. Already executed, too."

"Really?"

"Yes, indeed." I was, I knew, showing off – both for Susan and, I could tell, a little bit for Tracy, too. "Izzy set up the interviews and I conducted them this morning while you were getting your ID cards."

"What do these folks look like?" Max asked.

I shuffled through the paperwork on my desk to find their pictures – something that I should have known Max would want to see before the conversation went much further. Max reacted to people on a gut, composite level. Descriptions and analysis without a face to go with them were too disjointed for him to deal with. "Here. Paula Tate."

"Wow."

"Actually, double wow."

"Actually, triple wow," Susan said. She leaned over the desk to study the picture more closely. After a few moments, Susan looked up at me. "She's an interesting person, right?"

"Very," I answered, confirming her professional opinion. One thing Susan knew for certain was how to ferret out the potential chemistry between men and women. Paula Tate obviously had enough of that quality, too – enough for it to show up even in a photo.

"Did Paula Tate have lots to say?" Tracy asked. She, too, had glanced at Paula's picture – but I could tell from her voice that Tracy already knew all too well what Paula looked like. I had already suspected that Paula Tate was precisely the type that Tracy would have zero tolerance for. "I assume that Paula knew a great deal," Tracy continued. There was a barely concealed edge to her voice. "Her liaisons with Bridges were public displays. Displays of the worst type."

"Your assumption that Paula knows lots is probably correct, but she wasn't doing any talking." I went on to explain how that beautiful young woman had basically run all over me.

"Paula Tate's gonna be a tough one to squeeze," Izzy added when I finished. "My bet's on Zarrillo. He ain't got his cards stacked up neat as Paula-baby does."

"True." I fished out the photo of Zarrillo and passed it around. While everyone looked at his picture, I recounted the interview – including my feeling that Zarrillo had been uttering bold-face lies to me.

"Hey, that might be the break we need," Max said as he stepped between the two ladies and up to the desk. "What did this guy lie about?"

"For starters, everything. Most particularly, about his relationship with Jay Bridges. Zarrillo had flown most of his flights with Bridges for five of the last twelve months, yet he seemed to have trouble even remembering what his copilot looked like – never mind anything that Bridges might have said." I had already used the time between Zarrillo's exit and my troupe's arrival to convince myself beyond the heralded shadow of a doubt that Captain Louie would be our handle.

"Is there any chance that he was the guy that shot at us?" Max asked. "It was pretty dark when it happened."

"No, he doesn't look anything like that guy. But I think there's lots of chances that he knows who did. At least that's my feeling." The nice thing about this troupe of mine, I realised, was that I could be as open and up-front as I cared to be. My emotions were already in a relative state of disarray because of some of them. Was it Othello who had said that freedom comes when there's nothing left to lose? No, I now remembered, it was Janis Joplin. Othello said some other stuff.

"That's a pretty heavy accusation," Izzy injected in his deep voice, "that Zarrillo knows who shot at you."

"Do you disagree?" I asked.

"Hell, no." Izzy wrinkled his nose. "I think that both Louie and Paula-baby are, you should pardon the word image, up to their elbows in this crap." Izzy then gave a slight nod of apology towards the others in the room.

The group settled down for an amiable chat. After a while, Tracy asked, "What do we do next?"

"We want lemonade, we got to squeeze the lemon." Max shot a conspiratorial glance towards Izzy – a glance, I figured, that had to do with the fact that Izzy was the first to use that *squeeze* analogy a short while earlier. Izzy gave a small but perceptible nod back to Max. Poetic licence thus applied for and granted, Max continued. "We got to squeeze him on all sides – where he works, where he lives, where he plays."

The image of a lemon having separate sides that worked, lived and played was beyond my visualisation skills so I sat quietly. Everyone did. Half a minute went by. Susan inhaled loud enough for me to hear her. Izzy cleared his throat and everyone turned to him, but he said nothing.

"Wait a minute." It was Tracy who finally spoke. "I just realised that I know where Zarrillo lives." She reached over my desk and picked up Zarrillo's personnel file. "Yes, this is the address – a high-rise condo on Biscayne Bay. My girlfriend Pamela Nichols – she's a senior stewardess with us – lives in the same building. I remember that she mentioned it to me shortly after Zarrillo moved in."

"She a friend of Zarrillo's?"

"No. Hardly even an acquaintance. She just knows who he is, that's all."

"What does that do for us?" Max asked.

"Access to the building," I answered. Tracy nodded. "That means that we get beyond the doorman without Zarrillo knowing that we're around."

"Why should we do that?" Max asked. "Maybe we should go straight at him, let him know that we suspect him. If he thinks that we're on to him, maybe he'll make a mistake."

"No good," Izzy said. "Zarrillo scares pretty easy. Sounds like he'd already seen that ghost of Christmas past when Jack talked to him, but Jack didn't overplay his hand so Zarrillo just figures that his name came out of the computer because he flew with Bridges."

"Very true." I nodded in agreement – Zarrillo wasn't capable of being too deceptive, but he was certainly capable of becoming very frightened. If that happened, then he would – like Izzy was saying – probably go into full panic. What that would lead to was anyone's guess. Zarrillo's fears might be useful later on, but not quite yet when we had absolutely no idea of what we were looking for, and no other place to go if we scared our lone rabbit back into his hole.

"So where does that leave us?" Izzy asked.

"I'm not sure." I tapped a pencil on the desk a few times and looked around the room. Everyone was painfully quiet again.

"How about if we do a little scouting of our own," Susan finally volunteered.

"Scouting? Where?"

"Everywhere that Zarrillo goes. Starting with where he lives." Susan smiled at me with that beautiful look of hers that told me she knew what she was talking about. "This Zarrillo fellow that you're describing sounds like the type who might leave something interesting lying around. All we have to do is find it."

"I can probably get us past the doorman by calling my friend Pamela, but how are we going to get into his apartment?" Tracy asked.

Max stepped around the desk and laid his hand on Tracy's arm. "Don't worry about that, honey. Getting into a condo, once we're into the building, isn't gonna be much of a problem."

"Oh. Fine with me, if you say so," Tracy answered.

"Yeah, I do." Max squeezed her arm again, ostensibly to reassure her that his prowess with condo locks was nothing to have doubts about. Tracy smiled back, apparently convinced.

So, for that matter, was I. But I could see that Izzy had something to say. "Why the frown, Iz?"

"'Cause I outsmarted us." Izzy put his head down and shuffled his feet self-consciously. "I already didn't follow one of the rules. Damn."

"How?"

"Figured you might want Zarrillo available for the next few days, so I sent another check pilot down to take his flight. Made up a story about the copilot needing to be observed on a line trip. So Zarrillo left, probably went home. If he's not home now, he could be at any time."

"It's not your fault. You didn't know the rule until after you sent Zarrillo home. The question is, now, what do we do?" All of us went quiet again. Quiet seemed to be the recurring theme of our meeting. The vision of Zarrillo walking into his apartment while me and my gang were rummaging through his dirty socks was not a pretty picture.

"How long before Zarrillo's next trip?" Tracy asked.

"Not for a week."

"Too long," I answered. Without even asking, I knew that sitting on our hands for seven days was not what Elmer had in mind for our merry band.

Susan leaned over my desk and picked up Zarrillo's picture again. She studied it for a while. I could smell her perfume – that, and maybe the angle she was holding her head and the way her hair swayed across the nape of her neck, reminded me of an early trip we had taken together. Acapulco. She had hardly ever left my side the entire time. It was a long time ago, but it seemed like only yesterday. But it was a long time ago. "Susan, what are you thinking?" I asked.

"I'm thinking that if Captain Zarrillo is home, I might be able to find some way to keep him . . ." Susan looked away from Zarrillo's photograph, up at me, and smiled. It was her natural smile, a smile of sincerity and innocence – while also, somehow, being a smile that signified infinite wisdom and knowledge. ". . . to keep Zarrillo occupied. I bet I could do it."

"I bet you could," I answered neutrally. The palms of my hands had become sweaty, but I ignored that. I rose from my chair. Everyone was looking at me. "We'll give this plan a try, if we can work out the logistics. Izzy, you stay here to mind the store. Keep your eyes and ears open, maybe we'll start to get some growth from the fertiliser you planted with Ned Lange this morning."

"Okay."

"Tracy, you call your friend Pamela and see if she'd like a

few visitors for lunch. With our luck, she left yesterday on an extended flight around the world. If she's not in, we'll have to try to bluff our way past the doorman by using her name."

"No need, she's home – I spoke to her yesterday." Tracy reached for the telephone. "Pamela doesn't go out until the end of the week."

"Good. Maybe our luck is changing." I looked over at Max. "You need anything special to get us into Zarrillo's apartment?"

"Few things. I got them in the car."

"I need a few things, too," Susan said.

"Really? What?"

"Tools."

I took a step towards her and put my hand on her arm. Her skin was, as always, like a piece of fine, warm velvet. My fingers luxuriated at the touch. "What kind of tools?"

"Just a few things. I carry them in my car." She turned her head at an angle, she grinned at me. "You'll see. It's stuff I might need. Remember, we've got a bet going. I bet that I can get this guy out of his apartment long enough for you to look the place over."

"Sure, it's a bet," I answered, not bothering to point out that it was a bet I would never make in earnest – a fool's bet, of the worst kind. I was, in a sense, betting against myself. Worse yet, I had already been dealt a pretty bad hand. The sound of Tracy hanging up the telephone brought me back to the moment.

"Everything's set," Tracy announced. "Pamela's looking forward to meeting us."

"Then let's not keep Pamela waiting." I led the way out, with my gang following.

9

All four of us went in Max's car, a three year old Cadillac. Luck had smiled on us again, this time through Max's selection of car; Susan and Tracy both had two-seaters and I was afraid to use my white BMW for anything that resembled surveillance work. I was probably being overly cautious, but there was the outside chance that my car was already on the desperadoes' most-wanted list since at least one of their kind had seen it at the tennis courts. "Nice car, Max."

"Yeah. They don't make 'em this way no more." Max thumped the palm of his hand on the dash. The red leather was sun-bleached but solid, and was obliging enough not to cave in. "Nice riding car, too. It's comfortable to sit in, a guy can stretch out. And it's a good bet for undercover work 'cause it don't stand out."

"An excellent point." A three year old white Cadillac was more or less the Volkswagen of Miami, at least in the upscale sections of town. Even though the middle-aged nouveau riche did drive foreign machines, the hard core of condoville – the Jewish gentry, the retirees from the upper middle class – remained steadfastly loyal to the Cadillac emblem. It was a religious thing, I suspected; they used that symbol of solid Americana to ward off evil spirits, blacks and Latinos. "You should have no trouble selling *this* car," I said.

"I already had two offers on it." Max looked over to where I was sitting next to him. He smiled. "That's why I had to take it off the lot today, didn't want it snapped up too soon. Figured this car might come in handy for us."

"I like being chauffeured in a Cadillac," Susan said from the back seat where she was sitting with Tracy. The two ladies had been chatting in tones too low for me to hear them. "I just wish you had worn a chauffeur's cap."

"Naw. Don't wanna spoil ya." Max glanced up at me again,

in a way that spoke volumes about how my problems with Susan were caused by my inclination to treat her too well.

"Max, all women *like* to be spoiled," Tracy said. She leaned forward in her seat, her arm brushing against the back of mine. I had draped my arm casually across the car's giant front seat, and now Tracy was leaning against it. I let my arm lie.

"Yeah, they like being spoiled. But that don't mean it's good for them. Sometimes people don't know what they should have."

"Max, are you being serious?" Tracy asked.

"He sure is," Susan volunteered. She reached forward and ran her hand through Max's hair, mussing it up. "But it's not as bad as it sounds. He just doesn't believe that people should have quite as much latitude as I think they should, that's all."

"Yeah. Not so much latitude." Max was glancing over at me again, but this time I avoided his stare. Instead, I looked out front. I didn't have the energy to enter the debate, not in the direction it was headed in. A high-rise condominium loomed up, its uppermost floors poking out above the surrounding buildings. "That's the condo, isn't it?" I said to change the subject.

"Yes," Tracy said.

Max speeded up a bit, then wheeled around the corner and finally turned into the condo parking lot. We left the car and headed across the warm asphalt. Clear skies, a light breeze, and temperatures in the low eighties. A pleasant day to do scouting work. The four of us ambled casually, looking purposely nonchalant.

We had already agreed to act as two couples in our march to the apartment so as to avoid any suspicion of what we actually were – a gang of marauding thieves. The couples arrangement was that Max was with Susan while I was with Tracy. I was the one who had broached that delicate subject during our car ride, with the pronouncement that Max and Susan should stick together since they would eventually be wandering around the building. Part of my reasoning was that I didn't want Max spending his time hitting on Tracy when he should be paying strict attention to business. Max hadn't shown too much beyond mild interest in Tracy so far,

97

but I knew him well enough to expect that more was probably on the way.

Tracy's friend had already left word of our imminent arrival with the doorman, so we were ushered straight in. We rode up in the elevator in silence. Tracy led the way down the corridor.

Human beings are strange creatures, a fact that I was constantly reminded of through observation of others and, all too often, observation of myself. Today's lesson was courtesy of Max, who nearly did a backflip when the door opened to reveal the face and frame of one senior flight attendant Pamela Nichols. She was of medium height, thin, with a pleasant mane of dark blonde hair and a cute face. A nice-looking lady by anyone's definition. But to Max, she was obviously the Mona Lisa times two. Maybe times four. So much for my calculated plan to keep Max's mind strictly on the job.

"Pamela, let me introduce you," Tracy said after we all walked inside.

Everyone sat down. Pamela had drinks ready. I took a Heineken. Max had a frothy-looking pink concoction that Pamela was blending up for the ladies. Max also, naturally, insisted on helping. I could've screamed. Maybe I should've. Instead, I told Pamela a bare-bones story of why we were there, omitting nearly all the facts that mattered. It wasn't that I didn't trust her – she did look a little Mona Lisa-ish, even to me – it was just that there was no need telling more people than we really had to.

"I've got nothing much to do anyway," Pamela said after the pink drinks had been passed around. Max had manoeuvred the seating arrangements and was, *par conséquent*, sitting next to Pamela on the couch. "I'd love to help Tracy and you folks any way that I can."

We chatted a little more, learning some details about Zarrillo. Pamela really knew very little about the man, other than where his apartment was – two floors above us, on the tenth. Was he inside? No one knew. Should we call his telephone number to see if he answered? No, we all decided – it would only tip him off if he were at home, and, besides, even if he didn't answer that was no guarantee that he wasn't inside anyway. Zarrillo playing hard-to-get on the telephone could make our burglary attempt somewhat inconvenient. "Any ideas?" I asked.

"Yes." Susan stood up. She was carrying a small Gucci bag in her hand – her earlier-announced tools, whatever they were. "I need a place to change my clothes."

"In there." Pamela pointed towards what I assumed was the bedroom. Max assumed so too – I saw his eyes get a little beadier. He inched closer to Pamela on the couch. She, as far as I could tell, held her spot. In fact, if anything, Pamela had moved even closer to Max.

Why were these two total strangers suddenly on an apparent collision course of mutual interests? What was it that they liked about each other – and liked so much and so quickly? What does a used car salesman have in common with the Mona Lisa? I didn't know now, and, I now knew, I would never know. Not about them, not about me and Susan, not about me and Tracy. Not about anything and anybody at any time.

A few minutes later Susan returned. Even Max took his eyes off Pamela long enough to admire what Susan had brought in her tool bag. It was the nicest, sexiest blue and yellow one-piece bathing suit that had ever been created this side of the expanding universe. "Very nice," I managed to choke out through suddenly parched lips. I took another slug of Heineken, enough to empty the bottle. I sucked in a little air. "Are you going for a swim?"

"No. I'm going fishing." Susan smiled at everyone, then sauntered towards the front door. "The story I'll use is that I'm Pamela's old high-school friend, in from New York for a few days. I'll say that I saw him coming into the building, and Pamela told me his name and that he was a bachelor airline pilot who lives here. I'm intrigued by pilots, so I came up to meet him." Susan glanced at me, smiled, then turned back to Pamela. "By the way, where did we go to high school?"

"Sewickley, Pennsylvania. It's a nice suburb on the west side of Pittsburgh," Pamela answered. I could tell from her voice that Pamela was enjoying all of this – the intrigue, plus the attentions of Max.

"Okay, I've got it."

99

"What do we do next?" I asked.

"Keep checking the pool area. If Zarrillo's in, he and I will be down there in the not-too-distant future. If he's not, I'll come back to get you."

"Good plan," I mumbled. *Bad plan*, I said inside. I didn't like Zarrillo, and I didn't like the idea of Susan parading herself in front of him. For the ten trillionth time since I met Susan, part of me wished that I never had. "Pamela, I could use another Heineken, if you've got one."

"Sure." Pamela headed for the kitchen.

"Wish me luck," Susan said to me as she stepped out of the door and towards the elevator.

"Good luck," I answered automatically, knowing damn well that it wouldn't be a matter of luck at all. *Keep your mind on the job*, I said to myself. But all I could think about was that Louis Zarrillo had systematically lied to me, and he was about to get Susan's undivided attention. I now had two irrefutable reasons why I didn't like the guy.

10

I stood at the sliding glass door of Pamela's apartment and looked at the pool area below for what seemed like a week. It couldn't have been very long, though, because I had barely finished my second Heineken when Susan appeared. Even from eight floors above, her blue and yellow bathing suit was quite an eyeful. I watched her manoeuvre her way around the lounge chairs, with Zarrillo in tow, before she picked a spot that she knew would be within full view of Pamela's apartment. Smart girl. "There she is."

"Where?"

"Right there." Max had come up behind me and I pointed out where she was sitting. He nodded. "They look pretty settled."

"Yes, they do." Max watched a while longer. "I don't think they're going anywhere. If I was Zarrillo, I wouldn't be."

I tried to think of some witty comeback, but couldn't. I put my empty Heineken bottle down on a nearby glass table. "We should get going."

"Okay."

"I think it's best if Pamela stays here. We should use her as a lookout."

"How?" Max was visibly displeased with my suggestion that his new-found love stay behind.

"How? What kind of question is that? A lookout is some-one who *looks out*." I tapped my finger on the sliding glass door. I was getting a little testy with Max because of what I supposed was petty jealousy – his life was coming up roses, while my life seemed perpetually overgrown with weeds. Still, it felt so good getting my back up that I pushed aside any thoughts of apologising. I turned to Pamela instead. "Just keep an eye on them. If they go anywhere other than into the pool, come up and get us. You've got only two floors to go,

101

they've got to come up ten flights, plus Susan will be stalling him as long as she can. That should be more than enough time for you to beat them."

"I hope so," Pamela said. She sounded a little nervous. "But maybe I'd do better trying to head them off at the elevator? Susan's supposed to be my friend from New York, so if I ran into them we could talk. That'll look natural enough, and give even more time for you people to get out of his apartment."

"Yeah." Max took a step closer to Pamela. I could tell from his voice that he knew enough to be gentle with me. "Tell you what," he said, "I'll get Zarrillo's door open for you, then I'll come back here. If he and Susan leave the pool area, Pamela and me will both do something – I'll get you, she'll cut them off at the elevator. Like that we got it covered both ways."

Max was being gentle and, besides, I could tell that the negotiations on the assignment for Pamela Nichols might go on until the sun went down – maybe even until the new ice age began – if I didn't give in soon. "Okay. Fine. Great. Let's go." I motioned to Tracy, who had been standing quietly in the back of the room. She came towards me. Max, Tracy and I left the apartment, got into the elevator, and went up to the tenth floor.

"I already looked at the kind of door locks they've got in this building," Max said as we headed down the corridor that led to Zarrillo's apartment. "Shouldn't be too hard."

"Maybe you should've practised on Pamela's lock," I said, the double entendre intended.

"Naw. No need. These locks are simple. Besides," Max answered, his most irritating smirk aimed in my direction as he covered my second point. "She'll give me a key. Soon."

"A little cocky, aren't you?"

"Confidence, that's what it's called. Gotta have it, man, it's the secret weapon in this war."

"If you say so." *War?* Maybe. Maybe that was my problem, that I didn't realise it was a war. Or maybe my problem was that I was spending too much time fraternising with the enemy.

"Here we are," Tracy said. She stepped ahead of Max,

then knocked on the door. "If anyone's inside, I'll say we're looking for Susan," she whispered. But Zarrillo had no one hiding in his apartment, or, at least, no one who cared to admit publicly to it. "Okay, the coast, as they say, is clear," Tracy announced in a low voice. "Max, do your stuff."

Max pulled a couple of home-made tools out of his pocket. He bent over the lock and fiddled while Tracy and I watched the corridor. "Come on, hurry up," I said. "Someone on this floor is eventually going to get the urge to go out for a beer."

"Can't rush it, man. It's an art." Max never took his eyes off the lock. He took one of his handyman tools out of the keyhole. He inserted another one in its place. "Pretty soon, I think."

"Hurry up."

"Don't rush me."

Tracy was moving around nervously, swaying her body from side to side. "The people on this floor don't go out for beers, Jack. They go out for martinis. I could use one myself."

"A little early in the day for a martini, isn't it?" I answered, mostly to fill the empty moments with the sound of my own voice. Babbling was my substitute for whistling in the dark.

"Usually, yes. But there's something about the crime of breaking and entering that makes time fly. Right now, it seems pretty late in the day to me."

"I'll get you a martini as soon as we're done here."

"It's a deal."

"Got it," Max announced. He stood upright and pushed on the door. It opened. He flashed a big smile at Tracy, then a bigger one at me. "Go to it, boss. I'll head back."

As Max stepped around me, I grabbed him by the arm. "Just be sure that you watch Susan and Zarrillo. Don't let any distractions turn your head, if you know what I mean."

"Hey, no sweat. Strictly business."

"Business. Right." I let go of Max's arm and watched him gallop down the hall towards the elevator. *Business.* With a capital M for Monkey, I was quite certain. Still,

Max was probably responsible enough to keep Susan in view. Probably. I turned round and went into Zarrillo's apartment, closing the door behind me. Tracy was two steps ahead, looking into the kitchen.

"No one in here. That must be the bedroom." Tracy pointed towards the doorway to my right.

"I'll check it out." I moved forward cautiously to look in past the opened door. Empty. "Unless they're in the closets or under the bed, Zarrillo has no friends stashed up here."

"Now what?"

"I don't know. Look for anything marked *clues*." Tracy and I went our separate ways in the apartment – she, towards the kitchen and a hallway desk, me, towards the bedroom. The decor was sort of nondescript modern, with just enough aluminium and glass to prevent the overall effect from having any personality at all. Everything looked new, clean and distinctly middle class, as if it had all been recently transplanted, in its entirety, from a storefront display in the kind of shopping mall where little booths in the centre of the walkways sold keychains and monogrammed coffee mugs.

The bedroom itself had nothing to offer. I poked through the closets and discovered that I didn't like Zarrillo's taste in clothes. That made sense, since I didn't like Zarrillo. I went back to the living room. "Find anything?"

"Was that *clues* with a C or a K?" Tracy asked.

"Either will do. How are you doing?" She was holding in her hand some papers from, evidently, the hallway desk.

"A stack of bills. Thought maybe you might want to look through them. Nothing else of interest."

Tracy handed over the bills. "I was hoping for a signed confession," I said as I flipped through them. "Disappointing." A Texaco bill. A Visa bill, with an outstanding balance of $1,468.54. Good, it served Zarrillo right to have to pay one and a half per cent a month on the unpaid carry-over. An insurance bill for his car. "He drives a Buick. That's worth making a mental note of."

"I already know that – I've got his parking sticker paperwork."

"Oh. Right." I turned to the next bill. American Express. I could tell from the size of it that Louis Zarrillo seldom left home without it. I unfolded the sheet and ran down the list of charges, looking for God knew what. "Hey." Something on the page had caught my eye.

"What is it?" Tracy looked over my shoulder.

"Here." I pointed at the suspect line. "A charge for a round-trip airline ticket from Cleveland to Chicago on United Airlines. That doesn't make any sense. Why would Zarrillo ride on another airline when he could ride on his own airline for free?"

"And why would he pay full fare?" Tracy asked, pointing to the total. "We've got a pass arrangement with United, we get discounts on them. He could've gone for a quarter of that amount."

"Look at the date." It suddenly made sense to me.

"That's the night Jay Bridges was killed!"

"And he was killed in Chicago." I looked up at Tracy. "Zarrillo went to Chicago instead of being where he was supposed to be."

"Which was?"

"In Cleveland. He was on an overnight for the airline. He got into Cleveland in the late afternoon, and flew a trip out the next day. An eleven a.m. departure, if I remember correctly." I opened my notepad and flipped through it. "Yes, that's right. Zarrillo bought a full-fare ticket on United so that no one would know where he was. That's the only explanation."

"Then he killed Jay Bridges?"

"Possible. But there's got to be more to it than that. I don't get the feeling that Zarrillo was in this thing alone, whatever the hell it is. I just don't see him as the type of guy to do a lot of orchestrating."

"Maybe Bridges was the brains and the organiser, and, for some reason, Zarrillo decided to kill him. Maybe they had an argument about money, or something else."

"That still leaves the big question of what all of this is about. Other than the feeling that there's been murder among thieves, we don't know what these people have been doing."

"I also don't know what *we're* doing, standing around

105

chatting in someone else's living room. Are we *trying* to get caught up here?" As she spoke, Tracy took a step towards the apartment door.

"See? Now you know why I'm glad that I brought you along. I might've been inclined to sit down with a good book if you hadn't reminded me that we're not welcome guests." I had taken one step towards Tracy when the telephone rang. I froze in position. Tracy did, also. Neither of us spoke. The telephone rang two, three, four times. Finally, Zarrillo's answering machine clicked on. His monotone of a voice ran through the prescribed edict about leaving a message after the beep. When the recording ended, the caller's voice came across, real-time, amplified by the speaker on the answering machine.

"Hi, Louie-baby. This is Paula. Calling again just like I promised. I've thought over that lovely conversation we had a few hours ago. I've decided that, since I'm leaving my wonderful aerial hostess career at dear old Trans-Con, it's only proper that I get a little going-away present from one of Jay's good friends.

"Anyway, I figure that twenty-five grand would be a nice gesture on your part to help me forget my grief at losing a dear boyfriend. Before you bitch about the amount, let me also say that a gift of that magnitude would also help me forget the things that Jay told me – things about you and him, for starters. I think, all things considered, that twenty-five is a nice, round figure. I'm planning on leaving late tonight, so have the money ready. Jay told me that you've always got lots of cash lying around.

"If you need some extra justification for your generosity, you should consider the money as a travel fund to guarantee a hasty departure before that private investigator asks me more questions. That alone should make your investment worth it. Don't you think so, Louie-baby?"

The telephone clicked off and the answering machine stopped. Tracy and I looked at each other. "Paula Tate," I said. "Suspicions confirmed." Our timing, for a change, had been good – and the message more than informative. Yet inside, I had a gnawing feeling that there was something not quite right about what I had just been lucky enough to

106

hear. But there was no time to think about that now. "We've got to get out of here."

"Keen suggestion, Sherlock." Tracy took the stack of Zarrillo's unpaid bills from my hand, laid them carefully back on the hallway desk, then grabbed me by the arm and led me out of the apartment.

11

I'd been sitting in my car long enough for the first notes of Act III of *Rigoletto* to begin. The BMW's CD player tweeted and woofed through all seven speakers in marvellous resonance, and I allowed myself to be caught up in the musical exchange between Rigoletto and his daughter Gilda while I kept an eye on the entrance to the apartment building across the street from where I had parked. According to the information Tracy had given me, the old cream-coloured Toyota at the kerb belonged to Paula Tate, and the building behind it was where she lived with two other stewardesses. My car was reasonably hidden in the night-time shadows of the neighbourhood, as far between the street lamps as I could get.

Paula's apartment was on the north side of Coral Gables, very near to the airport and not very far from my own place in Coconut Grove. The apartment building was nothing to write home about but, then again, it wasn't too bad a place either. It was now a few minutes past ten, and I expected Paula to appear at any time if she were going to stick with her announced plan to pick up money from Zarrillo, then head out. At an airport like Miami International, a person could get a flight to lots of places even after midnight.

There was still no activity at Paula's apartment, but there was lots of activity from the CD player. The Duke of Mantua had begun to sing the most famous aria of the opera, "*La donna è mobile*". Luciano Pavarotti's rich voice sang the Italian lyrics in golden tones; I let the translation of those familiar words play through my thoughts:

> Woman is fickle
> as a feather in the wind,
> she changes her tune
> and her thoughts.

A sweet, pretty face
in tears or in laughter
always deceives us.

As Pavarotti was beginning the second refrain, the door to
Paula's apartment opened. It was her, suitcase in hand. She
walked briskly to her Toyota. I turned the volume slightly
lower on the CD player. I started the BMW's engine.

Paula Tate wheeled her Toyota away from the kerb. I
waited until she was half a block ahead before I followed.
She made a left, into the flow of traffic on Granada, and
headed north. I had to wait for the southbound lane to clear
before I could do likewise. By then, she had disappeared from
sight – but I knew that I could catch up by using some of the
BMW's superb performance. By paying enough money for
his wheels, a person could do a sterling impersonation of a
Grand Prix driver.

I weaved in and out of the moderate traffic. I was lucky
not to get caught at a traffic light, which I would've needed
to run if I were to have any chance of catching up. On the
CD, the Duke of Mantua was in an amorous exchange with
Maddalena – one that would end in the famous *Rigoletto*
quartet. Grand opera was just like real life – put four people
in a room and you get four differing views on what's happening.

The music was inspiring my driving. The BMW responded
as if it could read my thoughts; left, right, a jab of brake,
a touch of acceleration. The tail-lights of the Toyota were
three cars ahead, in the right lane. I swung to the right, to
stay a respectable distance behind.

My plan was to confront the two co-conspirators as soon
as the money was exchanged. If I did, I had a good feeling
that Zarrillo would break down right before my very eyes,
divulging the facts about this case that I had already strongly
hinted at knowing but which were actually still a total mystery
to me. I knew this was a high risk plan, but I had very little
to lose – after tonight, it was a sucker's bet that Paula Tate
would be a damned hard lady to find. Besides, something
about Paula's behaviour made me think that Zarrillo was
the proverbial missing piece to this puzzle.

The traffic light on Eighth Street turned red, and everyone slowed. The opera quartet finished with resounding brilliance. The BMW rocked to a halt in the right lane, two cars behind the Toyota. The Toyota was the number one car at the intersection, with its right blinker on. There was a continuous, heavy flow of high speed traffic eastbound on Eighth, which made the right turn impossible until the traffic light changed.

While we waited, Rigoletto sang the finishing touches to his plot with Sparafucile to have the Duke murdered. Overhearing, Gilda vowed to intercede, and volunteered to face certain death in order to save the man she loved. I wondered how she would explain that kind of pre-feminist decision on the *Phil Donahue Show*. Badly, probably. Anyway, Sparafucile then murdered Gilda, more or less by mistake. I glanced out at the cars ahead.

I couldn't quite make out Paula inside the Toyota, her car was too far away and it was too dark out. But as I was looking, something else caught my eye.

I sat further upright. An uneasy sensation filled me. In the background, I could hear the CD. Rigoletto has just discovered that the body in the sack is not the assassinated Duke of Mantua as he had thought. It is his daughter, Gilda, instead. I focused on the cars in front of me. *Something was wrong*.

Then I realised what it was. The car two ahead in the right lane – the car directly behind Paula Tate's Toyota, about three-quarters of a car length behind it – was a big, dark-coloured American piece of road-touring extravagance. But what actually caught my eye about it was the physical anomaly it displayed: *the car's side mirror was splintered and hanging from its mount*.

All my senses finally woke up; in less than a heartbeat I realised the obvious – that the car two ahead of me was the same car that I had shot at in the tennis court parking lot the night before!

There were two guys in the front seat of that dark-coloured American car, and the guy in the driver's seat had a striking resemblance to the one I had chased around the tennis courts. *Do something. Now.* But there was also a small

110

foreign pick-up truck between me and the American car, and the traffic had jammed in alongside and behind me, too.

I pulled my gun out of its shoulder holster and held it in my hand for what seemed like an eternity; it was probably no more than the count of five. During that time I thought briefly about jumping out and approaching their car on foot, but I dismissed that idea quickly enough – I would be exposed, totally out in the open, caught between traffic lanes. It would be suicide. But I knew that I couldn't just sit there. *Do something, dammit.* Out of desperation, I laid on the BMW's horn, figuring that maybe I could alert Paula, frighten away the two guys in the car, or maybe both. With all of us locked in our cars at a busy intersection, I thought we were as safe as we'd be for quite some time.

I thought wrong. As soon as I laid on the horn, the car with the shattered side mirror suddenly began to move. Its tyres screeched and it seemed almost to bend down on its hind end. I kept my hand on the horn, but my eyes were fixed on what was happening in front of me, on something I hadn't expected or anticipated. That giant American land boat was moving forward, gaining speed rapidly across the short open space between it and the cream-coloured Toyota ten feet ahead. It was headed straight for the tail-end of Paula's car.

Just then, I spotted something else in my peripheral vision. Barrelling eastbound on Eighth Street was a tractor-trailer rig. That big semi was accelerating as its driver tried to get across the intersection before the traffic light changed.

I turned straight ahead again, just in time to see the American car smash into the rear of the Toyota and send the Toyota skittering ahead by the force of the impact. A piece of the front end of the American car crumpled in and part of its bumper fell off as it bounced backward off its target.

The Toyota hurtled forward. The driver of the rig that was speeding east on Eighth jumped on his brakes with both feet. The trailer started to jack-knife sideways as the tyres on the front end began to dig in. But none of that was happening fast enough. Even with the wheels of the truck locked, its massive bulk was far too great to prevent it from running

111

down the Toyota. The entire scene seemed to be taking place in slow motion in front of me. Like an idiot, I still had my hand locked on to the BMW's horn.

In the glare of the truck's headlights I could see Paula Tate. Her hands had been thrown backward off the steering wheel by the initial impact from behind, and her head had snapped back, too. From what I could see, at the last moment Paula turned her head to the left – directly towards the onrushing truck, which was now no more than ten feet from the Toyota driver's door.

A hook on the front of the truck's bumper appeared to be the first part to make contact with the Toyota. It shattered the glass in the driver's side window, then impaled itself deeply into the vehicle. The Toyota was literally ripped apart by the impact of the far sturdier truck as the two vehicles – now an inseparable mass of folded, twisted metal – finally came to a stop against a lamp-post on the opposite side of the intersection.

I still leaned on the horn, out of pure reaction, not for any rational purpose. But the blaring noise I was making had the beneficial effect of getting the driver of the foreign pick-up truck in front of me to move to his right, out of my way. By now, the American car that had rammed Paula's Toyota had taken off straight ahead – through the empty intersection on Eighth, and into a backstreet on the far side. I floored the BMW and took off in pursuit, around several people who had abandoned their cars and were running towards the crash scene on the east side of the intersection. There was no sense in my stopping now: there was no way that Paula Tate could have survived that collision.

The American car had a half a block lead on me. On the straight-away, I was closing that distance rapidly. I laid my gun on the passenger seat, so that I could steer with both hands. We approached West Flagler. The American car took the turn on two wheels; luckily, no one was coming the other way. I also took the turn on two wheels.

Because the BMW turned and accelerated so much better than the car I was chasing, I was catching up quickly. The two guys in the American car must have seen that I was gaining on them. They made another right turn into a side street. I slammed on the brakes, yanked hard on the wheel, then hit the gas – all in nearly one motion. My car seemed to leap sideways as the pursuit continued; the American car was now only thirty feet ahead as I worked to close the distance between us. I tried to read the car's licence plate just in case I lost them, but both cars were bouncing and weaving too much to make that possible.

A few moments later I was happy for the bouncing and weaving as the first bullets from the passenger's side of the American car took out my right headlight. I flipped all the BMW's lights off – something I probably should've done sooner – and goosed the gas pedal enough to get tighter on my target. I was now a nearly invisible threat behind the two guys I was chasing. I rode tight on their tail-lights – lights that they had to keep on or they wouldn't have any headlights to see where they were going.

The American car turned left, right, left on several side streets in an attempt to shake me. After the last turn, the driver slammed on his brakes – trying, I suppose, to get me to drive into him and wreck my car. The BMW's brakes were better, though, so the cars never touched. I silently thanked God that Susan had kept up with the car's maintenance programme, just as I had. Before we came to a full stop, the American car was off again.

We came up to another intersection, a much busier street than the ones we'd played our game of tag on so far. There was now a traffic light to deal with. The light changed from green to yellow when we were still a hundred feet away from it; as both cars hurtled up to the corner, the light against us changed to red.

The American car skidded around in a right turn as it went north. I flipped on my BMW's headlights, laid on the horn and kept following. No matter what, I wasn't going to lose those bastards now.

The *no-matter-what* turned out to be a city bus. It was the first vehicle to move into the intersection, just as the car I was chasing sped past it. I could see the bus belch a cloud of black diesel smoke as the driver began his crawl from the light. The driver's face loomed up at me as I continued to close in. That bus driver and I, I now realised, were aiming

113

for the same spot in the intersection at more or less the same time. I nearly put my hand through the steering wheel as I pushed hard on the BMW's horn.

At the last moment the bus driver turned his head towards me – or, more specifically, towards the noise I was making. I could see his eyes pop open. He jumped on the bus's air brakes as I hit the BMW's gas, and the sides of our two vehicles passed within inches of each other. I could see an ocean of black and Spanish faces gawking at me in astonishment as I passed abeam the rows of windows and the big double doors, and I could see the stumbling, falling bodies of several of the folks inside the bus as I slid past its big, rounded front bumper.

The American car had got further ahead while I had been playing chicken with the public transportation system; I stepped harder on the gas to catch up. We were going beneath the Dolphin Expressway, and on to a road that I knew very well: the perimeter roadway on the southern edge of Miami International Airport.

The American car hung a left on the perimeter road. I did likewise. We were headed down a straight stretch that went past the old squat hangars that predated most everything else that still existed on the airport. Used by small cargo and non-sched operators, this part of the airport generated only a fraction of the activity that the main areas did. The road ran straight for nearly a mile; I held the BMW's steering wheel in both hands as we accelerated through seventy, eighty, ninety. To preserve my sanity, I stopped looking at the speedometer and just watched the car ahead.

The road curved right. We both slowed to stay on the blacktop. Luckily, no one was coming the other way. We approached a series of cut-offs that I couldn't remember anything about. The driver of the American car slammed on his brakes and turned right into the second access road. I followed as closely as I could.

The road narrowed to barely more than a single lane, with a high chain-link fence on both sides. A dark, rectangular shape was up ahead – it was one of the old, seldom-used hangars at this end of the field. Then I remembered that I had been here once before. *This is a dead end*. The narrow

114

access road I was on emptied into a wide apron of concrete surrounded by fencing. There were several gasoline trucks parked along the left side of the ramp, and the old, dark hangar was at the back end.

I stomped on the BMW's brakes and had the car skid sideways to a stop at the point where the narrow access road led to the ramp. The American car had raced ahead towards the hangar and around the far side, but I knew now that it would do them no good. There was a high fence around the back end that was always locked, and I was sure that the hangar itself would be locked, too. *Dead end, they can't get out.* I grabbed my gun from the passenger seat and jumped out of the car, leaving the BMW to block the throat of the only road in and out.

I began to sprint across the empty ramp, towards the deserted hangar. I figured that the two guys I was chasing would get out of their car and try to escape on foot when they realised that I now had them blocked in from behind. They would either try to break into the hangar to hide, or try to scale the high fence that encircled this corner of the airport. Either way, I stood a good chance of catching up to them, and I had the distinct advantage of knowing the territory.

I had run about fifty feet across the open tarmac when I realised that I was lots smarter than the two guys I was chasing – which, incredibly, made me lots dumber than them, too. I was *smarter* because I had already figured out that they had a better chance to escape on foot than by car once they had inadvertently got into this dead end section of the airport. But I was *dumber* because I didn't realise that those two goons didn't necessarily understand what a bad predicament they had got themselves into. What made all this obvious was the sight of their car turning around the old hangar and *heading straight back my way* – even though there was now no damned way out for them with my BMW blocking the access road!

Their car was a hundred feet away, and coming like hell. I had no place to run to, and no time to run in. The noise from their car's engine increased as the car's headlights grew in size. I knew they could see me now. They were

115

headed directly towards me. They were going to run me down.

My heart was pounding, my face was covered with sweat. *You idiot, you've outsmarted yourself.* I was in the middle of an empty ramp and, seventy feet away, two killers in a speeding car were intent on running me over.

I was holding my gun in my right hand. I raised it and aimed it at the car. For a moment I hoped that the sight of me aiming the gun at them would persuade them to head elsewhere. It took half a second of zero lateral motion from the headlights for me to realise that these guys didn't care what I was aiming at them. They intended to keep coming anyway.

Yet the lights from the car did give me an accurate idea of where the driver was. The engine noises flooded over me as I steadied my hand, held my breath, then pulled the trigger several times. I blinked as the rounds exploded out of the gun.

When I opened my eyes the car was still there and still coming at me. But within an instant, the car began to wobble a little and, then, to head unmistakably out of control. Rather than hit me, it passed several feet to my left. I saw the other man in the front seat grasping wildly for the steering wheel. The driver was slumped over the steering column, his weight evidently pulling the car to its right – straight towards the row of parked trucks.

Gasoline trucks. At twenty-five feet from the trucks the car's brakes began to squeal. At fifteen feet, a sharp right turn was begun. At ten feet the car looked as if it might miss the row of gasoline trucks altogether and hit into the chain-link fence behind them. At five feet I knew that it would be very close.

The first sound was a snap, followed by the thuds of metal-to-metal. Catching itself on the left front fender, the car was forced to spin inward. It crashed into the massive tank of the first gasoline truck in the line. The impact noises mingled together as the steel frames of both vehicles pushed hard into each other.

By now, the car had stopped moving. For several seconds, the only sound was a continuous hissing. But then there was a short burst of yellow light from beneath the twisted frame

116

of the car, and a small, muffled explosion – a sort of *thump* – that carried a bright fire rapidly over the entire length of the vehicles.

A big explosion came thirty seconds after. By now, I had backed further away from the burning wreckage – and, still, the force of the explosion knocked me to my knees. I watched the violent pattern of flames for a few moments, then allowed my head to sink down into my hands. The crackling noises and the continuous smothered rumblings from the inferno in front of me whirled around as I thought about how incredibly lucky I was to be alive.

12

By the time I had extricated myself from the police it was already after midnight. When I walked into Elmer's office at the Trans-Continental hangar he was at his desk and had, by evidence of the coffee cups, been there for some time.

"Been waiting for you," Elmer said as a manner of greeting.

"Unavoidably detained. The police wanted to chat, and I didn't want to look overly anxious to leave." I glanced at Tracy, who was sitting in a chair in the corner. She was the one I had called, using a telephone inside the locked-up hangar that the police had got me access to, soon after those two morons ran their king-size car into the gas truck. Tracy nodded at me and smiled – a half-smile that meant, I imagined, that I should be on guard, that Elmer was going to be a force worth reckoning with.

"How'd you leave it with the police?" Elmer asked. The angles of his face were chiselled into a monument of displeasure.

"Like I said to Tracy on the telephone, I didn't tell them much."

"Which means?"

"Concerned citizen, nothing more. Watched a hit-and-run. Chased the banditos, but lost them. Heard an explosion, saw the smoke and flame. By the time I got to the scene of the accident, their car was an integral part of the Towering Inferno. I said that I figured they must've lost control and piled into the gas truck when they tried to get out of the dead end they'd gone down."

"Is that what really happened?" Elmer asked.

"Basically, yes. Actually, no."

"Oh." Elmer strummed his fingers on the desk. "Well, did the police buy your story?"

"Absolutely." I thought they did, anyway. The old detective who interviewed me looked a little sceptical, but I attributed that to his professional curiosity. If he was really curious, he probably wouldn't have let me make my telephone call and wouldn't have let me go.

"Good." Elmer sat back in his seat, indicating slightly less displeasure than he had shown when I first came in. Not giving his name as part of my official explanation had evidently been the proper thing to do, as far as he was concerned. "And the cops didn't ask anything about why you were investigating the girl who got killed in the hit-and-run? Paula Tate's dead, by the way." Elmer nodded self-consciously at the mention of her name; he was a hard-ass, but that side of his temperament was displayed by caustic remarks and blazing memos – actual murder and mayhem were definitely outside his normal modus operandi. Mine, too, for that matter.

"Figured she was dead," I said, replying to his second point first. "That was a hell of a crash." I felt my guts turn upside-down as I remembered the crash scene. I quickly put it out of my mind, so I could continue to function. I was dead tired now, and the memory of Paula Tate was more than I could cope with. "As far as the police go, I didn't see any need to volunteer that I was an investigator. The subject never came up. I sure as hell didn't want to explain myself to them, or have to explain you people, either." I gestured with my hand towards Elmer and then Tracy.

"Good thinking. I hope your story holds," Elmer said.

"Me, too. I also didn't explain why I emptied my gun at that car just before it would've run me down. That happened micro seconds before the car swerved around me and into the gas truck." I could tell from their faces that detonating my verbal bombshell had got their full attention. The combination of my physical exhaustion and mental turmoil had been the motivation behind my melodramatic way of telling them what had happened.

Tracy stood up and took a step towards me. I had the feeling that she would've taken more steps if she hadn't suddenly remembered that Elmer was sitting there. "You

119

did what?" she said, as calmly as she could. There was a crack in the edge of her voice.

"Hold on a second." I was already regretting the way I had phrased it. "Before you start thinking that I'm into Clint Eastwood impersonations, let me say that it was pure self-defence." I ran over the sequence of events for both of them, including a confession as to how I nearly wound up as bumper-food for a Detroit monster machine.

I also volunteered that, once the car had exploded and that intense, fuel-fed fire had begun – a couple of thousand gallons of jet fuel make a wonderful bonfire – I realised that there wouldn't be enough left of the car or the two bodies for anyone ever to find evidence of the bullets I had used. That was when I had first got the idea of omitting some of the more incriminating details in my account to the police.

Part of my reason for not rushing from the scene had been to confirm that there were no clues left of my involvement. And just like I had predicted, the bodies were total ash and the car was a molten slag of steel. That was the break that would keep me on the case, and keep the police bureaucracy out of it, at least for a while.

"So where does that leave us?" Elmer asked. He was leaning forward in his seat again, showing me that he considered the situation close to being unmanageable.

"I can see that you're not taking this well." I decided to get right to the heart of the matter, since tip-toeing around issues was not Elmer's style, or mine either. "But there's no reason to feel in jeopardy."

"Oh, yeah? Jay Bridges, Paula Tate and two mysterious guys in a car. The bodies are piling up fast. At some point the police are going to take more than a casual interest in this whole thing."

"But *we* haven't done anything wrong."

"I'm not convinced."

"You should be." I paused for a moment while I sifted through my jumbled thoughts. "I shot at a guy who was trying to run me down with his car, right?"

"Yeah, but . . ."

"He was a guy who I had already watched kill someone a short time before. I do, by the way, have a licence to carry the gun that I used. It's all perfectly legal." I was, at best, using gobs of poetic licence in my interpretation of the gun laws. I knew it, but perhaps Elmer didn't.

"Yeah, but . . ." Elmer stopped again. He knew that he was starting to sound like a stuck record. "But not telling the police . . ." he continued, his words trailing off to nothing.

"Hey, if I had told the police what happened, at the very least they would've taken control of the investigation. They would've turned this place into a zoo. Whatever leads we've got, they would've been scared deep back into their holes. Worse than that, it wouldn't have been you, it would've been the Chief of Police calling the shots from that point on. That what you want?"

"No. Of course not." Elmer sat back in his chair, waiting to hear more.

I could see that he *wanted* to be convinced by me, which was, of course, more than half the battle. I wanted to convince him. I also wanted to lie down and go to sleep. I turned to Tracy. "There's still the Zarrillo question. Did you explain to Elmer what we found?"

"Yes."

"Okay, now you folks know as much as I do. Zarrillo was in Chicago the night Jay Bridges was killed – and he got there by buying a full fare airplane ticket on United Airlines. Pretty damned strange behaviour for a senior, full-time employee of a competing major airline, wouldn't you say?"

"Yes," Elmer agreed. He sat motionless, listening. Max would've labelled him as an eager buyer.

"Then Paula Tate calls while we're padding around Zarrillo's apartment. A break for us. But then Paula is set up by two goons who soon thereafter meet with an untimely demise themselves – a terminal condition they more than earned by trying to run me down. What does all of this tell us?" I pause to give them time to think it over – and to give myself time to think it over, too. At that point, I was more or less operating on autopilot, with my mouth several seconds ahead of my brain; I needed a few seconds to listen to myself, to figure out what I had just said.

"Zarrillo must've set her up, or told somebody to do it," Elmer volunteered. He was deep in thought, just about to say

121

more, when the telephone rang. Elmer yanked the phone off its cradle. "Hello?"

Tracy and I looked at each other. Twelve thirty-five in the morning meant that this was probably not a social call. I hoped to God that it wasn't the police. I was so tired, I probably would've confessed to the Jonestown massacre just to get it over with.

"Max? Oh, yeah, sure. Hold on, he's here." Elmer frowned, then handed the telephone to me.

I was too relieved even to smile in gratitude. "What's up, Max?" I said.

"I got news," Max said on the telephone to me. "Once Susan left Zarrillo at the pool, he went up to his apartment. He stayed there the entire time. Until thirty minutes ago. Then he left." Max paused for several long and ominous seconds. "Then I lost him."

My heart sank. More bad news. "Where are you? How'd it happen?"

"Pamela's apartment." Max stopped again, evidently considering whether he should explain why he was still at Pamela's or how he lost Zarrillo. He opted to concentrate on Zarrillo. "I stayed down the corridor from his place, just like you said. Pamela and Susan took turns keeping me company. Anyway, Zarrillo decides to leave. I set out to follow him in Pamela's car. But by the time we get her car keys and head down in the elevator, Zarrillo's already in his car and laying a yard of rubber out of the lot. Couldn't catch up. I wandered around a little, looking. Then doubled back here. Tried to call your place and Tracy's – this was the only other number I had."

"Okay, fine, you did your best." I stopped talking and looked at Elmer. Inside, I was a jumble of conflicting thoughts. But I knew that I had to do *something*. "Zarrillo was at his apartment, then headed out a little while ago. He left at light-speed and Max lost him. That means that his apartment is empty. Can you think of any reason why I shouldn't visit his apartment, maybe wait for him to get back?"

"It's against the law to break into his apartment." Again, Elmer was looking nervous.

"Murder – or conspiracy to commit murder, which is what I suspect your friend Zarrillo is involved in – is against the law, too."

"Maybe we do need the police," Elmer said.

"Maybe I need to lean on Zarrillo." What I knew, for sure, was that leaning on Zarrillo would be lots easier than being leaned on by the police. "Zarrillo doesn't impress me as a great underworld leader. I'm sure he's just a minor cog in this nasty train of gears we've got grinding away here. He's not going to want to take the heat alone. If I lean on him, he'll fold."

"I don't know." There was a line of perspiration on Elmer's forehead. "Very risky."

"We can always go to the police. That option's always open. Later." Much later. Much, much later.

"How do we account for the delay if we go to the police tomorrow or the day after?" Tracy had asked the question matter-of-factly, in a devil's advocate sort of way.

"Good thought." I found the energy to smile at her – I had every feeling that she was thoroughly on my side, which was the only good spot in my evening. As far as I was concerned, she and I had an uncanny empathy, a real melding of views.

"It's something that we should have an answer for," she said.

"I agree." On the other hand, maybe my male ego wouldn't allow me to see my expanding relationship with Tracy any other way but as an expression of *empathy*. *Empathy* was what I needed, so *empathy* was what I expected to get; it was the expectations theory in human relations. "Whenever we decide to bring the police in, we'll say that we just figured it out. Being slow-witted is not a criminal offence."

"Sounds good to me," Tracy answered. She nodded affirmatively, for Elmer's benefit – a vote of confidence in my behaviour and reasoning.

I looked at Elmer and made brief eye contact. I gave him a fraction of a second to stop me – he was, after all, the boss and he deserved at least that much. Elmer looked me straight in the eye, but said nothing. He had become the Sphinx of Corporate Administration – which, I decided, would make an interesting study in bronze. Maybe I should get the *Wall Street*

123

Journal to commission it. "Max," I said into the telephone, after remembering that he was still there and waiting for me to tell him what to do next, "hang out at Pamela's. I'm on the way back. I need you to get me into Zarrillo's apartment again. I'm going to wait for him to return, then I'm going to lean on him."

"Good. I'll be here."

I hung up the telephone. Now that I had direction and purpose, a little of my energy had returned. "Things are happening. We're close to really knowing something."

"Hold on. Maybe we know something already." Elmer stood up from his chair. He paced back and forth behind his big desk a few times. He glanced outside through the dark window, across the empty hangar ramp. Finally, he turned to me. "Paula Tate. Maybe she was the clue we're overlooking. If Zarrillo's not sharp enough to be the boss, maybe she was. Maybe that's why she was killed, maybe her connection outside the airline suddenly decided that she was better off dead."

"An excellent possibility, except that a few things don't fit."

"What things?"

"The way she handled Zarrillo, the way she was squeezing him for only twenty-five thousand."

"What about it?"

"Not enough." I had thought about this point on the drive back from the crash scene. "Unless I was wrong about Paula, the money she wanted was too small if she *really* knew something."

"Too small?"

"Yes. Paula was a consummate opportunist. Whatever this thing is – drugs, probably – the fact that she asked for only twenty-five thousand tells me that she had nothing to say. She was just trying to bluff Zarrillo out of some cash before she left."

"And her mistake was in not realising how scared Zarrillo really was," Tracy announced. All of it must've made sense to her, because she was taking the ball and running with it.

"That's probably true. Paula had more guts than Zarrillo, so she never appreciated how spineless he really is."

124

"Yes, that fits." Tracy nodded. "Paula hated the flight attendant job and was going to quit anyway. She decided to squeeze a going-away present out of Zarrillo, but Zarrillo panicked and jumped to the conclusion that Paula knew *everything*, that Jay Bridges must've told her everything about how this scheme of theirs worked. Zarrillo put the word out, and someone above him called in those two guys to deal with Paula. To Paula, it was an easy chance to make a little nest-egg out of a bluff, but to Zarrillo and whoever else he deals with, she was on the verge of exposing it all."

"Exactly." It was easy for me to admire Tracy's thought patterns and reasoning, since they invariably fitted so well with my own. Mirror, mirror on the wall, who's the smartest of them all? Me and my gal. In my rational mind I knew that Tracy and I had absolutely everything going for each other – except that my blood didn't seem to boil very hot for her. Why?

"Nothing else makes sense," Tracy said.

"I agree." My blood didn't boil for Tracy the way it had – and still did – for Susan, that much I knew. Even though Tracy seemed perfect in almost every way, I couldn't quite get the heat high enough. Not yet, anyway. But time was on my side. "Tracy, come with me. We'll go back to Pamela's apartment and Max will get me into Zarrillo's place. I could use you nearby if I come up with anything significant when I squeeze Zarrillo."

"Fine."

"Elmer, you go home. Go to bed."

"All right." He turned to Tracy. "But call me if anything happens."

"Of course." Tracy stepped over to his desk and scribbled out a telephone number. "This is where we're at, my friend Pamela Nichols who lives in Zarrillo's apartment building. She's one of our stewardesses. If I'm not up here in the office or at home, I'll be at Pamela's."

"Right." Elmer picked up the number and shoved it in his pocket. "Be careful," he said to me. "This is getting to be more than I imagined."

"At least you're getting your money's worth." I headed out of Elmer's office, with Tracy beside me.

The car ride to Pamela's apartment was quick; at one o'clock in the morning there wasn't a great deal happening in the streets of Miami, at least not in the streets that we were driving through. Pamela had already alerted the doorman to our arrival, and he quickly let us into the building.

Tracy held on to my arm as we rode up, in silence, in the elevator. Both of us were dog-tired – my little spurt of energy was beginning to fade – yet I knew we were too pumped up to sleep, even if we had the opportunity. Right now, there was too much that had to be done. Tracy let go of my arm just before we entered the apartment. Susan gave me a big hello. Max and Pamela were sitting close together on the couch, watching TV.

"Be careful," Susan said to me before I turned to leave with Max, after I had explained the plan to the rest of them.

"Be *very* careful," Tracy said to me at the door, just before I walked out to head for Zarrillo's place. "If you get killed, I'm really going to be mad."

"Me, too." I leaned over and kissed her on the cheek. I noticed that Susan wasn't watching. I hated myself for noticing that. "Don't worry, everything's under control," I said to Tracy. "Let's you and me go to dinner the first night we've got a break from this case, maybe go dancing, too. This way I can't get killed, I've got a prior commitment."

"I'll do it, but just to save your life. You bring out the humanitarian in me." Tracy leaned forward and kissed me on the other cheek. It seemed like the temperature of my blood had gone up a few degrees, or was I just flushed from exertion and fatigue? I couldn't tell. I turned and followed Max to the elevator.

"Tracy's a nice girl," he said, after the elevator door had closed.

"Yes, she is." *Nice girl*. Did I want a nice girl? Did I need a nice girl? Did I have enough brains to know what to do with a nice girl? That was too complex a question for that hour of the morning, so I let it go.

"Pamela's pretty good, too. We get along real good."

"So I've noticed."

"Yeah." Max smiled, although his smile seemed to be

126

more of a self-conscious grin than the flashy, toothy expression of the conquering male.

It occurred to me at that moment that maybe Max was, for the first time since I had met him, falling in love. On the other hand, maybe it was just another expression of the late hour and his own fatigue. I knew from experience that sometimes it was hard to tell the difference. "Once you let me in, go back to Pamela's apartment and wait. Tell everyone to catch a little sleep, but at least one of you stay awake by the telephone. Don't tie up the line either, so I can get a call down if I have to."

"Sure thing."

Max picked the lock with ease, and within a couple of minutes I was inside Zarrillo's apartment again. Everything was just about the way we had left it, except for some scattered clothes on the bed and a drinking glass in the sink. I poked around the periphery of the room, looking at everything, while I ran through my mind my plan for getting Zarrillo to cave in.

I checked my gun several times, although I had no real expectation of needing it. At least I hoped not. I put the gun back in my shoulder holster and purposely left my sports jacket unbuttoned so the weapon would be obvious. The only gigantic fly in the ointment would be if Zarrillo showed up with an armed escort – a possibility that might turn my little scenario of intimidation into a major gun battle. That, for sure, I didn't need.

A table in the corner had a stack of airline material on it. Bulletins, revisions to manuals, a vacation bid award. I glanced at each piece. I took out my notepad and wrote down what Zarrillo's vacation dates were – useless information, no doubt, but at least it gave me something to do to occupy the time and keep me awake.

The sheet under the vacation form was an inter-office memo to Zarrillo. The signature on the bottom caught my eye. Captain William F. Davenport, the irritating Trans-Continental chief pilot. He was rescheduling Zarrillo to take his six month simulator check-ride in March rather than in February. I opened my pad and made a note of that date, too. Then I glanced at my wristwatch. A little over an hour had elapsed since I had arrived in Zarrillo's apartment. I hoped that Zarrillo made it back soon, the thought of his big, soft bed was becoming more enticing every passing minute.

There was a low knock at the door, a knock that sounded much louder than it actually was because of the thick silence in the room. I quickly moved away from the desk and across the apartment. I took my gun out of its shoulder holster and edged towards the front door. A knock at the door at nearly three o'clock in the morning? Inexplicable.

I heard a muffled, whispering voice once, then a second time before I recognised who it was and what he was saying. It was Max, and he was asking me to open the door. I did.

"Hey, you gotta come with me."

"What?"

"Yeah. Right now." Max stood in the doorway and looked around the room behind me. "Is everything just like you found it? There's no way that anyone can tell that you've been here?"

"No, but . . ."

"Listen, man, come on." Max gestured for me to step towards him, into the corridor. "Probably not, but there's a chance that the police might be coming up here any time now."

"Police?" I stepped into the hallway. Max took out his handkerchief and carefully wiped off the hardware on both sides of the door. "Did you touch anything else in the room that you could leave fingerprints on?"

"No."

"Good." He closed the door.

"What's this all about?" I asked.

"Elmer just called. The police called the airline a little while ago, 'cause they found his company identification card at the scene."

"Card? Whose?"

"Zarrillo, man."

"Zarrillo?"

"Yeah. He's dead. Shot. A robbery attempt is what the police are saying."

13

For a change, I had no music on. I walked slowly around the confines of my apartment, glancing outside at the late morning sky, then turning back and looking into the room at nothing in particular. I had a cup of coffee in my hand, and every now and then I took a sip of the tepid brown liquid.

I was wrestling with the problem of feeling uncomfortable and unsettled. With Zarrillo's death – a robbery that was too coincidental to be anything other than staged, probably by the people that Zarrillo and Bridges had been dealing with – the case was closed. Elmer had called this morning to congratulate me, to say that the job was done. As far as the airline was concerned, it was all over, he said. Elmer had thought it over and had decided during the night that Zarrillo and Bridges had, by themselves, been in some kind of deal together and that the deal had gone bad. With both of them dead, the airline was no longer involved.

But I didn't agree. Oh, at first I was happy to have Elmer sing my praises, but in my gut I knew better. Zarrillo was not the main man; no way, he couldn't be. He was too spineless, too flaky, he wasn't the type. Without someone around – someone at the airline – to keep pushing him, he would have quietly blended into the walls as soon as Bridges had been killed. Besides, Zarrillo had been in Chicago the night Bridges' pseudo-accident had occurred. Was Zarrillo the one who had killed Bridges? I didn't think so. He didn't have the courage or, probably, the wherewithal. There was someone behind Zarrillo, but I hadn't the faintest idea who it was. Should I leave well enough alone and keep my sterling reputation as an investigator intact? Probably. But I couldn't do it.

I walked over to the telephone and dialled Elmer's number. Tracy answered. She, too, began to sing my praises. In

129

her voice, the accolades sounded even sweeter – but I cut her off. I told her that I didn't think it was over yet, that there were too many bad vibrations about this apparent solution. She sounded as if she were on the fence, unsure. She handed the telephone to Elmer.

"Yeah? What?"

"It's not over. There's got to be more." In my mind's eye, I could picture Elmer's frown. I was glad that modern technology had yet to force the picture-telephone on us.

"That's bullshit."

"The only bullshit is what we're spreading among ourselves, that Louis Zarrillo was the man in charge. We sound like a big city police department – we find one guy with a cap pistol, we want to make him responsible for World War Two. Clean up our files. Very neat, but pure bullshit."

Elmer paused on his end of the line. Finally, after our mutual silence had got to the depths of the Mariana Trench, he spoke again. "Well, what do you want from me? What's your point?"

"I want to stay on the case."

"How long?"

"Until I figure out where we are."

"Sounds like job security for you."

"Probably is." I could tell from his tone that Elmer had a shade of doubt in his mind, too. He was taking a shot at the messenger, not the message. "You hit the nail on the old head. I need the dough. How about it?"

"It's a damned waste of time – and airline money, for that matter. But maybe we owe it to you. Okay. You can have another week, a little paid vacation courtesy of Trans-Continental. You did, after all, do a good job keeping the airline out of it. A week's retainer for not getting our names in the newspaper is a fair enough bargain."

"What if one week isn't enough?"

"One more week, period. Then it's done, no matter what."

"Okay." I hung up the telephone. I looked around my apartment again. I shuffled my feet. *One more week*. I didn't know where to begin. With what in Shakespearian circles would be known as a heavy heart, I walked over to my desk. I sat down and began to look through my notes on the case. I had to start my final week somewhere and my notebook, by default, was that place. I had been at that seemingly pointless task for just a few minutes when the doorbell rang.

Susan was at the door. She looked as good as ever, although she had a little bit of a pout on her face. I let her in. "What's up?"

"I've come to turn in my deputy's badge."

"Quitting our merry little band of cat burglars?"

"Have to. My . . . boyfriend's . . . back." She had paused at the inane label that grown, middle-aged females of the species are compelled to place on their sexual encounters outside the sanctity of marriage. "I'm going to pick him up at the airport in an hour."

"He wouldn't approve of you working for me?" I knew that I had gone to the free-throw line on that one but Susan had, after all, fouled me more than once during our life together. At least that was my excuse for the little jibes that I occasionally took at her.

"He doesn't care if I work for you, he only cares what I'm doing for him. But if I'm working for you, I'm not *doing* for him." She turned her hands palms up to me and smiled, in a gesture that spoke of the finality of her statement. "You know how men are."

"I can appreciate that. Come and sit down. While I'm repossessing your detective's status, I'll fill you in on what Elmer and I were talking about this morning."

"Okay, but just for a minute. I've got to get to the airport." Susan stepped past me, into the living room, and sat on the couch.

"Can I get you anything?"

"No, thanks."

I sat at my desk again. I grabbed a handful of my notes and paperwork and held it up. "I'm so desperate, I'm reading my own material."

"What are you desperate for?"

"I don't know." I explained to her Elmer's congratulatory call and my gut feeling that the case wasn't over, that there was still someone at the airline behind what Zarrillo and Bridges had been up to. Susan nodded sympathetically but ventured no opinion one way or the other. "So I've got one more week to figure out who it is and to trip him up. That's all I've got."

"Not a great deal of time." Susan stood up and walked over to me. She put her hand on my shoulder and looked down at the pile of debris on my desk that I had the audacity to call data. "You think this mystery person's done something to have their name in your notes?" she said as she ran her other hand across the stack of papers.

"Could be, but what I'm really looking for is a connection." Susan still had her hand on my shoulder, and I liked it. The fact that she was headed out to pick up Mr Mercedes at the airport made her gesture even more significant, to my deluded way of thinking. Optimism runs rampant in some types of mental illness, I had once read.

"What kind of connection?"

"I don't know." I looked up at her, then back at the papers. One of the sheets caught my eye. I glanced at it. The flight operations file for Captain Louis Zarrillo. Dates of his medical exams, his last recurrent ground school, his last Boeing 737 simulator check-ride. None of it meant a damn, yet I was poring over it like it was the Dead Sea Scrolls, examining the nuance of every line, every letter, every number . . .

"Jack, what is it?"

A proverbial shiver ran up my spine, just like it's supposed to. I blinked, then looked at the line of data again – a line I had read a dozen times before, but I had systematically managed to miss its importance until just now. "Look at this."

"What?" Susan leaned over closer to where I was pointing. "Where?"

"Here. The simulator check-ride date."

"What about it?"

"The date. It's January 15th – less than a month ago." I stood up, but my eyes were still on the paper.

"And?"

"And another piece of paper I've got says something else." I rifled through the data on my desk until I found the note I was looking for. It was a note that I had made for myself in Zarrillo's apartment. "Chief Pilot Davenport had sent

Zarrillo a memo saying to call his office to reschedule his simulator check-ride. To reschedule his *February* check-ride to *March*."

"Yes?"

"Yet Zarrillo had just taken a check-ride the month before. *Nobody* takes simulator checks more often than they're required to – it's every six months for the captains, period." I took a step away from the desk; I finally had something, a place to start from.

"But what does all that mean?"

"Davenport. It means that Davenport was sending Zarrillo some kind of signal, because the message itself – change a non-existent check-ride to another date that he also didn't need – was pure fiction. The memo I found in Zarrillo's apartment was a signal from Davenport, it had to be. He's the link I was looking for, I'm sure of it."

"Oh." Susan sounded unconvinced, but she smiled encouragingly. "Well, at least you've got someplace to start."

"Yes, I do."

"I'd like to help, but I really do have to go." She took a step towards the door.

"Give me a call tonight or tomorrow, I'll let you know if I find out anything. That's if you're still interested, of course," I said, hedging my bets.

"I'll call when I can." Susan leaned towards me, gave me a light, brushing kiss on the lips, then opened the door and left.

I watched her get into her red Mercedes and drive off, although my thoughts were, for a change, on something else. Davenport. That pompous bastard had, more than likely, been in with Zarrillo and Bridges from the very beginning. It made sense that it would take someone at or near the top to keep a tight rein on whatever the hell those clowns were up to. Davenport. He was up high enough at Trans-Continental to make almost anything happen.

I closed the door and headed back for the telephone. I dialled Elmer's number again. Tracy answered. "This is your favourite detective. I'm calling with another instalment to make Elmer proud of how he's spending airline money," I said.

"A new idea so soon?" she said. "I thought you didn't have anything to go on."

"I was overlooking the obvious."

"Really? Like what?"

"Like Davenport."

"Oh, oh." Tracy paused. "I could tell from the first minute that you didn't like him. I hope that this is more than just a gut feeling. I know that you're prone to them."

"It is." I fumbled with my sheets of notes while I wondered for myself whether I was making more out of that memo than was warranted. No, I wasn't, I finally decided. It was too much of a coincidence that Davenport was sending erroneous, cryptic messages to Louis Zarrillo, of all people. "I've got proof that Davenport was communicating with Zarrillo."

"About what?"

"It's some kind of coded message between them. But the important fact is that Davenport sent it."

"I think you better talk to Elmer."

I could hear Tracy saying something before she handed the telephone over. For the first time since I had met her, I wasn't sure that I knew what Tracy was thinking – or was I just being paranoid? The only word I could make out from the comment she made to Elmer was that one name: Davenport.

"You better have something pretty damned good, you're on dangerous ground," Elmer said as he came on the line.

"Dangerous? Why?"

"Because William F. Davenport is the next man in the line of succession for my job. If we make a stink about him and we're wrong, it'll look like I'm trying to railroad my only competition to get him out of the picture. I can't imagine that the Board of Directors will think kindly of me for that."

"Is Davenport really a threat to you?"

"At this level of corporate politics, everyone in the line of succession is a threat. I've made some enemies, Davenport's made some friends. All I'm saying is that it won't look good. Not at all." Elmer paused. I could almost hear the synapses in his brain as they connected. "Now, what have you got?"

I explained the memo I had seen in Zarrillo's apartment. My explanation was greeted with silence. I then went on quickly to explain what, from my point of view, it all meant.

134

"How about a simple mistake? Isn't that a good enough reason for him to send the memo? I know for a fact that our scheduling departments make more than just a few errors," Elmer said gruffly. Clearly, any investigation of a connection to Davenport was something that Elmer was very, very nervous about. He probably had a right to be.

"Too much of a coincidence. A memo to Zarrillo *this week*. Come on, Elmer, give me a break. Besides," I said, "why should the chief pilot get involved in a simple scheduling matter? Isn't that like calling the fire department to put out a glowing marshmallow?"

There was a pause on Elmer's end. "I suppose," he finally answered. He stopped again for several long moments before continuing. "You've made a good point. I guess that it's enough of a reason to look – *very carefully* – at any possible connection between Bridges, Zarrillo and Davenport."

"And Paula Tate, too," I threw in. The all-too-graphic memory of her car wreck was still very much with me.

"Yes. Her too, of course." Elmer exhaled audibly into the telephone, leaving little doubt that he was far more fond of the idea that the case had already been closed. But he knew what he had to do. "What is it that you want?"

"Since you've made an excellent point about my being careful, we'll go slowly. Maybe it's even better that I don't go back to the hangar, so that no one will see me."

"Okay, fine."

"Ask Tracy to assemble whatever files and data she has on Davenport. Come over to my place. We'll review them here."

"What kind of files?"

"Everything and anything with his name on it. I won't know what we're looking for until we find it." My thoughts were racing ahead in the various directions I could take the investigation. No direction seemed any better than any other – it was all guess-work, a long shot. But now, at least, I was back at the gaming table.

Elmer spoke to Tracy for a moment, then got back with me. "She says it'll take a while. The files are in various buildings. She'll get to your place as soon as she can – late this afternoon, probably."

"I'll be here."

"And you'll be careful, too – right?"

"Very careful, very gentle."

"Thank you," Elmer said sarcastically.

"Sure thing." I hung up, sat back and listened to the silence in the room for a few moments while I analysed the situation. Things were not great yet, but they were getting better.

I got up from my desk, walked over to the stereo and pulled out the Herbert von Karajan edition of Beethoven's Symphony Number Five. I put the compact disc in the player, turned up the volume, then pushed the play button. Those four thunderous, familiar opening chords would set the keynote for the afternoon while I thought about what William F. Davenport had been up to and why in God's name I hadn't realised it sooner.

14

I pored over the meagre data on the case that I had already compiled at the apartment, then I made lunch. I made a steak, put it in a kaiser roll, and had a beer. I figured that I played enough tennis to keep my arteries clean of cholesterol and, besides, I needed the protein as brain-food. Maybe that's why I hadn't figured things out yet, I'd been eating the wrong foods.

The steak was good, the beer even better. Chock full of protein, I gazed at my paperwork like some Eastern mystic searching for a vision. All I got was eyestrain. By three o'clock I was weighed down by twenty subliminal reasons why my Davenport connection was fatuous at best. Depressing. I had another beer.

Beethoven had made way for several chamber music discs, strictly background stuff. The doorbell finally rang. I jumped up from my desk and rushed to the door to meet Tracy, as much to get away from the stifling situation at the desk as to see her. But it wasn't her at all.

I opened the door to a dapper, well-dressed man in his mid-fifties. He had a thin but relatively friendly face, and black hair that was well greyed at the temples. He looked like a banker; no, that wasn't quite right – he looked more like the *owner* of the bank. Behind this distinguished gentleman, in the driveway, was Susan's red Mercedes. Susan was nowhere in sight. "Yes?"

"My name is Allan Lyle. A good friend of," he said as he turned slightly and gestured discreetly towards the red sports car, "Susan." Lyle turned back to me. For a moment he said nothing. Finally, he cleared his throat and spoke again. "I'd like to talk to you. May I come in?"

"Sure." I stepped aside to let him enter. I closed the door after him. We stood in the entranceway.

"I obviously know who you are, and I think you know who I am," Lyle began. He looked casually around the room, then back at me.

"You're the Mercedes-man, would be my guess."

"Pardon?"

"Susan's new *friend*." The word had come out a little nastier than I had intended; to Lyle's credit, he seemed not to notice.

"That's correct." Lyle looked into the living room. "May we sit down? There's something I'd like to discuss with you."

"Susan's an adult, she can do whatever she wants to. Even though I'm not happy about it, we're separated. I've got no quarrel with you." My openness and generosity were shocking, even to me. What I had hoped for, at some basic animal level, was more of a natural macho response – like knocking the guy down with a left hook. Instead, I found myself amicably smiling. Nauseating. I could imagine that if Max were here, he'd be throwing up in the corner just about now.

"I'm glad you don't have a quarrel with me. A lot of men would."

"Don't give me too much credit, I'm usually much more childish than this."

"I doubt that. However, it's all academic since none of this is about Susan – or, more accurately, only indirectly. May we sit?"

"If you'd like." I followed him into the living room. He was wearing a smartly tailored grey pin-striped suit. I had always wanted to get one just like it but had never got around to it. "That's a nice suit," I said, making chit-chat. "Where did you get it?"

"This suit? It was custom-made." Lyle turned and looked at me. "Would you like the name of the tailor? He's very good, he's up in Palm Beach."

"Forget it." At that moment, I couldn't afford a custom-made pair of socks. I pointed to the living room couch. "Make yourself comfortable. Would you like a drink or anything?"

"No, thank you."

"Well, I need another beer." I detoured into the kitchen, grabbed another Heineken, then headed back to the living

138

room. Lyle was already seated on the couch. I sat in the chair opposite him. "As you probably expected, you've got my full attention, not to mention my curiosity. Begin wherever you like."

"I'm an arbitrageur, a deal-maker," Lyle began. His tone was easy and casual, and had a haunting ring of sincerity about it. He spoke for a few minutes about his work, which had, evidently, been quite successful the last few years. Begrudgingly, I could see what Susan liked about him. "I'm here for two reasons," Lyle said as he finally got nearer to his point. "First, because of an obligation that I feel I have to set something right. It's something unpleasant that has happened that, unfortunately, I was the motivating party behind. That aspect of what I've come to talk about has nothing whatsoever to do with Susan."

Lyle looked directly at me to take a reading. I felt neutral, so I suspect that I must have appeared that way. "Go on."

"The second reason for my being here is the payment of a debt. I feel very strongly about paying my way as soon as possible, about not owing anything to anybody."

"Yeah, I know the feeling. I once found out that American Express feels exactly the same way."

Lyle ignored my little joke and continued with what I suspected was a rehearsed speech. Still, he was presenting it rather well. "Actually, for what I'm talking about today, it's not so much the payment of a debt as the payment of the interest." Lyle squirmed in his seat ever so slightly; this was obviously the part of his carefully mapped-out explanation that he was least comfortable with.

"This is the me-and-Susan angle, right?" I volunteered. My comment came out rather positively because, for some reason, I was trying to help the guy off the horns of his dilemma – whatever in God's name it was. I had, for some reason, already taken something of a liking to him. In addition to speech-making, I had to give Lyle high marks for pure courage, or pure stupidity. They were both traits that I could easily identify, since experience had shown me that they seemed often to flow from the same river of blind faith in oneself – a river that I had been known to fish in from time to time.

"Yes, you're right. Susan and you. I know a lot about you. Incidentally, you're very well thought of by your wife." Lyle smiled in a friendly way.

"Nice to hear."

"And the reason that I'm here – the second reason – is that there are no bad guys in this little morality play between you and me and Susan. I know that this is going to sound absurd to you, but I'm here, in part, to pay to you the interest you've more than earned on your loan of Susan to me."

I was stunned. I sat in silence for what must have been a full minute. In the background, the chamber music players on the CD fiddled away at their task. Finally, I spoke. "You either think that you know me pretty well, or you enjoy taking big chances. Could be you're just stupid, although you certainly don't give that appearance."

"I . . ."

"Don't interrupt me, I'm on a roll. Now, where was I?" I smiled, somewhere between maliciously and amicably. "Oh, yes, now I remember. This might come as a surprise to a sophisticated gent like yourself, but some men might not take too kindly to what you just said. I feel an obligation to warn you that I'm sometimes known to be armed and dangerous." Just the potential in that verbal threat made me feel a little better.

"Oh, I think I know you pretty well. Susan talks about you often, talks about your relationship with each other." Lyle smiled himself, and there was not the slightest trace of anything other than openness and sincerity in his manner. Lucky for him there wasn't, because I can't imagine how I might have reacted if I had thought that he was mocking me. Also to his credit, Lyle didn't appear to be the slightest bit nervous. He leaned forward in his seat. "I've got lots of money, so something like a Mercedes is not really a big deal to me. Susan is a wonderful woman, and I very much enjoy my time with her. But I'm a married man myself."

"Oh, really?" That was an intriguing angle.

"Yes, although I'm sad to have to say that it's not much of a marriage. I mostly live apart from my wife. Because of that, and for other reasons, it's safe to say that Susan

140

will be moving on at some point. Hence the concept of the *temporary* loan of her."

"Interesting. When she moves on, do you think that she'll be coming back to me?" I wanted to add something like a pronouncement that I might not consider taking her back – but I found that I couldn't even say it, never mind actually consider it.

"I wouldn't know. That's strictly between you and her."

"When she moves on, will it be with the red Mercedes?" I asked. Here I was, negotiating with her current lover to make certain that she was getting a good deal. Incredible. In my mind's ear, I heard Max gagging.

"The car's in her name. Of course she'll keep it."

I took a long draw on the Heineken. "Anyway, Susan's not mine to loan out, so what you say about temporary or permanent doesn't matter to me."

"Oh, it's true that she's not a possession of yours – but it's also not true, in a manner of speaking." Lyle waved his hand in a motion of dismissal. "Yet all of that is quite beside the point. In my mind there's a loan, so in my mind I'm paying the interest on that loan. The payment will take the form of valuable information, something you'd want to know."

"I'm listening." There were seldom times in my life when I had absolutely no idea what a person was about to say to me. This was one of them.

"And as I said before, I'm also getting something out of this myself. I have an obligation to set something right. Fulfilling that obligation is going to give me peace of mind." Lyle took a deep breath, exhaled slowly, then began. "When Susan picked me up at the airport today, she told me how your investigating for Elmer Woodruff has been going. Before you protest about confidentiality, let me add that Elmer is a friend of mine – in fact, I'm the one who had introduced him to Susan."

"Yes, I already knew that." There was no way I could allow this guy to run through an entire Socratic dialogue without me getting in at least one pre-emptive remark. My ego was at stake. "Your introduction is what eventually got me the job at Trans-Continental." Saying it out loud made me feel a little better about it, although I didn't know why.

"Yes. Anyway, about a year ago I had brought some acquaintances of mine to a party that Elmer was giving. Some of his airline people were there, including a William Davenport."

I must have raised my eyebrow at the mention of the name because Lyle lifted his hand in a gesture for me to let him say it all before I interrupted.

"Susan has told me about your current suspicions of Davenport. That's what all this is about. One of the acquaintances I had brought to Elmer's party was a man named Joseph Tazik. Mr Tazik has lots of money, and I was helping him with legitimate investments. Since then, I've stopped working with Mr Tazik because I've come to learn that his primary business for raising capital is, more than likely, drug smuggling. Thanks to the Republican Party, I simply make far too much money legitimately for me to consider tainting myself with those kinds of associations."

I set my Heineken down on the table. So far, the only thing Lyle had told me that I could have predicted was that he was a Republican. "You introduced Tazik to Davenport?"

"Unfortunately, yes. Since then, I've been told that they've spent quite some time together." Lyle slowly shook his head. "You have to appreciate that I didn't realise any of this at the time, or all of it until today. It didn't completely come together in my mind until Susan filled me in on the details of your investigation when she picked me up at the airport. Now it seems, in hindsight, that I might be the original source of the introductions that eventually became Elmer Woodruff's problems."

We each sat quietly for a while. The CD player shut itself off. I looked at Lyle. For some reason, I believed him emphatically. In a sense, Susan had become Allan Lyle's character reference. "Anything else?"

"That's everything I know." Lyle rose to his feet and stuck out his hand. "I just wanted you to know this. It makes us square, pays off any debt that I might have to you. I'm sure that you'll be able to use what I've told you. Good luck with your investigation," he said as we shook hands. He turned to go.

"One more thing," I asked. "Does Susan know everything? Does she know that you came here?"

Lyle turned back to me. He nodded. "Of course she does. As you know – better than anyone, I would suspect – with Susan, being totally truthful is the only way."

Lyle had passed the final litmus test – he was indeed a genuine Susan-aficionado. "Thank you for the information."

"You're most welcome." He let himself out the door and, a minute later, I heard the Mercedes drive away. I sat on the arm of the couch for what seemed like five minutes; it turned out to be forty-five. It was the doorbell once again that brought me out of my trance.

Tracy. She was bubbling over with news when she walked in. We hadn't even sat down yet when she pulled out a paper and handed it to me. "Guess what this is."

"Your Christmas list?"

"Better. *Your* Christmas list. It's Davenport's expense account. I've circled one item. Look at it."

I did. Immediately, the date caught my eye. "That's the day Bridges was killed."

"Yes."

"What's Davenport's expense entry for?" I asked. The sheet Tracy handed me had some numbers on it, but it must have been a cross-reference to some other paperwork since it didn't make sense by itself.

"Take a guess. Be good to yourself while you're doing it."

Tracy had a broad smile on her face, and it made her dimples stand out. Lately, every time I saw Tracy, she looked better to me. Was she on a trend, or was I? "Take my best guess, something that would make me happy?"

"Yes."

"Chicago."

"Go to the head of the class."

"Really?" This was nearly too good to be true. Zarrillo and now Davenport, both in Chicago on the same night Bridges had been killed. "Why was Davenport there?"

"An air safety meeting. Three days. It was held at a hotel not far from the airport. Bridges was killed on the second night that Davenport was in Chicago."

15

The room wasn't totally dark because I had left the drapes partially separated. The glow of the rising sun was showing through the window, and when I opened my eyes the first thing I did, out of habit, was to glance at the clock on the nightstand by the bed. It was ten minutes to seven – a little too early to get up, a little too late for me to fall back to sleep.

The second thing I did was to roll over quietly and look at the supine figure beside me. Tracy's blonde hair was nearly iridescent in the red tinting from the scattering of morning sunlight. The blanket was wrapped casually around most of her, with just enough of her arms, shoulder and back showing to remind me how pleasant to the touch her skin was.

Last night we had found out that, just as we fit together conversationally, we also fit together sexually. Easy, natural, rewarding, satisfying – those were the words I'd have to use if anyone made me describe what we had done. I'd had more exotic sexual experiences in my life, but never a more pleasant one. Tracy and I melded so well together that it was, frankly, a little frightening.

"Don't you dare," Tracy said in a low, flat voice. Her eyes were still shut and she hadn't moved a muscle, but she was evidently fully awake. She was one of those instant-on people, just like me. "I know that it's too early to get up. It's a crime against nature."

"How did I wake you? I tried not to." I laid my hand on her arm; her skin was warm to the touch. Tracy had a way of bringing out all sorts of good sensations in me. As yet, she had not brought out any of the bad ones.

"Frankly, you were thinking too loud."

"The sound of gears meshing?"

"More like the sound of atoms whirling." Tracy opened

one eye, looked up at me and smiled. "Hey, big boy. Sunlight becomes you," she said. "It goes with your hair."

"And you certainly know the right things to wear," I answered. I had added the obvious tag line as I ran my hand down her bare back and across her hip.

"Naked makes an interesting fashion statement, don't you think?" Tracy had opened her other eye by now. She was still smiling, looking at me fully. She turned slightly and propped herself up on one elbow. "Well? What were you thinking about? Confess."

"I guess I was picking up where we left off last night, before you diverted my attention by being too sexy. As I recall, I was thinking about Davenport and company."

"Oh, them." Tracy put on an exaggerated pretend-frown. "So I suppose it's time to get up and get back to business, huh?"

"Probably."

"Okay, but my heart's not in it. We've been working too hard, we need time to ourselves."

"You want to be the one to tell Elmer?"

"Not a shot." She laughed, ran her hand through my hair, then jumped out of bed and headed for the bathroom. "Okay, you win. Back to work. If you start the coffee, I'll be out of here in no time. Then I'll make us breakfast while you get ready."

"Deal." I threw on a shirt and a pair of bluejeans and headed for the kitchen. The first order of business was getting the coffee pot going, then dealing with the remains of last night's Chinese take-out dinner. The fortune cookie that had predicted excitement and romance for her – the excuse we had used for me to put my arms around her and begin what we both knew we both wanted – lay on the counter. I placed it carefully on the side, before finishing with the empty cartons.

Tracy was true to her word. She was out within a few minutes of when the coffee pot had started pouring out the black elixir that I required to get my heart started. She was barefoot, her blonde hair was shiny-wet, and she was wearing one of my shirts. Far as I could tell, she was wearing nothing else. She looked gorgeous. "You're making another fashion statement," I said.

145

"Since I didn't pack anything, it was either one of your shirts or your black raincoat. I figured that the raincoat would've made me look like a guy from a porn movie, so I picked out a nice shirt."

"Nothing could make you look like a guy."

"Thanks." She smiled. "What do you want for breakfast?"

"I don't have much in stock. Eggs, I think some bacon. Maybe some English muffins in the freezer."

"Okay." Tracy opened the refrigerator and began to reconnoitre.

"Be back soon." I went into the bathroom, shaved and showered, combed my hair, brushed my teeth, put on decent pants and a clean shirt and came back out. All the while, especially when I was facing the mirror and looking myself in the eye, I struggled with the concept of how far we had got with the investigation and where we should go from there. The most amazing part of our discoveries was that we now felt like we knew who the perpetrators were – but we had no real proof of what they had done, what crime they had committed beyond the one of eliminating each other in rather systematic fashion. Finding some link between Davenport and an actual crime was obviously going to be the next item on the agenda.

Tracy and I had breakfast in the kitchen. Her hair had dried but, other than that, she looked the same – ravishing. I knew that I had to get my mind out of that track or we'd never get out of the apartment, never get back to work. The idea of needing to tell Elmer that we hadn't accomplished anything was the equivalent of my cold shower, and I set aside any thought of resuming our tryst until we had put in at least a few hours of honest labour.

Tracy had made scrambled eggs, and they were good. Over the second cup of coffee we shared our ideas concerning what in the world Chief Pilot Davenport and his dwindling band of conspirators had been up to. Drugs, of course, with this Joseph Tazik angle added by Mister Mercedes. But how, when and where? We collectively decided to go back to the Trans-Continental flight department. There, maybe Izzy Reese could help us get started in the right direction.

When we had just about finished eating, Tracy and I descended into a mutual silence for a few moments. "Do you miss your husband?" I finally asked to fill the void; I was changing the subject to something else that was also very much on my mind. It was a topic that we had briefly hinted at the night before, a little while before we began to get seriously turned on to each other. Dealing with the sensation of losing a person who meant a great deal to you was a topic close to home to me.

"Carl was very special. It was a horrible loss. You get over it after a while."

"I'm not sure that's an honest answer," I said. I thought I could tell that what she had told me was a pat, rote reply – the kind of answer that you used at cocktail parties and family functions. I wanted more.

Tracy blinked a few times. She looked down at her plate and poked her fork through the scattering of scrambled eggs that was still there. She looked back up at me. "You know me too well."

"Only because you let me."

"Only because you want me to." She gave a half-smile of resignation. "Truth. Okay, we'll try it. Truth is, I miss Carl so bad that it aches, that the emptiness burrows right through me. It was like the doctors said about his cancer, that it was burrowing right through him. For the longest time afterwards, I thought that Carl had passed along some kind of variant of the cancer to me because I now had this giant hole inside."

"Maybe I shouldn't have brought this up."

"No. I'm glad you did." Tracy paused for a moment, then decided to add more, to say everything. "But the whole truth – which you probably have already figured out – is that I feel that hollowness just about all the time, day or night, rain or shine. The only exception is when you're around."

"Really?" I didn't know if I deserved the credit for figuring it out yet, but I did know that I was evidently competing for top prize in the category of the most inane, innocuous response to a meaningful statement. On the other hand, uttering anything was probably better than sitting there with my slack jaw wide open, which was my first inclination. At that moment, Tracy was reminding me that it was a very nice feeling to be very significant to someone.

"Yes. When you're next to me, it's like a new life altogether. Honest Indian."

"That goes for me, too," I answered. My mother had told me years ago that when you can't think of a really good lie, you might as well tell the truth. "The most frightening thing about you is that you make me forget how unhappy I've promised myself I would be."

"Is that good?"

"Damned if I know. I think it is. I hope it is." Being absolutely, impeccably honest with Tracy was easy. Everything with Tracy was easy. We were too much in tune, in concert, to be otherwise. "Now that we've said all of this, what do you suppose we should do about it?"

"I don't know. Whatever comes to mind."

"Lots of things come to mind. Going back to the bedroom comes to mind."

Tracy laughed. "A great idea, except that if we do, then we're not working. Let me remind you that you're the one who brought up Elmer."

"Elmer. Oops. Forgot."

"A tough man to forget."

"Very true. The memory of his face has the potential of dousing the fires of my romantic instincts."

"Mine, too."

"Then how about if we just clean the dishes, then go to work? Time for other stuff later."

"Dishes. A very good thought. We can't have a pleasant relationship or a pleasant investigation with egg on our plates." Tracy got up and began clearing the table.

I scooped up a handful of utensils and put them in the dishwasher. Tracy was at the sink, next to me. I put my arm around her. "You look great in my shirt. Much better than I do."

"I wouldn't say that. You look pretty good yourself." Tracy kissed me on the cheek, then stepped away. "Okay, let's conjure up the image of dear Elmer so we can get down to business. What are we going to do about Davenport?"

"We're going to let Izzy be our guide."

"How?"

"Pardon me for repeating myself, but damned if I know."

148

I patted Tracy on the backside; she had a shape that was worth writing home about. "Get dressed. We'll go to the airport. We'll snoop around until Izzy arrives, then we'll see if he has any ideas."

"Other than the part about me getting dressed, your plan seems pretty vague."

"Vague, hell. It's non-existent."

"I thought so." Tracy disappeared into the bedroom.

I fiddled around at my desk for a while, sorting through piles of meaningless papers. As I could have predicted, my shufflings produced nothing. Tracy appeared, dressed and ready for action. We took my BMW, since there was no reason to suspect that anyone was on the lookout for me any longer – the suspects were, after all, dropping like flies.

Tracy and I used the time in the car to hypothesise what kind of dealings Davenport and his clan were involved in. Drugs were a broad cliché that really didn't tell us anything. Besides, Trans-Continental had no international routes. The idea of smuggling drugs from, say, Denver to Des Moines seemed ridiculous at best. Maybe, contrary to what Allan Lyle had told me, it wasn't drugs after all – maybe it was something else. By the time we had pulled into the hangar parking lot, we had got absolutely nowhere.

We took the employee bus to the terminal building and went upstairs to the flight department. Since it was only eight thirty, the place was pretty much empty. The exception to that was Izzy Reese, who was already at his desk.

"The early bird," I said as we walked in. Tracy took a chair as I slid on to the corner of Izzy's desk.

"Yeah, man. We early birds do get the best choice outa da chitlin buckets," Izzy said. He gave me a full-face grin, then turned to Tracy. "Good morning, Missis. You are sure looking fine today."

"Good morning, Iz. Thank you."

"Wait a minute," I said. "What's going on here? No paisley tie?" Izzy was wearing a plain-looking brown and blue number with an off-white shirt.

"Naw. There's a limit to how cool a dude can be, even me. The rank and file can only stand so much *très magnifique* from us minority folks. We got us an image to keep up. Besides,"

149

Izzy continued, pointing to my open-collar sports shirt, "you got no right to talk about my neckwear. How come you slumming it today?"

"Undercover work. I figured that no one would recognise me without a jacket and tie." I wasn't wearing my jacket since I wasn't carrying my shoulder holster – I was operating on the assumption that William F. Davenport wasn't going to gun me down in the hallway, especially since he didn't know that I was on to him. But just to be sure, my pistol wasn't far away; it was locked in the glove compartment of the BMW.

"Undercover, huh? Now that you mention it, I'm not too sure that I know who you are." Izzy gave both of us a nose-flattening smile. "Okay, so everything's cool. What can I do for you?" he asked.

"I'll fill you in." I brought Izzy up to speed on what had happened with Allan Lyle and what we had learned from Davenport's expense account. When I mentioned Davenport's name, Izzy snorted audibly and gave me an *I-told-you-so* look. It was nice to know that both of us were less than enthusiastic about the innocence of William F. Davenport. Our suspicions wouldn't hold up in a court of law but, then again, this wasn't a court of law.

"Now that we're seriously lookin' at the big daddy rabbit, I'm beginning to enjoy this case even more," Izzy said.

"It does have its pleasant moments." None of us really knew anything concrete about Davenport, but we all had the unmistakable feeling that he *had* to be up to no good. He was, from our point of view, a no-good type person. Still, in Davenport's defence, associating with a person who is *reputed* to be a drug smuggler is not even vaguely a crime.

"So where do we go from here?" Izzy asked, when I finished my presentation.

"I've come to you for guidance. We need a good paisley-tie man to take the point on this issue. What's your feeling so far?"

"My feeling is that we got big problems if we don't come up with some idea of what this here crime is. Gossip about hanging out with drug pushers don't mean nothing. We got lots of suspects, but no particular crime that I see."

150

"Tracy and I were talking about that very thing just before we got here."

"Okay, that's cool. We all agree," Izzy said. "We need a crime. We should probably make our plans figuring that it's drugs, considering what you've been told. But *figuring* ain't *knowing*. The airline don't fly much international. That seems to put a serious stranglehold on our theory that all of this adds up to some kind of pipeline to Colombia and points south."

"Hey, wait a second." I stood up from the desk. "How come you said the airline doesn't fly *much* international? The route map says that you don't fly international at all."

"Charters, man. A few to the Bahamas now and then. A weekly trip to Cancún, in Mexico."

"I'd forgotten about that," Tracy said. "Sorry."

"It probably doesn't mean anything," I answered. Yet, for some reason, I thought that it might. "A weekly run to Cancún, huh? How long has that been going on?"

"I could check for the exact dates. Over a year, I know that for sure. It's a contract with a travel agency. Tourists in, tourists out every week, a seven day package of sun, sea and bad drinking water." Izzy sat back in his seat and eyed me suspiciously. "It's the regular *weekly* bit that gets you, right?"

"Right."

"And a contract."

"Which means a predictable schedule that can't be altered without notice. Something that a syndicate of bad guys would like to have in their favour." I shook my head a few times; maybe we were on to something. "What's the schedule?"

"From Miami to Cancún on Saturday night. Layover. Return on Sunday morning. One airplane."

"What kind of equipment?"

"737."

"Bingo."

"Why do you say that?" Tracy asked.

"Boeing 737. It's a common thread between the parties who have got our attention so far. Bridges and Zarrillo were both pilots on the 737."

"Double-bingo, man. So is Chief Davenport," Izzy said.

"He is?" I asked. My antennae were up because it didn't seem right. "You sure?"

"Absolutely. I know for a fact that Davenport allowed his other qualifications to lapse, but he made a point of staying current on the 737." Izzy glanced at Tracy, then at me. "That's kind of strange for a man who could stay qualified on anything in the fleet."

Tracy shook her head. "I don't understand what you're saying."

"Davenport should be on the big iron," Izzy said.

"I still don't get it."

"It's simple," I answered. "It's customary for the chief pilot to stay current and qualified on at least one piece of the airline's equipment, so that he can leave his desk once in a while and see what's happening out on the line. It's like the king getting on a horse and riding around the countryside with his troops, so he can see what's happening, get a feel for things."

"Okay. And that's what Davenport's doing, right?"

"Yes. But he's doing it in the 737, which is a little unusual. Being the chief, he could get himself qualified on any of the airplanes that the airline operated – like one of the widebody jets that fly the non-stops to the Coast. Flying around in the 737s – which are purely the workhorse fleet – in preference to sitting in the company's biggest and most prestigious equipment is odd. Worse yet, it just doesn't seem like Davenport's style. Our king has voluntarily chosen to ride a mule rather than a stallion."

"Yet that's exactly what big daddy is doing," Izzy added.

"I see." Tracy glanced between me and Izzy. "So it seems to add up to this – that every one of the people we've been looking at was pilot qualified on the Boeing 737s, and that's the kind of airplane we use on our only international service, the weekly charter to Mexico."

"None of it by itself means anything," I said, mostly thinking out loud. "And all of it together could be nothing but a coincidence. But there sure as hell seem to be a lot of coincidences going on here. I bet that if we looked up the records, we'd discover that Zarrillo and Bridges both flew lots of those charters. Maybe Davenport, too."

"Here. We can check." Izzy turned round and faced the crew management computer on his desk. He typed in several codes, retrieved some numbers, then typed again. Soon the screen was full of names and dates.

"What have you got?" I asked.

"Man, exactly how much was that bet for?"

I could tell from Izzy's voice that I wasn't going to like his news. "Not enough to make a difference to a highly paid airline pilot. What do you see?"

"Crew names for all the Cancún charters, going back for more than a year." Izzy looked up. There was a frown on his face. "Something don't add up here."

"Why? How many times did our boys fly it?"

"Zero, man." Izzy swivelled the screen so that it faced me. "Absolutely zero."

"Strike out." The three of us sat in silence.

"I hate to bring this up," Tracy said, "but what do you think about the chance of someone else being involved? There's lots of names here that flew those trips several times." She ran her hand down the list on the screen.

"Bad vibes on that one," Izzy said. "Lots of pilots like the charters, gets them out of the usual routine. Flying them a few times is not enough to go on."

"Besides, we didn't have the slightest indication that anyone else was involved. We'd be going against everything we've already learned if we head down that road. The crime-stopper's handbook says that's not a good idea."

"Okay, then what is?"

"Search me."

"Hey, man, while she's searching you, I'm going for a stroll," Izzy said. He got up from his chair and headed for the door. "I'm going to poke around Davenport's office. His secretary should have a list of all the flying he's done. Maybe when he bought those trips he didn't bother – on purpose – to put his name in place of the scheduled captain's."

"Good idea." I watched Izzy walk out and close the door behind him. "That's our only chance, that Davenport actually flew the trips but didn't sign into the computer."

"Explain how that works, I don't follow it," Tracy said.

"The regular line pilots bid on their flying in seniority and

153

are awarded their trips accordingly – just like your husband used to do."

"Yes, I know that much."

"Check pilots, chief pilots, people like that, when they want to fly a scheduled flight they have to replace the regular pilot whose trip it was supposed to be. They just call the regular pilot and tell him to stay home, but the airline pays the regular pilot for the trip anyway."

"Oh, yes. I remember Carl having trips bought from him every now and then. That was the expression he used."

"That's it. They pay the regular pilot to stay home that day so that the supervisor can fly the trip with a brand new captain, or just to get some flying in himself. Most airlines do it that way."

"Okay. We'll just have to wait until Izzy finds out if Davenport had been flying any of those trips."

"Yes. Wait and see." The minutes ticked by. Tracy and I talked casually. We made tentative plans to do some things together – movies, theatre, symphony, opera. By the time Izzy walked back into the room, we had made enough tentative plans to take us into the fourth or fifth year of our relationship.

"Another piece of the puzzle, man. I just hope that it's *this* puzzle," Izzy said. He looked at the two of us. "Strange stuff."

"Did Davenport fly any of those charters?"

"Naw. Not that I could tell. But while I was poking around, I saw a note that said he was going to do some training – some flight training for new copilots. Can you imagine that?"

"New copilots?"

"Strange," Izzy repeated. He turned to Tracy. "A guy like Davenport, going out late at night to give new copilots some takeoffs and landings."

"That's not the kind of thing a chief pilot ever does, not if he has a choice," I added, as a matter of explanation.

"Hell, man, that's not the kind of thing that *I* go out to do if I have a choice," Izzy said. He wrinkled his nose and snorted. "So Davenport left this message with the training captain to stay home, that he'd take out the new copilots himself. Very weird."

154

"When did this happen?" I asked.

"Hey, you like coincidence, right?" Izzy said. "That's what you're going to like the most about this."

"When?" I asked again. The image of Chief Pilot Davenport doing night takeoffs and landings with new copilots, and in a Boeing 737, was enough to cause all the sensory alarms in my head to ring at once.

"Tonight, man. Nine o'clock. From the hangar."

16

We had spent the entire day carefully poking around, trying to learn more about what was happening. It was nearly 6 p.m. and we were back at the hangar offices. We had, so far, learned absolutely nothing else. We were like a record stuck in a groove and, frankly, I was getting tired of the song. "Izzy should've been here already."

"You keep saying that." Tracy glanced up at the clock above her desk, then back at me. "He'll get here when he can. Maybe it's good news that he's late. Maybe it means that he's come up with something we can use."

"Maybe." I had my doubts. The only thing we knew for sure was that the airline's chief pilot was going to waste an evening of his life by giving two new-hire copilots the practice takeoffs and landings they needed in order to be officially qualified. Since it didn't make a damned bit of sense for Davenport to be doing that, it also meant that nothing else we knew made any sense either. The consistencies in our position were comforting – nothing plus nothing ciphered up to a grand zero.

"Be patient. Izzy won't let us down." Tracy smiled and tried to look encouraging. Instead, because of our non-stop efforts, she looked tired and was beginning to look nervous.

"I know that Izzy won't let us down. I'm only hoping that Davenport won't be the one to change his mind about whatever the hell all of this means. I've got a feeling that we're close, real close, to finally figuring out what it's all about."

"Yes, I think so, too." Tracy got up from her desk and walked over to me. She put her arms around my neck and looked me straight in the eye. "I've also got a feeling that things are going to begin happening pretty quick now."

"It's about time. My pacemaker's about to stop from lack of exercise."

"Listen to me. Be serious. This could start to be real dangerous now. You've got to promise me that you'll be very careful."

"Sure." I decided not to remind her that Max and I had already been shot at, and that Paula Tate was no longer around to smell the flowers. Ditto Bridges and Zarrillo. "But you'll have to stand in line for a promise like that."

"Stand in line? Why?"

"Because I've already promised myself exactly the same thing." I slipped my hands down around Tracy's waist and pulled her closer to me. "Don't tempt the gods by asking for too much. The gods get real nasty if you get greedy. Let's be thankful for the good breaks we've already had."

"Breaks? That's a joke."

"Just like a woman." I rolled my eyes in an exaggerated display. Meanwhile, I was keenly aware of how her body felt in my hands. "You're overlooking our moments of good fortune."

"Like what?"

"Like Elmer being out of town today so we could stand in front of his office and fondle each other." I nodded towards the opened door and darkness that was the Grand Inquisitor's inner sanctum. I *was* thankful that Elmer had left on an early morning flight to go north for meetings. That meant that I had nobody to check with and nobody to have to answer to – not until tomorrow. By then, with any luck, I might have something to say.

"I'm not fondling you." Yet Tracy kept her hands around my neck, and her eyes riveted to mine.

"Okay, you're not fondling me. Then what are you doing?" The curves between her waist and her hips were a tantalising part of her, and I had no intention of removing my hands until there was an absolute need to.

"I'm giving you encouragement and support. They taught me to do that at management trainee school. Since Elmer is gone today, I'm the only company representative around who can show you how satisfied we are with the investigating work you've done for the airline."

157

"Thanks for the encouragement." I leaned over and gave her a gentle kiss on the cheek. "Now, as an official representative of management, would you please answer me a question?"

"Sure thing."

"Where the hell is employee Ishmael Reese?"

"Right behind you, man." Izzy had just walked in, on cue. He was carrying a paper bag in his hand.

Tracy and I stepped apart. I had already figured on trying to look angry, but one look at Izzy changed all of that. He had the kind of face that was hard to be mad at. "You're late," I mumbled, hoping a lack of volume from me could be interpreted as my being in a bad temper.

"Couldn't be helped." Izzy nonchalantly put the bag down on Tracy's desk. "I was too busy. Couldn't boogie any quicker."

"You should've called."

"Naw. Tension's good for guys like you and me – gets our blood moving, our brains perking."

"We'll debate our emotional proclivities later. What's in the bag?"

"Hallowe'en, man. Your costume."

"Could you be a little more specific?"

"Here, see for yourself." Izzy reached into the bag and pulled out a jumpsuit-type uniform. "Company threads, man. A technician's outfit."

"What for?"

"For you. So you and me can walk around the hangar ramp without anyone thinking a thing about it. It'll look like I'm doing some kind of consulting with the maintenance and engineering department. You, my boy, are the maintenance and engineering department."

"Okay, I get the idea. That also tells me that you found out more." I picked up the technician's jumpsuit and looked at it. It was khaki-coloured, with the airline name on the back in red letters.

"Yeah. I found out a little more. By hanging around the dispatch department I found out the ship number that's scheduled for tonight's copilot training. I did it without

158

asking anyone, since we're still not absolutely sure that we know all the players in this game."

"The ship is still one of the 737s, isn't it?" Tracy interrupted.

"Yeah," Izzy said. "Ship 263. It finished up its last scheduled flight early this afternoon, it's on the hangar ramp already. But better yet is what I learned about where that ship was last weekend."

I didn't know if it was the look on Izzy's face, or his words, but suddenly the whole picture became perfectly clear to me. It was now absolutely obvious. If I had been in a more personally hostile mood, I would have kicked myself for not having figured it out sooner. Fortunately, my spirits were on the rise. "Iz, stop right there."

"Huh?"

"Please, say no more. Let me take a stab at it. Truth is, I'm trying to impress the lady with my clairvoyance."

"Oh. Sure thing, man. You want three guesses?"

"Hell, no. I'm trying to *really* impress her." I smiled at Tracy. "I only need one guess."

"Puttin' it all on the line, huh?" Izzy grinned at me. "Go ahead, if you think you're man enough."

"Ship 263." I closed my eyes and held my fingers to my temples, as if I were trying to conjure up a mystic image. "Ship 263. Yes, the fog is burning away. I can see it now. Ship 263 . . ."

"Come on, Jack, stop fooling around," Tracy said. "Tell me already."

I pretended that I hadn't heard her. "I see ship 263 . . . I see enchiladas . . . I see castanets and conquistadors . . . I see beer bottles with limes stuck in them . . . I see ship 263 in Cancún last weekend." I opened my eyes.

"Hey, right on."

"*Right on?* Iz, I'm truly surprised at you."

Izzy laughed at his own gaffe. "Oops. Pardon the expression. And don't tell the brothers that you caught me using yesterday's jive, will ya?"

"Your indiscretion's safe with me."

"Praise be to Allah. Anyway, you're right. Cancún, less than a week ago. Maybe you oughta enter the Florida

159

lottery, you seem to have a good feel for these kinds of things."

"Sure thing. I'd be great at guessing the numbers from last week's lottery."

"Okay, I see it now, too," Tracy said. "Whatever they were smuggling is stashed somewhere on that airplane. We kept thinking it was a *person* doing the smuggling, when actually it was just the airplane that was the focal point. The people involved could catch up to the airplane a few days or even a week later, when it was safer and more convenient, as long as they knew which ship it was. Where do you think they could hide the stuff so it would go undetected for that long?"

"Everywhere. Airliners are big. Full of lots of places where people hardly ever look."

"That makes sense. Anyway, that's why Davenport is going out tonight to do this training, to pick up whatever it is."

"Maybe." I held the airline jumpsuit up to me; it was a little too small. Instead of just putting it over my clothes, it was probably going to be tight enough to make me take off my pants and shirt first. Even then, it might be tight. "All of this sounds good, but we're still doing a lot of guessing."

"Come on, Jack, don't be a wet blanket. Guessing is what we've been doing all along," Tracy said. "At least now the guesses are beginning to make a good deal of sense."

"Right. They are." I put my hand into one of the jumpsuit's side pockets. The pocket was big enough for my gun, which I had brought up earlier and which was now lying on Tracy's desk, suitably masked by a pile of paperwork just in case anyone unexpected had shown up. We were now at the stage when I wasn't going to do anything without the gun somewhere near me. That compact piece of pig iron was, from this morning, my indispensable security blanket. "What about these new copilots that Davenport is going to train? I can't imagine that they could be any part of this."

"More information, courtesy of me." Izzy flashed us one of his biggest, broadest grins.

"Speak, brother Iz."

"I had the same thought that you did, that the copilots

160

didn't fit the picture. I decided to call the copilots myself, just to check out the schedule that they'd been told. I did it a little while ago, so that we'd know about any last minute changes." Izzy paused.

"And?" He looked at both me and Tracy before he spoke again; evidently, the news that he had was major enough to demand a little dramatic interlude. If I were any good at imitating a drum roll, I would've done one.

"And guess what."

"No more guesses from me, I did that before. I don't want to burn out such a fine-tuned psychic machine."

"Miss Tracy, you wanna turn, you wanna try to impress this guy with your guess-work?"

"Iz, truth is I'm trying to impress him in other ways." Tracy looked over at me with a pleasant but neutral expression on her face, a fact that we could both be proud of.

"Aw, you folks is too easy." Izzy opened his hands in a wide, expansive, what-else-could-it-be gesture. "So Davenport calls the two copilots at their hotel a little while ago. He tells them to forget it, that the training is cancelled."

"Really?"

"Yup. But then right after that he calls the dispatcher to make sure the training is still on and that the airplane – ship 263, of course – is going to be ready."

"My, my," I said.

"We've got him," Tracy said. She turned to me. "We should call the police. Have them here for when Davenport shows. When he grabs the stuff from wherever it's hidden in the airplane, then the police can grab him."

I took a deep breath. I exhaled slowly. The amazing part, to me, was how much I wanted to go along with Tracy's idea even though I knew better. My guts wanted me to make a beeline towards resolution. But, like I said, I knew better. "Can't call the police yet, it's too early."

Tracy blinked a few times. She looked at Izzy, then at me. "Why?"

"Because it's too hypothetical. If we bring the police in now and we've guessed wrong, or something else happens to change things, then we're going to look bad. Worse than

161

that, Elmer's going to look bad when it comes out that it was Davenport, of all people, that we were suspecting."

"Oh."

"Something else, too," Izzy said. "Just finding stuff on the airplane ain't enough. We've got no real tie with Davenport – or even Zarrillo or Bridges, for that matter. Unless we see him with our own eyes pulling stuff off the airplane, I think any two-nickel lawyer could get him off."

"True." I took a few steps across the room and sat on the edge of Tracy's desk. I looked to my left, towards the opened door and the darkness where Elmer's empty office was. "We've got a responsibility to Elmer to make this iron-clad. We can't have any holes in it, or any slip-ups. I'll have to be out there when Davenport shows, and I'll have to see him take whatever it is off ship 263. If I grab him then, we've got the kind of case that Elmer needs."

"It's dangerous, and you know it," Tracy said.

"It has that potential, that's true," I admitted. "But remember, I've already made a promise to both you and me. I'm going to be very careful."

"If you say so." Clearly, Tracy was not happy.

"Unfortunately, I do. It's the only way." I couldn't think of anything else to say, so I picked up the airline jumpsuit and stepped into Elmer's darkened office to change. If the truth be known, the situation was a little too open-ended; I wasn't very happy with my immediate prospects either.

17

The ramp behind the Trans-Continental hangar was, like most airport ramps, a study in stark contrasts. The big floodlights that covered the area were unnecessarily bright, and they washed everything in irritating streaks of brilliance. Between the shafts of light, or behind some intervening object like a parked airplane, there were deep pockets of long and gloomy shadow. Izzy and I walked around ship 263 twice, me with a clipboard, him with a sheaf of papers in his hand. We were trying to look diligent and peremptory, but actually all we were doing was marking time.

The airliner was dark and quiet, its electrical power shut down. It loomed above us, its hundred-foot-plus length and nearly forty foot of height appearing even larger on the bare expanse of concrete. Other than Izzy and me and ship 263, the ramp was totally deserted – it was relatively late for the afternoon shift to be starting any serious work, and it was far too early for the night shift to begin shuffling airplanes around and fixing problems. All our posturing to make me look like an airline technician was, evidently, for an audience that was conspicuous in its absence. "Nothing out of the ordinary out here," I said.

"A real shame. I was hoping for a good clue."

"Like what?"

"Like one of the maintenance access panels on this flying Trojan horse labelled as *drug storage* or something like that. That would make life real easy." While he spoke, Izzy continued to amble slowly around the Boeing jet while he led us in something of a mock inspection; he casually rubbed his hand on the exterior of the left engine's thrust reverser as we walked past it.

"Yes. That would be nice." I glanced at my wristwatch. Seven forty-five. Davenport was due to show in a little more than an hour. So far, we had had no indication that he was going to do anything except stick to that plan. I was walking stiffly because the airline jumpsuit was too small, even though I had taken off my own pants and shirt before putting it on. Like most big guys, Izzy evidently had a propensity to evaluate other people as being much smaller than they actually were.

"No news from Tracy is a good sign," Izzy said.

"Sure is. Maybe Davenport will keep his appointment with destiny."

"He'll show." Izzy looked up at the large aluminium slats at the leading edge of the left wing, then back at me. "Around this company, Davenport's been calling the shots for a long time. When he makes a plan, I get a feeling that he figures that it's written in stone."

"The commandments according to Davenport."

"Something like that. 'Cepting that this time he forgot about the commandment not to steal."

"And not doing other bad stuff, too."

"Yeah. He forgot about a lot of things. But maybe he's not a bad guy, maybe he's just forgetful." Izzy grinned.

"Maybe." I stopped at the base of the airplane's extended airstairs, and Izzy stopped next to me. I peered up the stairs, into the darkened cabin. "I might as well go up now," I said.

"We still got time."

"No. I don't want to take chances. I go up now, then you can get out of here before he shows." I pointed up the stairs, towards the interior of the Boeing jet.

"I still think that I should stay with you," Izzy said.

"Iz, we've already been over all that. I need you to be between us and the airplane, so that you can watch things from a different angle."

"But . . ."

"But nothing. There's not a damn thing you can do to help me out here. I need help over there." I gestured towards the hangar.

"That's the dugout, man," Izzy said. "Pinch-hitter shit." He scowled. "I don't like flunkey work."

"Me neither. But if you don't haul your ass out of here and post yourself over in one of those dark corners by the hangar,

164

Davenport's going to spot you, or some other stupid damned thing is going to happen. If it does, then Elmer is going to make flunkeys out of both of us tomorrow morning.''

"Okay, man, I give up. You win.'' Izzy still had a frown on his face, although he seemed somewhat more reconciled to the plan. ''But just remember to be careful. Davenport might be carrying a gun.''

"I doubt it.'' I took a step up the Boeing's airstair. "He's playing this cool, and he has no idea that we're on to him. There's no need for him to take a chance on carrying a gun. He'll just come out here, grab the stuff off the airplane, then try to beat feet.'' I took another step up. "Then I'll grab him. You'll be on the hangar side of the ramp if he tries to make a run for it.''

"Right. I'll stop him if he does.''

"I bet you will.'' I turned away from Izzy and continued climbing the short set of airstairs that reached up to the airliner's main entrance door. As I stepped inside the dark cabin, I turned and saw Izzy trotting briskly towards one of the deep shadows at the corner of the hangar. For a man on the heftier side of average, he moved quickly. I turned again and entered the airliner's cockpit.

Everything was dark, but the shapes were very familiar. After having spent a few years in the copilot's seat of one of these Boeing 737s, I knew what switches did what. The panel layout on the Trans-Continental airplane was only slightly different from the ones at Air East, so I felt sort of at home. After a minute of standing in the companionway behind the cockpit centre pedestal, I let the urge to do the obvious take hold of me; I slid into the copilot's flight chair.

The perspective from that angle was frighteningly familiar, as if I had never left my airline pilot job. What I had vowed to wash out of my thoughts and memory was evidently very much there – an understandable reaction since I had spent several years of my life sitting in an area that was, in reality, no bigger than a small closet.

As if it were only yesterday since my last airline flight, I laid my hand on the copilot's control column. My hands fitted comfortably on the black wheel, the inside edges of my thumbs felt sensually alive as they caressed the complex curves of the smooth plastic. Smooth plastic, complex curves. Sensual. I had to laugh to myself at the aeronautical pornography that the moments of nostalgia were bringing to the surface.

It was aeronautical porn of the first order, a sort of Orville and Wilbur sex shop. Yet the image did truly fit, because most pilots were both in love with their airplanes and made love to them, too. That was why the job itself was so entrapping, so enticing – because it was more than a job, it was a way of life. Steering big machines through the sky had a way of becoming an integral part of yourself, even when you no longer wanted it to be.

I kept my right hand on the control wheel as I slid my left hand off the column and placed it on the twin engine throttles on the pedestal between the two pilot seats. My fingers wrapped around the curves of those knobs; another sensual reaction to the mysterious relationship between man and machine.

So why, I asked myself, did I walk away from it all if it was so damned tantalising to me? Truth was, I didn't. Just like Susan, Air East had left me, deserted me, divorced me. And, just like Susan, I didn't think I'd have enough energy to go through the courtship routine again. Not with another woman, not with another airline. That was probably closer to the whole picture than any of the other lies that I had cleverly crafted for myself.

But then Tracy had entered my personal life, and I discovered that in reference to women I had more energy, more resilience than I had thought. Now, this. Was I discovering that, deep down, I really wanted to, in a manner of speaking, be remarried to a pilot's job?

Who knew the answer to metaphorical questions like that? Not me, that was for sure. I felt like Hamlet, racked with indecision – or like Faust, making a pact with the devil. All I knew for certain was that at this moment it felt damned good being back in the cockpit. But I also knew that if I didn't get myself out of the cockpit and hidden in the back end of the airliner pretty soon, then Davenport would see me and all hell would break loose.

I looked out of the cockpit window and scanned the ramp outside. Still empty. Even Izzy was out of sight, hidden, I imagined, in one of the shadows alongside the hangar. My career and life expectancy questions would have to wait, it was now time to set the final trap for William F. Davenport. Ah, how sweet was a dedicated life of direction and purpose. I slid out of the cockpit seat and stepped back into the airliner's cabin.

Since the Boeing's electrical system was totally shut down, the only light inside was what came through the cabin windows from the ramp floods. I walked through the small first class section and headed further aft, towards the very back end of the cabin. I had already given some thought as to where I might hide myself and, much to my amazement, discovered that a hundred-foot-long airliner was pretty thin on good places to hide.

At the very back end of the fuselage was the rear galley and the lavatory. The problem with using either one of them to stay out of Davenport's sight was that the likelihood of one of those places being the spot where the drugs were hidden was pretty high. If Davenport came aboard and made a beeline to the rear galley, I would be trapped there with no way to get out. Not good.

Strictly playing percentages, I went three-quarters of the way aft and slid into one of the seats on the left side of the cabin. Even though the drugs could presumably be hidden beneath the floor panels in any of the rows, the chances of me picking the wrong row out of the twenty rows of seats in the airplane seemed pretty slim. If Davenport was that lucky and I was that unlucky, he probably deserved to get away with it.

I sat in the centre seat of the row of three, keeping back far enough from the window to make myself invisible in the darkened cabin, yet with a good view of the ramp that Davenport would have to walk across. I took my gun out of the pocket of the airline jumpsuit and laid it on the adjacent seat. I glanced at my wristwatch: eight twenty. I waited.

Twenty minutes later Davenport appeared out of the shadows, interrupting my thoughts about Tracy. He was a hundred feet away on the ramp, dressed in his airline pilot's

167

uniform. I sat further upright and watched him; he was headed straight for the stairs of the Boeing.

But then behind him, from the shadows, came another figure: another man in a pilot's uniform. For an instant I thought it might be Izzy, and I cursed him for being so dumb as to follow Davenport so closely. Yet even before the first epithets formed on my lips, I realised that it wasn't Izzy – the guy was too thin, and he had a different walk, a different bearing.

I laid my hand on the gun. This was a wrinkle that I hadn't thought about, that Davenport would have yet another accomplice. I don't know why I hadn't thought about that, but I hadn't – probably because we hadn't the slightest clue that there was anyone else involved and I was a firm believer in not flying in the face of the evidence I had already gathered. Maybe I should really consider becoming an airline pilot again, because my career as a detective was going to be foreshortened if I kept making those kinds of assumptions and errors.

I crouched down on the floor between the seats to make myself as inconspicuous as possible. I peeked out of the window and watched Davenport and the other man as they approached the airstairs. The other man – shorter than Davenport, but powerful-looking and with a puffy, unfriendly face – was totally unfamiliar to me. Once they had got within a dozen feet of the base of the stairs I lost them from view, but by then I could make out their voices in the quiet night air. The words were unintelligible, but it sounded like Davenport's voice giving some instructions as they mounted the stairs. I could feel the vibrations of their footsteps as they walked up the stairs and stepped into the Boeing's entranceway.

Next, there was a half a minute's pause without anything happening. After that, a sprinkling of cabin lights came on as, evidently, Davenport turned on the ship's battery. Even though the lights were widely scattered and quite dim – only a few lights were designed to work when the airplane was purely on battery power – I crouched even lower between the rows. Now was not the time to be seen.

The next sound I heard startled me because, even though

I knew exactly what it was the instant I heard it, I hadn't expected it at all. My record tonight was, so far, totally intact – nothing whatsoever was going according to plan. I was increasingly becoming a member of the audience of this play, not the director of it like I had hoped to be. The sound I heard was the airplane's auxiliary power unit being started – the little turbine power-plant in the tail that provided the electricity and air-conditioning for the airplane while it was sitting on the ramp.

Why wasn't Davenport – and whoever he had brought with him – simply taking the drugs from wherever they were hidden and getting out of here? Why were they powering up the ship, as if he were really going out on some kind of copilot training flight? I didn't have a clue. Maybe they needed a little additional light to get the drugs from wherever they were hidden, and they figured that there was no risk since they were supposed to be here anyway. I hoped so.

I shifted my position and peeked up the aisle as much as I dared. One of the men had moved into the centre of the entranceway. From where I was positioned, and because of the angles, I could see only the man's legs and back. I couldn't make out for certain if it was Davenport or the other guy, but what I did see caused me to worry: he was standing in the entranceway in a familiar location, doing a familiar thing – raising the airplane's airstairs. Once they were fully up, the man stepped out of sight towards the aircraft's main door frame. The slight pressurisation bump in my ears and the change in illumination on the entranceway floor told me that the main cabin door had been closed.

In the dim lights of the cabin, I took a chance by coming more fully out into the aisle to watch what would happen next. I caught sight of the man who had closed the door – it was Davenport, for sure – stepping back into the cockpit. Davenport slid into the captain's seat. The other man was already in the copilot's flight chair. With the cockpit lights on bright and the cockpit door only partially opened – it had swung halfway towards closed after Davenport had walked by it – I knew they couldn't see me. I stepped out into the aisle and carefully made my way forward.

By the time I reached the first class section, my worst

169

fears proved to be true. I could hear the flow of the cabin air-conditioning being shut off and, a few moments later, the whine of engine-starting as it began. Within a minute both of the Boeing's engines were running. The airplane's brakes were then released. I swayed under the sudden motions of the airplane, holding on to the back of the first class seat beside me.

As the airplane turned on the ramp, the cockpit door swung shut of its own accord. I took a few steps ahead, into the forward galley. I held my gun in my right hand and braced myself against the irregular motions of the taxiing airplane with my left. The jet was being taxied rapidly. I glanced out of the small window in the main entrance door just in time to see us exit the Trans-Continental hangar ramp and roll down a taxiway that I knew would lead towards the runway.

I stood with my back against a fibreglass panel and wondered what in hell was going on and what in God's name I should do about it. We were evidently headed towards the runway to go flying, although I didn't have the slightest idea why.

What to do about it was even further from my thoughts; I felt like a passenger wanting to go to Miami who suddenly discovers that he somehow boarded the flight to Toledo. Not good, not good at all. Maybe I had been right all along – that I was a modern day combination of Hamlet and Faust. Maybe in my oversights and indecisions, I had already sold my soul to a devil. To a devil named William F. Davenport. And maybe the guy in the copilot's seat was Mephistopheles himself. I had a feeling that I was going to find out if any of this was true in the very near future.

18

We waited in line for takeoff for about ten minutes, then rolled down the runway and, from the features below, I could tell that we were headed west. The air was mostly smooth. Davenport was evidently a little rusty at his stick work, because the Boeing waddled from side to side and had an annoying tendency to pitch down abruptly at each altitude level-off point. The Miami ground lights faded quickly behind us.

From what I could tell by looking out of the small window in the entrance door, we finally levelled off at about six thousand feet and were holding that as our cruise altitude. That meant that we weren't going very far – possibly only to the outlying training field that was forty miles northwest of Miami International. The Dade-Collier strip, a single ten thousand foot runway in the middle of the Everglades swamp, was used strictly for training purposes. It was, in fact, precisely the airport Davenport would've used if he did have two new copilots aboard. From that point of view, Davenport was playing it very smart.

I watched out of the entrance door's window while my mind raced through the possibilities of what might lie ahead. I realised now that Davenport had set this job up even better than I had given him credit for. Not only had he given himself an official excuse to be on board ship 263 so that he could unload whatever the expensive cargo was, but he was also taking the airplane to a remote strip where his covert activities would stand a much better chance of being totally undetected. Smart. My congratulatory hymns to Davenport were interrupted by the sound of the jet engines being brought back to idle power as the descent began.

The idea of bursting into the cockpit and forcing Davenport to fly back to Miami occurred to me, but I dismissed

171

it immediately. I wasn't sure who the guy in the copilot's seat was – no new-hire copilot, that much was certain – but, regardless, at that point all I had on Davenport was wasteful use of his company's airplane. Taking a friend for a joyride, no matter how expensive it might be to Trans-Continental Airlines, was hardly an indictable offence. I had to let Davenport do something far more overt and discernible with the hidden cargo; I had to catch the guy, literally, with the stuff in his hands.

The Boeing continued its descent. I heard the flaps being let out, then the landing gear go down. Outside, the terrain was pitch black – the ground below us was nothing but swamp and alligators. The airplane's landing lights came on, the long, bright wands of white slicing through the darkness. Like it always did during an inky-black night, the airplane felt as if it was suspended in the sky and completely motionless.

I edged closer to the window to try to catch a glimpse of the airport. We were, I imagined, landing straight in on the west runway, so I had no chance of spotting the field out of the south-facing window on the side of the ship I was standing on. The gun in my hand was causing my palm to sweat. I shifted the gun to my left hand while I rubbed my fingers along the leg of my airline jumpsuit to dry them.

I knew we were getting close, but I couldn't really tell how near the runway was until the landing lights suddenly reflected off the terrain below. A couple of hundred feet to go. I braced myself against the wall for the touchdown, not knowing how well good old Davenport was going to execute this night landing.

The Boeing crossed the threshold of the runway; I saw the green edge lights flash by. Then we floated, about ten feet in the air, for half an eternity while our stalwart skipper hunted for the ground – a typical error from someone who hasn't flown recently and often.

With half the pavement behind us, Davenport finally found the concrete with a thud. We had arrived at Dade-Collier training field. Davenport stomped on the brakes and pulled the engines into reverse. We exited the runway at the end, then manoeuvred slowly down a parallel taxiway.

Once again, I didn't know exactly what to expect next, although, for a change, I did have some ideas. I stayed close to the window to see what was happening outside. More than likely, Davenport would bring the airplane to a stop somewhere on the deserted apron in the centre of the training field – an apron that was occasionally used to park an airplane during crew changes and training breaks. Then he would do his unloading from wherever the stuff was hidden, and probably just lay it in the cabin for the short return flight. I would make my move when we touched down back at Miami.

As I expected, he steered the Boeing on to the dark patch of blacktop to the south side of the taxiway that led back to the single runway. There was nothing on the apron other than the paved surface itself and some blue taxiway lights; not a structure of any sort, not even a floodlight. The training field had no control tower, either – very seldom did more than one airplane inhabit the traffic pattern at a time. On those rare occasions when two or three showed up to do practice landings, the pilots spoke directly to each other on a common radio frequency to give each other a turn at the runway.

The only illumination in the ramp area was of our own making, from the airplane's powerful landing lights that Davenport had left on. Even more than before, I really began to appreciate how the spartan environment of this training field was custom-made for what was shaping up as Captain Davenport's smuggling business. That was a catchy title: I made a mental note to mention it to the District Attorney, maybe he'd like to use it in the official paperwork.

I had started to walk away from the window and head back towards my hiding place in the rear when I spotted something out of the corner of my eye. A flicker of light. I stepped closer to the window again. A light in the distance. A pair of headlights. A car. No, it was a truck. *Damn*. A medium-sized van. It had been driven on to the empty airport ramp, and was being steered off to the Boeing's left side.

The van came to a stop. The doors opened. Four guys got out. I could see them clearly from the glow of the airplane's landing lights. Big guys, less than friendly looks. One of

173

them waved at the airplane. Davenport blinked one of the landing lights off and then back on. The guys stood where they were while Davenport manoeuvred the airplane slowly around them so that the Boeing was facing back towards the taxiway again.

Decision time. Four unfriendlies on the ramp, plus two in the cockpit. I had six bullets, total, in the gun. I hadn't expected a Mexican standoff, so I hadn't brought a case of ammo. I probably should have. As it turned out, I hadn't left myself a great deal of room for manoeuvring.

I thought over the entire situation for maybe ten seconds. Options were narrowing. Well, in the vein of what the famous homespun philosopher Max Bergman once told me, when life gives you lemons, you should consider making lemonade. I put my hand on the cockpit door and turned the knob. It was, thank God, unlocked. I pushed the door open and rushed into the cockpit.

"Freeze," I said. "Don't touch a thing. If you do, I'll blow your damned heads off." When Davenport saw me, his jaw dropped wide open. The guy in the copilot's seat looked at me less with fear or surprise than with dislike. Disdain, even.

"Don't be an asshole," was the opening line from the guy in the copilot's seat.

"If you move one inch, you're going to have a new one." I moved the barrel of the gun back and forth between Davenport and the other guy, although I had the good sense to leave it pointed mostly towards the fellow in the copilot's seat. The guy to my right was, without a doubt, going to be the biggest threat to my plan – a plan which, unfortunately, I had yet to come up with. But what I knew for sure was that I couldn't let those other four goons get on board the airplane. Like it or not, two against one was going to be tonight's best odds. "We're getting out of here," I said.

"We can't do that. We need to get fuel." Davenport looked scared, and he sounded scared, too. But his brain was working, and he was trying to come up with some way to stop me.

"Don't give me that bullshit." I pointed to the fuel gauges. "You've got ten thousand pounds in each main. That's enough for four hours."

"I . . ." Faced with the fact that I obviously knew what I was talking about, Davenport had run out of words.

I glanced outside. The guys from the van were milling around, looking concerned. Clearly, something was not going according to plan. They didn't look like the types to weigh their options discreetly before acting. While I was watching, one guy aimed a handgun towards the cockpit, although I could see that he wasn't quite sure what to do with it. With the airplane's landing lights on, and us inside the darkened cockpit, I could clearly see the guys on the ramp but they couldn't see me. "Push up the engine power. *Right now*," I said. I stuck the barrel of the gun into Davenport's ribs.

He pushed up the engine power. The Boeing began to move forward. "Hurry. Down the taxiway. To the end of the runway." I pulled the gun out of Davenport's side and aimed it at the other guy, who had edged closer to me. "I can see that you're back on the asshole programme," I said. "That's not a smart choice."

"Fuck you." He turned away to face out of the cockpit window.

We were already halfway down the taxiway; I could see the turnoff to the departure end of the runway a few hundred yards in front of us. "Okay, Mister Chief Pilot, it's your turn to dance again. Get this aluminium sled off the ground."

"I can't. Not this quickly."

"You'd better. Get the flaps out. Everything else we can live without." I watched Davenport pull the flap handle down to the one degree position, an acceptable setting. With the flaps lowered and both engines running, there was nothing else critical enough to stop us from getting off the ground.

"I've got to do a cockpit check. What you're asking me to do is suicide."

"I'm not asking you, I'm telling you. Get on the runway. Push up the power. *Go*." As Davenport wheeled the Boeing around the taxiway turn, I could see the headlights of the van coming towards us in pursuit. I didn't know what kind of arsenal the four goons had on board with them, but I didn't really want to find out, either. "Make the takeoff. If you do anything stupid, I'll put a bullet through the back of your head." I leaned forward and shoved against the engine

175

throttles; I grabbed hold of the collar of Davenport's shirt to maintain my balance. The lightly loaded jet accelerated rapidly as the engines spooled to full thrust.

We lifted off in the first quarter of the runway. Davenport held the nose of the jet lower than usual, and airspeed built rapidly. Still, with as light a load as we had on board, the Boeing climbed quite well. We were through a thousand feet before I spoke. "Get the gear up," I said.

"I can't reach it."

"Bullshit." But then I made what must have been my fiftieth error of the evening by reaching over the centre pedestal myself and pulling up the landing gear handle rather than arguing with Davenport. It was in that two second span that the gorilla in the copilot's seat made his move.

The guy flung out his left arm towards me. His clenched fist hit me in the side, just below my right arm. He was a powerful man but, fortunately, he didn't have much leverage from where he was sitting. Still, the force of the blow pushed me sideways and I lost my balance for just an instant. While I pressed my left hand – the gun still in it – against Davenport's ribs to steady myself, the guy to my right followed his first motion with a right cross that caught me squarely in the chest.

Again, he hadn't been able to get his weight into the punch, so it didn't have the effect that he would've liked. But what it did do was knock me slightly backward, adding another dimension to my growing instability; I had no choice but to grab Davenport's shoulder with my right hand to stop myself from falling.

"Christ – stop!"

With me yanking on Davenport, he started to yank on the airplane. The Boeing suddenly reared up, its nose pitching fifteen, twenty degrees higher than normal. We would have been in deep trouble immediately if it hadn't been for the extra airspeed that Davenport had let the ship build up during its initial acceleration after liftoff. "Get the nose down!" I shouted.

"Let go of me!" Davenport was pushing forward on the control wheel, but I was still pulling back on his arm to keep myself upright. The conflicting forces were a sort of wash and the airliner kept its nose pointed far too much up. "Let go!"

Throughout all of this, the Sumo wrestler in the copilot's seat was working with perseverance and diligence on only one thing: getting me off my feet and the gun out of my hand. Of the three of us, he seemed to be the only one not to notice that we had become a jet-powered carnival ride – a carnival ride with a rather finite lifespan, if somebody didn't do something pretty quick about the pitch attitude that the airplane was taking.

"I'll kill you," the guy shouted. He had grabbed me with his left hand and was hitting me with his right. None of the blows was lethal in itself, but, I'll confess, I was beginning to notice that the cumulative total was approaching my threshold of endurance. I knew that I'd have to do something soon, because if the guy landed one good shot against my head, I'd be down.

I put all my strength into one forward push against him. Not only was I fighting the Wild Man of Borneo, but I was also fighting against the aerodynamic forces that were trying to get me to fall in the other direction. I grabbed the guy around the neck with my right arm, and tried to smack the butt of the gun into his face.

But he had obviously been in those kinds of situations before; he was too fast for me. His left arm locked on to my left wrist. We struggled above the centre control pedestal for several seconds, my body all the while bouncing off Davenport's, and Davenport's motions causing the airplane to do something akin to the rumba. My technician's jumpsuit ripped at the shoulder.

I felt the guy's powerful fingers groping along my wrist and on to the gun. There was nothing I could do about it except to keep hitting him and yanking on his head and neck. From what I could tell, I was having about as much effect as a mosquito would against an elephant.

"Can't control the airplane – stop!" Davenport shouted. The motions in my gut and the tone in his voice told me that he wasn't bluffing, either.

But, at that particular moment, I had my own problems. The guy who was wrestling with me had got his hand on the gun – we were, in fact, now sharing the weapon. My finger was still on the trigger, but I had only a tenuous hold on the

177

butt itself. For that matter, I could no longer tell if the barrel was pointed up, down or sideways.

A gunshot in a confined space as small as a Boeing 737's cockpit is a shattering noise; it gives the sensation that the entire universe has exploded. Somehow, by pulling too hard and too often, the guy had mashed down on my hand in such a way as to pull the trigger.

For just an instant after the shot was fired, nothing happened. Then all at once all hell – aerodynamically speaking – broke loose. Davenport fell against the control column. The airplane pitched violently downward.

"Look out!" My head practically hit the ceiling as the floor dropped out from under me. I felt the gun slip out of my hand; the guy to my right now had it completely away from me. But while the idea that he now had the gun was not comforting, the view out of the cockpit windshield was even more disconcerting: we were pointed thirty degrees down, straight towards a dinner engagement with the alligators.

I dived, literally, over Davenport's limp body and got hold of the control wheel. Using the seat itself for leverage, I managed to pull back hard enough to begin reversing the airliner's descent path. The forces from the pull-up were draining the blood from my head. Boeing, I prayed, did in fact make strong airplanes.

"I'll kill you," the guy in the right seat said. He now had the gun pointed at my head.

Without even looking at the instruments, I could tell that I had finally managed to stop the descent. I glanced at the altimeter, since the view out of the windshield was nearly total blackness: two hundred feet and climbing. We had come within a single wingspan of hitting the swamp. But now I was one trigger movement away from being dead anyway. Suddenly, something occurred to me. "Don't pull that trigger. Not unless you know how to fly. Your buddy's dead," I said, when I was finally able to catch my breath.

"Huh?"

"He's dead," I repeated. I continued to fly the jet from my position behind the captain's seat, my arms over the limp body between me and the control column. I wasn't immediately sure that Davenport was dead, but it was pretty obvious to both me and the guy to my right that Davenport had seen healthier days. That was, I was certain, the only reason I didn't already have a couple of bullets in me.

"Dead? You sure?" The guy had a quizzical look on his face – it was his equivalent of fear.

"Yes. Dead." I would have said yes in any event, but I could now see that I was probably right. There was a hole through the middle of Davenport's chest the size of a half dollar, and the control column, seat and floor looked like someone had dropped a few gallons of red wine on it. If Davenport wasn't dead yet, he would be dead very soon. "Dead. Finished. You shot him when you pulled the gun out of my hand." The airplane was under enough control for me to glance over at the guy. "He's dead. So it looks like we need each other."

"What?" The guy blinked a few times. There were a lot of subtle nuances in this situation, and one by one they were becoming increasingly clear to him. "Just shut the fuck up. Let me think."

"Don't burden yourself. We need each other, period. You need me to fly. I need you not to shoot me." Although not exactly to my liking, there was a certain neatness in this quid pro quo.

"Shut up," the guy said again. But I could tell from his voice that he had suddenly come to realise how much each of us was now dependent on the other. We had, in our aeronautical perch a few thousand feet above the Everglades swamp, become a classic example of the symbiotic relationship.

19

The Boeing 737 climbed slowly into the black night sky. I reached towards the centre glare shield panel. The guy in the copilot's seat jammed the gun into my ribs. "Hold it. What are you trying to do?"

"Relax. I'm trying to turn on the autopilot. I can't keep flying from behind the seat like this." I tried to keep my expression neutral, to keep the guy from doing something that we would both regret.

"Autopilot?" He blinked again, then let his eyes glance up in the direction that I was pointing. Unfortunately, the two paddle switches were labelled only as "Channel A" and "Channel B" – a little too cryptic for his liking. "It don't say nothing like that." He pressed the barrel of the gun – my gun – harder into my side. "Don't try nothing."

I shook my head. "Look, I don't have time to give you a flying lesson. We're both going to be dead if you keep this up. Spinning in from a few thousand feet isn't going to be a pleasant way to die." I didn't mention the fact that being shot in the ribs wasn't too pleasant, either.

"Don't bullshit me. I don't trust you."

"I don't trust you either. We're even." The technician's jumpsuit had torn a little more, and most of my right shoulder was now exposed. For some illogical reason, my mind was focused on the fact that my shoulder was now cold, that I was going to get a stiff neck from the air-conditioning that was incessantly playing against it.

In the strange sequence of my parallaxed thoughts, the next piece of data that floated through my brain was that my serve would suffer and that Max would win our next tennis match. I guess it was more comfortable to think about my shoulder than about the gun in my ribs. "We don't have a lot of options here. If we don't start trusting each other at least a little, we're going to die."

The guy thought over what I said for half a minute. While he did, I continued to lean over Davenport's body, my arms stretched out, while I used the jet's control wheel to keep the airliner more or less upright. We were still in a shallow climb, which was all right by me because there was a certain level of safety in altitude.

"Okay," the guy finally answered. "You do what you need to. But remember, I'm watching close." He pushed the gun into my body again, as a way of italicising his spoken words.

"Gotcha." I smiled amicably, then reached up and flipped on the autopilot. Much to my relief, the "A" channel held immediately. I was able, finally, to let go of the control wheel.

"Now what you gonna do?"

"Now I've got to get your buddy Davenport out of the seat. I can't make a landing from back here."

"Okay. Do it slow."

"You can bet on it." I reached down, hit the track release on the captain's seat, and slid it backward. With my other hand, I held on to Davenport by the neck so that his body wouldn't slouch any further forward. His body was already beginning to cool off – in a manner of speaking, William F. Davenport had already achieved the ultimate in a stiff neck. I released the seatbelt from around him, grabbed him under the arms and pulled his inert bulk out of the captain's seat. I laid his body on the floor, behind the centre control pedestal. Davenport's eyes were wide open, and his gaunt face was frozen in an expression somewhere between annoyance and panic.

"Okay. Now you get in the chair. Careful." The guy waved the pistol menacingly.

"Sure." I stepped over Davenport and into the captain's flight chair. My shoes squished through the puddles of blood on the floor. Matter of fact, I had blood all over the technician's jumpsuit. I wondered if Izzy was going to make me wash it. I wondered if Elmer was going to insist that I be buried in it. Out of pure habit, I put on the captain's seatbelt, then pressed the track release mechanism and pulled the chair to a more comfortable flying position. "Okay, now what?"

"You take us somewhere to land."

"Okay. I'll head back to Miami."

The guy laughed. It was the kind of laugh that even Don Giovanni would have been proud of. "Don't be an asshole. Nowhere like that. No talking on the radio. Just find a runway and put this crate down."

"Back at Dade-Collier?"

"Huh?"

"The training field where we were." I motioned over my shoulder, towards the tail of the airplane. We were headed west, cruising at five thousand two hundred feet, which just happened to be the altitude that the autopilot had levelled us off at. The Dade-Collier training field was behind us, probably thirty, forty miles.

"No. The guys must've left already. Maybe all that shit we did got the police out." He shook his head while he continued to think out loud. "Someplace new. Without a control tower to ask any questions. Marco."

"Marco Island?"

"Yeah. That's good. Real good."

"It's too small." I had been in there a great deal during my occasional bouts of light airplane flight instructing, as recently as just a month ago. The single runway was five thousand feet long, which was long enough for the Boeing since we were very light. It had runway lights, too, but no control tower – just a small operations building, which was probably closed up this time of night. Marco Island was enough of an airport for me to get the Boeing into, but I was still hoping for something a little more crowded, where I stood a better chance of coming out of this experience alive. "It's not enough runway, we'll get killed."

"Bullshit." Once again, the guy pushed the gun into my ribs. "I know you're lying, you bastard. Davenport and me talked plenty about Marco. It was our second choice, if that training field back there didn't work out."

"You're Joseph Tazik, aren't you?" I said. It suddenly became clear to me that this must be the guy that Allan Lyle had come to my apartment to tell me about.

"Yeah."

He seemed to have no opinion, one way or the other, about

182

my knowing who he was. "I'm afraid I can't say that it's nice to meet you."

"Fuck you." Tazik waved the gun. "Keep your mouth shut and fly the airplane. Get us down or I'll put a bullet through your head."

"Wrong, prick-face." I felt a certain need to speak Tazik's language if I was going to make myself clearly understood. "If and when I get us down, that's exactly when you intend to put a bullet in my skull. Until then, I get the continual but rather dubious pleasure of your company."

"I'm telling you for the last time to shut the fuck up."

I pretended that Tazik hadn't said anything which, in essence, he hadn't. "So you listen to me, Mister drug kingpin. If you don't want your guts smeared all over the crushed remnants of this cockpit, you'd better come up with some method of guaranteeing both our safeties. Otherwise – to quote your limited and rather pointed but effectual verbiage – you can go fuck yourself, since I'm a dead man anyway."

This time, Tazik said nothing. He nodded his head a few times, as if my words were percolating through his brain at the same rate that water drained through solid clay. Finally, it had all got down to his level. "Okay, I get it. We gotta come up with some idea where you know I ain't gonna kill you as soon as we land."

"An inspiring, altruistic thought. The only answer is if you unload the gun. Then I know you're not going to kill me as soon as I get the airplane into Marco."

"No way, asshole."

"Think about it. It's the only way. I've got to land the airplane if I'm going to save me, too – I'm not going to crash it just for revenge. You having the gun is the only real threat here."

"Well . . ."

"It's the only way." I didn't want to push him too hard but, on the other hand, I didn't want to leave Tazik alone to his own devices. Without some restraints, he was capable of arranging things like Paula Tate's traffic accident and Louis Zarrillo's mock robbery. Up ahead, through the cockpit windshield, I could make out the distant lights of what was probably Marco Island and, to the right, Naples. "We're getting close to Marco. We've got to do something soon if you want to get down. Unload the gun."

"No." Tazik waved the barrel in my direction. "You must think I'm a fucking moron. I ain't." He smiled. "I got a better idea. I keep the gun but go in the back. You can lock the door." Tazik gestured towards the cockpit door behind us. "When you land and stop, I jump out the main door and get away. I keep the gun so I know no one is gonna try to stop me."

"It's a deal." I had to give the guy credit, he had come up with something of a solution to our standoff. But I did see a few holes in his plan – holes that were distinctly in my favour. "Go ahead, get in the back. I'll start down for the landing. Once we're on the ground, you open the main cabin door and leave."

Tazik released his seatbelt and slowly rose from the co-pilot's chair. He was careful to keep the gun pointed at me the entire time he edged past the centre control pedestal. He was standing behind me, straddling Davenport's body, when he finally spoke again. "And now I'm gonna show you that I'm a good listener, too, asshole." Without another comment he pumped two bullets into the radio controls that were mounted on the centre console.

"What the hell did you do that for?" I said, after the ringing in my ears had finally subsided. I knew damn well why he had done it, but I wanted Tazik to think that I hadn't figured it out.

"Don't play dumb with me. I didn't get to where I am by underestimating a prick like you." Tazik laughed again. "Our pilot friend showed me where the two radios were." He kicked his heel into Davenport's limp body. "So now you can't call for help, can't tell nobody where we're going. Just another guarantee that there won't be no cops waiting for me when we land."

"I don't give a damn whether you get away or not, I just want to get out of this alive." What I wanted to do, of course, was to pump the three remaining bullets in my gun into Tazik. Unfortunately, it didn't look like I was going to get that chance. Not tonight, anyway. "Get in the back, I'll get us down."

184

"Okay. But if we ain't on the ground in five minutes, I'm coming back up. I ain't afraid to die, just so I got company."

"That's understandable. The ride to hell can be a lonely one."

"Fuck you." Tazik left the cockpit and slammed the door shut behind him.

I quickly found the electronic cockpit door lock on the centre pedestal, the same place it had been in the Air East Boeings. I pushed the button and heard the bolt click shut. For the time being, Tazik and his gun – my gun – were locked on the other side of the cockpit door.

I pulled back on the engine throttles and began a descent. I shut the autopilot off and did a few shallow turns to get the feel of the airplane again. It all came back to me very quickly, as if I had never left the business of driving big jets. The ground lights ahead of me grew rapidly in size and clarity. Soon I spotted the beacon that I knew must be the airport at Marco Island.

Sitting on the left side of the wide Boeing cockpit rather than on the right gave me a different perspective from what I had been accustomed to, but it wasn't enough of a difference to really matter. I fumbled a few times as I looked for particular switches and levers that for years had been on my left but were now on my right, but other than those few awkward moments, the approach to Marco went normally.

There was no other air traffic in sight. I turned on all the airliner's exterior lights, lowered the flaps, dropped the landing gear, lowered the remainder of the flaps, then turned on a long final approach to the single northwest runway. Since the radio controls had been smashed beyond recognition by Tazik's gunshots, I didn't even bother to try to call anybody – the radios probably wouldn't work at all, and, besides, I was too busy just trying to get the Boeing down. Tazik's threat to kill both of us if I dallied was also a very real consideration – he seemed crazy enough to do whatever he had vowed, no matter how illogical.

The night sky was clear, the wind was nearly calm and the air was smooth. All those factors made it easy for me to get back into the saddle again; by the time the ship was a quarter mile from touchdown, our altitude on descent was perfect and the airspeed was just a few knots above my target. It was too bad that Chief Pilot Davenport was already dead, I could have impressed the hell out of him with my flying prowess.

I made only the slightest flare for landing and allowed the airliner to touch down moderately hard, so that I wouldn't use up precious runway that I really didn't have to spare. The automatic wing spoilers came up while I jammed on the wheel brakes and pulled back on the reverse thrust handles. The Boeing ground to a halt in about two-thirds of the available length. Out of habit, I lowered the spoiler handle, cancelled reverse thrust and raised the flaps to their takeoff setting – the customary procedures that I had followed at Air East for so many years.

I taxied to the end of the runway, then wheeled the Boeing around so that it faced into the landing direction and I could see any inbound traffic. I set the parking brake. I left all the exterior lights on, so that we would be quite conspicuous – maybe some cop would wonder why a big airline jet was sitting on the end of Marco's relatively small runway, all lit up like a Christmas tree. But the odds of some cop getting nosey in the very near future were pretty slim.

I reached over to the right side of the overhead panel and shut off the pressurisation system to get rid of the aircraft's internal air pressure. I picked the PA microphone off the rear of the centre pedestal. "Okay, Tazik. I've done my end of the deal. We're holding at the end of the runway. You can open the main door. You can get off."

But instead of hearing the sound of the main cabin door being opened, the next noise was another shattering repetition of what I had nearly become accustomed to. Tazik had fired the gun again, this time into the locking mechanism of the cockpit door. I could hear the metal shatter, and I could hear Tazik pounding against whatever fragments of the electronic lock were still in place. In fifteen seconds at the very most, Tazik would be up in the cockpit – and he still had two bullets left in the gun.

My response was not a conscious one. I was reacting purely on the instinct that, for me, safety was up, danger was down. I shoved the engine throttles full forward. Both power-plants, which were still running, spooled rapidly up from idle to full power.

The takeoff warning horn began to blare, filling the cockpit with yet another loud and distracting sound. What the equipment was trying to tell me was that something important for the takeoff was not set properly. I couldn't afford the luxury of figuring out what it was. Tazik burst into the cockpit, waving the gun, just as the Boeing reached takeoff speed.

"Stop!" he yelled. He shoved the gun into the back of my neck.

I yanked back on the control column. The lightly loaded Boeing literally jumped into the air. Now that we were off the ground, the takeoff warning horn finally stopped – but the reason for its having sounded became more than obvious: during the landing, I had set in far too much nose-up trim for the subsequent takeoff. We were now rocketing skyward like the Space Shuttle but, unfortunately, we had no solid rocket boosters to help us keep going up. I laid my thumb against the tailplane trim button and pushed hard against the control wheel. I needed to stop our upward pitching motion before the airplane totally ran out of energy.

Just on the verge of stalling, I managed to get the ship's nose down enough to keep us flying. We were through a thousand feet already, and still hurtling upward – although now at a diminishing, controllable rate. The airspeed indicator was still pointing to the end of the scale that I would rather not have been looking at, but at least now it was rising to a more respectable portion of the gauge.

I pitched the airplane level at two thousand feet, then pulled the throttles back to a moderate setting. The landing gear was still down, the flaps were still in the takeoff position. I glanced over at Tazik, who was holding on to the bulkhead behind me. The acceleration forces had rolled Davenport's body out of the opened cockpit door and back into the galley area beside the entranceway. "You stupid bastard." That was all I could say, after I eventually caught my breath.

"Fuck." For the first time, Tazik looked damned scared. He had allowed a sense of revenge to put him back into total jeopardy; there was something about being involuntarily subjected to the forces of a wildly bucking airplane that had the potential to make even macho guys feel like Shirley Temple.

"Now what are we going to do?" I asked, as if I wasn't the one who had total control of the situation – at least now that we were airborne again. I began a circle to the left. The lights of Marco Island were beneath us, the airport a few miles further inland. I began a slow, gradual descent.

"Shit." Tazik looked around, bewildered. Clearly, he had now decided that he did not want to die inside this cockpit. "You got to get us down."

"Not a chance, you prick. You can die with me."

"No. I'll let you go this time. Really."

"Fuck you." It was my turn to display my opinions in a contemporary, emphatic fashion. "We'll both die, you bastard. There's some satisfaction in that." I shoved forward on the Boeing's control column, pushing the nose straight down towards the dark water of the Gulf of Mexico beneath us.

"No! Stop, for chrissake!" Tazik was holding on to the bulkhead to keep himself on his feet, otherwise the aerodynamic forces would've put him against the cockpit ceiling. "Stop! Damn!"

I yanked hard on the column the opposite way. The Boeing ended its descent abruptly. We were down to five hundred feet, but were now holding altitude. "You better make a suggestion fast, you son of a bitch," I said to Tazik. "You've got ten seconds to live, if you don't come up with some guarantees for me."

"Okay, hold on." Tazik stood in the rear of the dimly lit cockpit, trying to think. Ten seconds came and went without him coming up with anything.

"Time's up." But I didn't actually do anything yet because, naturally, I didn't want to push the issue. Getting killed with Joseph Tazik might have got me the Trans-Continental Purple Heart or even their Medal of Honour with the coveted Elmer Woodruff Cluster, but it wouldn't do much for my date with Tracy tomorrow night, my next tennis match with Max, or my tickets to what was left of this year's opera season.

"I don't know what to do," Tazik said. "I can't give you the gun."

"And I can't let you keep it." I began another slow orbit

of the Marco Island airport, gently turning the Boeing east, then north again. "But I tell you what. We can compromise."

"Huh?"

When I had looked over my shoulder, even in the dim light, I had noticed two things about the cockpit door – that Tazik had completely destroyed the electronic lock, and that there was a simple slide bolt, intact, above it. "You've got two bullets left in the gun. You take one out and give it to me, that leaves you with one. Then you go back to the cabin. I'll lock the cockpit door again, this time with the mechanical bolt. Just like before, I'll land the airplane and you can get out the main cabin door. But if you decide to shoot the lock off the cockpit door again, you'll be using the only bullet you've got."

Tazik thought over my proposition for a while. I turned the Boeing west, then south again. The altitude had drifted back up to a thousand feet. The lights of Marco Island slid by beneath the left wing. "Okay," Tazik said. He unloaded one bullet from the chamber and laid it on the centre control pedestal. He turned and walked out of the cockpit, back into the cabin.

As soon as he left, I flipped on the autopilot, climbed out of the captain's seat and closed the cockpit door. Just as it had appeared, the mechanical slide bolt was still in good shape – I pushed it shut. I tried the door. It was locked. Tazik was on the other side, but now with only one bullet left. Safety, as they say, is a relative term.

I climbed back into the captain's seat and busied myself with the approach and landing. The airplane was still unpressurised from the last takeoff, and all the rapid manoeuvring had blocked my ears slightly. But I had enough to worry about just then without fooling around with the pressurisation system, so I left it off.

Setting up for landing had become the routine part of the evening for me; in short order we crossed the threshold of the Marco Island runway. Touchdown was a little smoother this time, rollout just as short. As a precaution, I quickly wheeled to the other end of the runway, then spun the jet around so that we could be ready for another takeoff if it became necessary. It was just about that time that the idea struck me.

Without thinking of the millions of reasons why I shouldn't, I set the parking brake, then hurriedly reached over for the airplane's pressurisation controls. I pushed all the switches on, then cranked the setting for the cabin altitude for something far below sea level. With the engines still running and supplying air, the cabin pumped up immediately – I could feel the big pressure bump in my ears as the inside of the airliner packed itself with air. We were now a completely sealed entity, with lots more air pressure inside than out.

I could hear Tazik rattling around back there, working on the main door handle. But now, unknown to him, I had an ally in my efforts to keep him on board until the folks from officialdom showed up to see what the hell a big airliner was doing on the small runway at Marco Island.

My ally in the battle against Tazik was hundreds of pounds of air pressure inside the ship, holding the plug-type doors rigidly shut in their mounts. That much internal air pressure was far too much even for a muscle man like Tazik to overcome – or anyone else, for that matter. As long as the jet's engines kept running and the air kept being pumped in, there was no way for anyone to override the air pressure to get any of the doors or emergency windows open. Tazik and I were, literally, trapped inside.

As predictable as day following night, Tazik used his last bullet to blast the cockpit door's mechanical lock away. This guy, if nothing else, was proving to be tough on the airline's hardware. Tazik stormed up to the cockpit. I had already taken the precaution of grabbing the crash axe out of its holder. I held it in my right hand, its sharpened blade aimed directly towards him. It would have made an awkward weapon at best in the narrow confines of the cockpit, but any weapon was better than none at all. "What do you want?" I said in all innocence; there was no sense making Tazik think that I had something to do with his new dilemma – he was potentially irrational enough to do almost anything. "I did my part. Now you can leave."

"The fucking door," he said. He aimed the gun at me, but then realised that it was empty. In disgust, he threw the gun on the floor behind him. It rolled backward into the cabin. Tazik had, evidently, forgotten that I had one of the bullets inside the pocket of my jumpsuit. "The fucking door. It don't open."

"Must be jammed. Buckled by the manoeuvres," I lied. I shrugged. "Beats me," I said. I was his buddy now, trying to help him. "Maybe one of the other doors is okay. Or the emergency windows."

"Right." Tazik spun round and ran back into the cabin. I saw him beginning to work furiously on the emergency window above the right wing. He pulled and tugged but, naturally, it wouldn't give. Every few seconds he looked towards the cockpit. I sat quietly in the relative darkness.

I was biding my time until I could go back and hunt for the gun before Tazik remembered that I still had one bullet left. Although I couldn't see it, I guessed that the gun had rolled underneath one of the rows of seats on the left. Tazik was still working on the emergency window, and I was still working on appearing casual and unconcerned when something finally caught my full attention. The thing that caught my eye was neither Tazik nor the gun, but something even grander – the powerful lights of a big airplane on final approach for the runway that we were sitting at the opposite end of.

I shut down my airplane's external lights. I watched, in awe, the view out of the cockpit window. The target kept coming. Since I was parked at the far end of the runway, I wasn't worried about a ground collision. In reality, all I was doing at that moment was hoping and praying that the lights represented what I thought they might.

I was right. It was another Trans-Continental Boeing 737. It touched down on the opposite end of the runway, then rolled carefully to a complete stop about fifty feet in front of where I had parked the Boeing we were in. That mirror-image airliner, with its silver body and red striping, was a beautiful sight.

Just a few moments after it came to a stop, the other Boeing's main cabin door opened. The internal stairs popped out. A gang of about a dozen men, some in suits, some in police uniforms, stormed down the stairs. They surrounded my airplane. Last, but certainly not least from my point of view, Izzy Reese came down the stairs. He stood on the tarmac below me, looking up. I instantly fell in love with the sight of his big, flat nose and his curly hair.

I smiled and waved. Izzy waved back. I reached over and shut down my airplane's engines. As soon as they began to unspool, the differential air pressure inside the cabin began rapidly to bleed off. With the electrical generators now also off the line, most of the internal lighting went out, leaving on only those few lights still connected to the ship's battery power.

The airplane became eerily quiet. I got out of the captain's seat, then stepped back into the entranceway. I grabbed the main door handle. It moved easily in my hand without the air pressure fighting it. "Hey, Joe," I called out into the darkened cabin, although I couldn't see where he was at that moment, "don't be bashful, come on up. Looks like we've got company."

20

I was in Elmer Woodruff's corner office with my feet up on his desk. The morning sun was shining across the Trans-Continental hangar ramp, and there were a couple of airliners parked on the blacktop. One of them was ship 263, the star of last night's drama. Even from where I sat, I could see a bevy of mechanics working on the Boeing jet and several official-looking men strutting around it.

Tracy was sitting on the front edge of Elmer's desk, telling me a few of the details that Elmer had skipped over in his explanation of what the police had found so far. Elmer himself was showing marvellous restraint by sitting back in his chair, smiling, and saying nothing about where my shoes were placed.

"So, basically, we were right," I said. "It was the airplane, not the men, who were the focus." Not being a guy to push things to their ultimate limits, I cautiously swung my feet off the desk and sat upright.

"Yes," Tracy answered. She was wearing a yellow knit dress that hugged her curves quite well. "The airplane was the focal point. There's no way to tell now how often it had happened, but it appears as if periodically the airplanes that overnighted in Cancún would have drugs hidden on them. Then, at some point, one of the pilots in on the deal would take the drugs off a few days later. We've got a computer printout that shows that either Zarrillo or Bridges would pick up whatever trip the Cancún airplane flew shortly after the Mexico overnight."

"Makes sense." The sight of Tracy in her yellow knit dress was making me want to hug her curves again, even though we had done exactly that for a good part of the evening. Once I had got back from the excitement of Marco Island and the return flight to Miami, Tracy and I had gone to her apartment. I was exhausted this morning, in the best sense of the word. So, I could tell, was she. "Did Tazik finally tell the police where the stuff on ship 263 was hidden?" I asked.

"I don't think I should repeat the things that Tazik kept telling the police." Tracy shook her head. "He's a tough character. He doesn't seem to realise that it's all over, that there's nothing to be gained by cursing at everyone and being uncooperative."

"Yes, indeed, that's my friend Joe." I laughed.

"Anyway, a couple of hours ago they found a few hundred pounds of cocaine," she said. "It was hidden inside several of the hydraulic reservoirs and pump housings in the wheel well. The police are guessing that it was probably the biggest shipment that Davenport and company had made so far. That's why it was hidden so well inside the airplane's equipment. There might even be more."

"Then those guys who met us at Dade-Collier must've had tools with them to get that stuff out."

"Sure," Elmer said. "Lots of tools." He leaned forward. "It took our own mechanics a couple of hours to break into all those places to find the cocaine. That's why Davenport couldn't remove the stuff unless he had the airplane away from peering eyes for a few hours at least. If they tried to remove the cocaine here at the hangar, one of the supervisors from maintenance would've spotted them and begun asking questions."

"Questions that Davenport and, especially, my friend Joe weren't in a position to answer."

"Exactly."

"Okay, that part seems pretty well under control. Is our arrangement with the police still the same?" I asked.

"Yeah. Our arrangement still stands." Elmer shook his head; unhappiness was creeping back into his persona. "You'll find out for yourself how good that arrangement is when they get here at ten o'clock." Elmer glanced up at the wall clock. It was nine twenty. "According to what they told me on the telephone, the Chief of Detectives is going to want to have a nice, long chat with the three of us."

"I figured he would."

"You did? Why?"

194

"The guy's a little upset that we didn't cut him in until late in the action."

"Damn. I knew that we should've. I told you so."

"Elmer, calm down. The man is no fool. The case is closed, and we more or less finished it off together."

"More for you, less for them," Tracy volunteered. She had a look of admiration in her eyes that most guys would've been happy to pay a hefty amount for, if it could be bought. Which, I was sure, it couldn't. And it was mine for free. "That was one incredible job that you did."

"It worked out okay." I shrugged. Modesty aside, I knew that I'd been uncommonly lucky, too. The bullet that hit Davenport could have been inside me instead. So could any of those bullets that were left in the gun once Tazik got control of it. And that's not to mention any of the problems with the flying or the airplane. Now that I was listing all the ways that I could've been killed last night, it made me shiver inside.

"Yeah, it worked out okay." Elmer took a sip of his coffee, then leaned forward. "But what about the Chief of Detectives thing?" Elmer now had the customary frown on his face. With the main action behind us, we were returning to business as usual. I realised that putting my feet up on Elmer's desk from now on would be unwise. The man did not like unresolved dilemmas hanging over his domain; those kinds of yet-to-be-resolved situations tended to remind him that he was the king of this particular fiefdom.

"The Chief of Detectives is coming here to make sure that we don't make him look bad, that's all. That's why we were told last night to hold absolutely no press conferences before they got back to us this morning. The police could have insured against that possibility, of course, by taking us all into the station house straight from the airport."

"I never thought of that."

"It would have been customary. Instead, they let me go home with Tracy and you go back to bed. There's a reason for it. They're playing a gentlemen's game here. The Chief of Detectives is showing us that he'll take us at our word. That way, he's establishing a certain bond of cooperation between us."

"By the way, the press has been driving us crazy. We finally scheduled the press conference for noon," Tracy said. "Right here."

"But what, exactly, will this Chief of Detectives be looking for when he gets here?" Elmer asked. He strummed his fingers on the desk. "I still think we're a little too exposed with the law on this whole thing."

"The police will be looking for a coordinated statement that doesn't make them look like they were asleep at the switch, which of course they were. That's all they want, some good press. While it's true that they can give us a hard time on legal technicalities, they know that we can turn up the heat on them for their lack of imagination and for letting the whole damn thing go on for so long right under their noses."

"How do we give the police what they want?" Elmer asked. "We'd be crazy not to cooperate."

"Of course we would. The reason they put the police interview off until this morning, I imagine, is to give us a chance to think things through, to coordinate our stories. They're giving us a chance to be sure that we don't embarrass them or ourselves. If need be, the Chief of Detectives will let us know what we should and shouldn't say, but he's hoping that we can figure it out for ourselves. That way, they can pat us on the back, say we were good boys and girls, and close the case completely."

"What part of the story do we have to coordinate?" Elmer leaned forward even further – he was paying strict attention now. In a sense, he knew there was going to be a test on this material at ten o'clock.

"Only that we never really had any factual information. Without knowing anything conclusive, we had no obligation to turn any of our sketchy information over to the police. That was why we didn't call them, and why they didn't act. You hired a private detective to follow up the Jay Bridges accident. Since the police already know that I was at the scene, I'll say that I was following Paula Tate that night only because she was Bridges' old girlfriend and I thought she might have somehow been involved with him. I'm going to leave the Zarrillo aspect out completely – I'd rather not have to explain when and how I got into his apartment.

That'll also leave out the need to explain Susan, Max and Pamela. We didn't suspect anything about Zarrillo until he turned up dead, then we decided that he must've been part of the action."

"That's wise."

"Anyway, I'll stress that I simply guessed a possible connection to someone higher in the company. The fact that Davenport was then scheduled to give copilot flight training seemed strange to me, so I followed him to the airplane. That was our lucky break. I got on board while Davenport was getting the airplane ready. All the rest comes out exactly the way it actually happened."

"What about Izzy Reese?" Tracy asked. "Should we say that we spoke to him? I've already told Izzy to say absolutely nothing without checking with us first."

"Sure, we spoke to Izzy. That's how we found out about Davenport's intention to do copilot training last night. Izzy couldn't understand why Davenport was doing something like that, so he alerted me."

"I've got to give Reese credit," Elmer said. "He stuck his neck out by grabbing another company airplane, getting the police out here, then going after you. If he was wrong, he would've had a tough time explaining himself."

"He may have stuck out his neck, but he sure as hell saved mine."

"Absolutely. He did what needed to be done. That's a wonderful trait in a man – he's a natural leader. He did get one break, though, that Miami air traffic control still had your airplane in radar contact, so that they knew exactly where you had gone. That's how Izzy found you so quickly."

"I was wondering how he figured out that I was at Marco. I didn't get a chance to ask him last night, I was too busy kissing the ground."

"You'll be able to sit around and talk to him all you want this afternoon. You'll find him in Davenport's office." Elmer allowed a brief hint of a smile to etch into the corners of his mouth. "I promoted Reese to chief pilot this morning, replacing the late William F. Davenport."

"Nice touch."

"I've got a few other nice touches, too." Elmer stood

up. He was on a roll, enjoying himself immensely, now that the investigation he had single-handedly authorised had been completed so successfully – and now that he felt secure about the upcoming police interview. The next company board meeting was going to be a stellar occasion for Elmer Woodruff. "I remember you saying that you wanted more work from us, didn't you?"

"Sure thing. I need work. A man's got to eat, a man's got to join tennis clubs, buy opera tickets. All the essentials of life take money."

"Good." Elmer smiled. "Just to be on the safe side, I've authorised a thirty day extension of your duties here, at full pay of course. You can use that time to wrap things up."

"Another nice touch. But to be honest, there's not thirty days' worth of work here."

"Then work slow." Elmer gave me a conspiratorial glance for a moment, before his serious expression returned. "Now, in addition, here's another offer I have for you – if you're interested."

"Let it rip."

"Thirty-five days from now, I'm told we've got a new copilot class scheduled to begin. I don't have to tell you that you've already impressed everyone in this company with your airmanship abilities, not to mention some other ingredients of your character as well. I've got your name down for that copilot class. Think it over. If you accept the job, I'll still be able to use you now and then for consultation on security matters. For those kinds of duties, there'd be extra pay."

"Elmer, that's a very generous offer. I'll let you know very soon." I didn't want to make a rash pronouncement so I held myself back, but I had to admit that the proposition sounded very, very good. I guess that last night showed me that I did actually care more about flying than I had allowed myself to believe. Lately, I'd learned that I cared a lot more about lots of things than I had allowed myself to believe.

Elmer glanced over at Tracy. "Okay, I'm finished. Do you want to tell him the other part?"

"My pleasure." Tracy had the cat-ate-the-canary expression on her face. She gave me a heartfelt, warm smile. "After examining the entire situation," she began, "Elmer felt that

198

in order for you to do this thirty day wrap-up properly, you should do some travelling around on the Trans-Continental system to get a good feel for the company. Here's a stack of first class passes." She handed me a booklet.

"Thank you," I said.

"Naturally, since we'll want you to visit several of the company's outlying stations – Los Angeles, San Francisco, New York – it would be best if you had someone from the company as your personal guide."

"Naturally."

"So I've gotten some first class passes for myself, too." Tracy waved another booklet at me. "The itinerary I've got mapped out should take about ten days."

"It sounds like a great deal of work, but I've always been a glutton for punishment. I'll do it."

"Yeah, I thought you would." Elmer stepped forward. I rose from my chair. He handed me an envelope. "And we sure don't want to overwork you on this trip, not after you've done so much for us. So we added something else to the itinerary. A little entertainment. Here's a list of where we've got tickets – two tickets – on reserve for the things I understand that you'd like to see."

"Like what, if I might ask?"

"Like the symphony in San Francisco, the opera in New York."

"The opera we've got tickets for is *Pagliacci*," Tracy said. "I hope it's one that you like."

I put my arms around her. Even though Elmer was standing beside us, we pretended that he wasn't. The two of us stood quietly, looking straight into each other's eyes. "I enjoy *Pagliacci* a great deal," I finally said. I could feel the blood in my veins as it went from simmer to full heat. Wisps of Tracy's blonde hair were falling across her forehead. I brushed them aside with my hand. "That opera is full of great music, but it's also a historical piece."

"Historical?"

"Yes. At one time, *Pagliacci* was the story of my life."

"It's not any more?"

"No. Not any more."